FROM RICHES TO RAGS

Constance felt as if everything were slowly swimming away from her and someone had gripped her by the throat. She started her car and threaded her way through traffic, a strange dull horror in the back of her mind. She wasn't Constance Wetherill anymore, she was just a poor girl with almost nothing left in the world, and her grandmother to care for, and what was she going to do about it?

She was not as calm as she had appeared to the old family lawyer, neither was she uncomprehending. The fact remained: her fortune was gone.

She had yet to even imagine the riches that lay ahead. . . .

Bantam Books by Grace Livingston Hill
Ask your bookseller for the books you have missed

#43 DAWN OF THE MORNING
#49 THE ENCHANTED BARN
#52 TOMORROW ABOUT THIS TIME
#57 HONOR GIRL
#62 THE CHRISTMAS BRIDE
#63 THE MAN OF THE DESERT
#64 MISS LAVINIA'S CALL
#65 AN UNWILLING GUEST
#66 THE GIRL FROM MONTANA
#67 A DAILY RATE
#68 THE STORY OF A WHIM
#69 ACCORDING TO THE PATTERN
#70 IN THE WAY
#71 EXIT BETTY
#72 THE WHITE LADY

The White Lady

Grace Livingston Hill

BANTAM BOOKS

TORONTO · NEW YORK · LONDON · SYDNEY · AUCKLAND

This low-priced Bantam Book
has been completely reset in a type face
designed for easy reading, and was printed
from new plates. It contains the complete
text of the original hard-cover edition.
NOT ONE WORD HAS BEEN OMITTED.

THE WHITE LADY

A Bantam Book / published by arrangement with
Harper & Row, Publishers

PRINTING HISTORY

J. B. Lippincott edition published in 1930

Bantam edition / March 1986

ISBN 0-553-25573-8

Published simultaneously in the United States and Canada

Bantam Books are published by Bantam Books, Inc. Its trademark, consisting of the words "Bantam Books" and the portray-
al of a rooster, is Registered in U.S. Patent and Trademark Office
and in other countries. Marca Registrada. Bantam Books, Inc.,
666 Fifth Avenue, New York, New York 10103.

PRINTED IN THE UNITED STATES OF AMERICA

H   0 9 8 7 6 5 4

The White Lady

Chapter I

"Then you mean that there is only about five thousand dollars left?"

Constance drew the rich furs about her throat and stood up to try to still the tumult of her heart.

"Yes—about that. Understand, it may be a trifle more, perhaps a thousand; but that is doubtful. There may be some other small accounts that have not been settled."

He looked at her keenly and drew a sigh of relief. He had expected a scene and she had made none. Some girls might have fainted at hearing such news so unexpectedly, but Constance Wetherill had not fainted. Had she fully understood what a change this meant in her income? The old lawyer drew his shaggy brows together fiercely and tried again. He must do his duty fully.

"You understand, Miss Constance, that this means five thousand dollars capital, not income. It does not mean you will have five thousand a year, but only the interest on five thousand. If well invested it ought to bring you about——"

But the girl cut him short with her clear comprehending voice that made further calculations unnecessary.

"I quite understand," she said with a quick little catch in her breath. "We shall have but five thousand dollars in all. And now, if that is all, I think I must go as I have an engagement in a few minutes."

She was gone and the lawyer looked after her half bewildered, half sadly. Surely she could not comprehend the relative value or figures or she never would have taken

his news so calmly. Why, it would mean an utter change
in her way of living. It meant absolute poverty after a
life of luxury from her birth.

He had intended to ask some questions about her
prospects and offer some aid; but she had left him no
opportunity. The keen lawyer who led juries about at his
will, and was apt to tell clients exactly what he pleased,
had been held at a distance by this mere child with the
patrician face and the costly garments.

"She's of the old stock. Her father over again!" solilo-
quized the lawyer, as he sat for an idle moment reflecting after the office door closed behind her, and her
footsteps echoed down the corridor to the elevator. "If
she's like him through and through, nothing can down
her. But there are very few women like that, and she's
a mere slip of a girl. She doesn't understand or else she
knows where she can find plenty of money, that's certain. I suppose perhaps she's engaged to Morris Thayer,
or as good as engaged, and that will make everything all
right. He has plenty."

He turned with relief to a knotty case that was awaiting his attention.

Constance, in her car below, felt as if everything were
slowly swimming away from her and some one had
gripped her by the throat.

She started her car and threaded her way through traffic, a strange dull horror in the back of her mind. She
was not Constance Wetherill any more, she was just a
poor girl with almost nothing left in the world, and her
grandmother to care for, and what was she going to do
about it?

She was not as calm as she had appeared to the old
family lawyer, neither was she uncomprehending. She
had a clear knowledge of figures, and she knew just how
much money seemed an absolute necessity to keep life
running comfortably, and she felt that the lawyer might
as well have told her that there was not a penny left as
to speak of the paltry sum of five thousand dollars. She
knew that it was as nothing beside the annual income
that had been hers since her father died, a trifle less than

ten years ago. She did not trouble her mind with raging at the poor, incompetent uncle whose ill-advised care had allowed this state of things to come about. He was in his grave, and it did not matter whether he had been simply incompetent, or whether he had also been a rascal; the result was the same. The fact remained that her fortune was gone.

She looked out through the car window and tried to realize what it would be to live without a car.

Suddenly she caught sight of a familiar face coming down the avenue, Morris Thayer, her life-long friend, and he was stopping at the curb and signaling her to stop. She drew a breath of relief. Life could not have suddenly gone blank, for here was Morris, smiling and friendly, and the sun was shining. There must be some mistake. The lawyer would discover it and telephone her tonight—or tomorrow.

Constance drew herself up smartly and resolutely shut back the thoughts that had been surging over her. At least, she was not utterly penniless yet. There was still the five thousand between her and poverty. She need not let any one know just yet—not at least till she herself fully understood what it all meant, and knew what she was going to do. The paltry five thousand seemed suddenly a wall, a shield between herself and an unpleasant future. She would be herself for this one afternoon and forget that there were such things in the world as stocks and bonds and failures.

She leaned forward with her own charming smile and welcomed the young man. Here at least was a friend, one who had been devoted to her for years. After all, what matter did a few dollars more or less make in life?

Perhaps there was a tinge of more warmth than usual in her smile, for Constance was an independent young woman, and not given to showering her favors broadcast.

"Are you going to Mrs. Graham's tea, Morrie?" she asked. "Get in then for that's where I'm bound."

The young man sprang in eagerly, and they had not gone a block before the meager fortune of five thousand dollars was forgotten for the moment in eager discussion of the interests of the young group to which they both belonged.

The afternoon was lovely. Just enough snow on the ground to make the world glisten with beauty. The brown branches that arched over the avenue were touched with a feathery penciling of white that made an exquisite lace work against the blue winter sky. Everything was bright and comfortable and familiar, just as it had been for years along the avenue since Constance had taken her airing as a child under the care of a smart nurse maid, in the open park, or aimlessly rolled her doll carriage from day to day. There was the old church where the élite worshiped God. There were the houses of her father's friends, their richly draped windows speaking eloquently of the luxurious life lived within, a life that had belonged to Constance ever since she could remember. It was easy to forget that there was such a thing as poverty. And yet, in the back of her mind was that strange sinking feeling that something dreadful had happened, but it gradually faded in the comfort of the moment.

Morris Thayer insisted on stopping at a florist's shop and purchasing an enormous bunch of violets; their fragrance fastened among her rich furs dispelled the last memory of a looming trouble. Then suddenly it was recalled to her in that sharp, quick way that trouble has when it is new, and there is a sensitive victim upon which to play.

"Well, I suppose you've heard about the Van Orden failure," said Morris Thayer in a comfortable tone as he retailed the last delicious bit of social gossip.

Constance felt a heavy load drift down upon her heart, and a sudden tie between herself and the Van Ordens whom she had never quite liked.

"They say the old man has all gone to pieces, had a stroke or something. Hard lines for Alice, I'll say, she's worked so hard to get a social footing. But it came just in time to save Harry Bishop. He thought he was marrying a great heiress."

"What do you mean, save him?" asked Constance

sharply, turning a face suddenly white toward him. "Aren't they engaged?"

"Oh, yes, engaged I guess, but that's not married. Harry will find an easy way out of it now, you may be sure. He's not the kind to let any one put anything over on him."

If Morris Thayer had not been so altogether satisfied with himself and his surroundings he might have noticed the sudden look of astonishment and pain that dawned in the eyes of the girl beside him, and the involuntary scorn that settled upon her lips as she turned her head away from him. That look might have given him the key to some things that happened afterwards. But he did not see and talked on.

Something seemed to have gripped Constance's soul. There came a great sinking of heart, and a whirling of her head again, as when the lawyer had first told her the astonishing news of their great loss.

Morris Thayer talked on, but she did not hear a word he said, and when he finally paused, she said suddenly:

"You think then, that a man has a right to desert his friends because they have lost their money?"

"Oh, not desert, of course," said Thayer lightly, "but he could scarcely be expected to marry her. The utopian days are past when such deeds were done."

Constance turned her gaze upon him suddenly, critically, with a new understanding of the smallness of his soul. Somehow his mouth seemed to have taken new lines of weakness since last she had looked at him, and there was something about his eyes that suggested lack of principle.

"I think," she said gravely, "that Alice Van Orden should surely be congratulated——"

"Congratulated? *Alice* congratulated? Why? I don't quite understand," said the young man in puzzled tones. "Why should she be congratulated?"

"That she has been saved," said Constance freezingly.

"Oh, has she indeed?" said Morris Thayer, quite misunderstanding. "Nice thing for her. Had a private fortune of her own, did she? Good thing to have. Glad you told me. I might have said something about his escape to Harry; and it would have been awkward, you know. Well, I always thought Alice Van Orden was a nice sort of girl, though I didn't know she was a great friend of yours."

"You don't understand me, Morris," said Constance, "I mean that Alice is to be congratulated that she has escaped marrying a man who simply cared for her money. She is not an intimate friend of mine and I know nothing of her affairs, but if I were in her place I'd be glad I'd escaped."

Then the car drew up before the old brown stone residence that was the scene of the afternoon's function and Morris Thayer was diverted from his puzzlement and said no more.

Constance was at once claimed by groups of welcoming friends. Thayer tried once or twice to get near her, but she seemed constantly surrounded, so he had to content himself by gazing at her from across the room.

He hovered near when she was leaving, and hoped to get another invitation to share the car with her; but she took an elderly woman away with her, with only a distant smile of absent-minded good night. It made him quite miserable. Somehow he felt that he had been given an unusual opportunity that afternoon, and not embraced it, though just what he had done to shut the door of the opportunity he could not have told.

The sun was slipping out of sight, and the many checkered windows in the tall buildings of the city's heart flashed into view in one magnificent conflagration, when Constance was at last alone. She had taken the elderly woman to a dinner appointment, having offered to do so in order to escape any further talk with Morris Thayer. Now she felt the sudden relief of being alone, followed by the quick grip of her new trouble on her consciousness. In the sweep of it all Morris Thayer was forgotten utterly. He would return to memory soon, and have a part in the general whole; but now he did not count for much.

Unutterable weariness seemed to be the most prominent thing in her mind, and a wall of blackness was settling about her, burnt through with those brilliant, burning windows that flashed at her from every building. She must get calm somehow, and try to think what she should do. What *could* she do? Oh, that she might just lie down and sink to sleep, forgetting it all! Her world was broken, and how could she longer live?

To be put into the same category with that vulgar Alice Van Orden, and to be pitied as she was being pitied, and called "a nice sort of girl," and have men discuss her, and say that some man had "been saved" from marrying her! How her soul revolted at the thought! How she despised people who could talk that way. How she longed to show them that she despised them, now, before it was too late! Now, while there was yet five thousand dollars between herself and poverty! Now, while no one suspected but that she was worth her plentiful fortune!

The car was at her own door. Mechanically she stepped out and stood a moment on the sidewalk, like one awaking out of sleep.

A tall young man with a suit-case came by. He looked at her out of the twilight, and she looked back at him, as two ships sight one another, come near for a moment in the lifting of a fog, and then pass on. His face gleamed white against the soft darkness, and there was something about his eyes that held her gaze for an instant. They seemed deeply earnest. It came to her that a man with a face like that would never turn away from one in any kind of trouble. Then the shadows of the street swallowed him and she went into the house alone.

There was nothing unrestful about the home into which she had come. There was quiet order everywhere and utmost plenty, though no gaudy display of luxury. Respectful attention to her wishes met her as she crossed the threshold, and struck her with a new pang that this, too, which had been so long a matter of course to her, was bought with money, and that now she would no longer be able to command it. She realized keenly what it would be to give it up.

A stately old lady with white hair and a placid face sat awaiting her in a great easy-chair, with a bit of fancy knitting in her fingers. A pang struck deep into Constance's heart. How would grandmother bear the new state of things?

They went down to dinner together, and sat through the courses, Constance eating little, her grandmother talking gentle society gossip mingled with reminiscences of the past. She did not go out much, except for a ride in the car on pleasant days; but she loved to hear about the old families, and questioned Constance about every detail of her afternoon. The girl held her breath once or twice lest her grandmother should discover her talk with the lawyer. It seemed as if that subject was a newly acquired wound that could not bear to be touched.

At last, coffee was over, and grandmother had gone to her room with her maid. Constance was free to put aside her mask and think. She went at once to her room. None too soon had she escaped, for Morris Thayer's card was brought to her within five minutes with a most urgent request that he might see her if possible for just a few minutes.

Constance almost groaned. It seemed as if she were pursued, and would never get a chance to be by herself and think.

"Tell him I have a headache, Susanne," she called from the couch where she had thrown herself, "and I have retired for the night." She pressed her throbbing temples with her cold finger tips, and felt momentarily glad for the headache that had excused her from going down.

She listened for the door to close and the echo of his footsteps on the pavement; but it was a moment before she heard them, and then Susanne came back, a great bunch of English violets, almost large enough for a pillow, in her hand. She gave her message, arranged the flowers on the table under the shaded light and went out.

The strong, subtle fragrance stole forth, as the donor had meant it should do, and tried to speak to the girl on the couch in his behalf. But the odor only irritated her. She did not wish to be reminded of him now. What he had said that afternoon seemed to put him outside

the circle of true friendship, and it only brought pain to
be reminded of him.

But, try as she would, instead of being able to consider what she ought to do in a practical way, her mind
was beset with angry, fruitless thoughts of what she
should like to say to such as he. Indignation towered
high. If he had stood before her now with his violets,
and offered them, she would have flung them back. The
sight of them was hateful to her; the thought of him had
become a disappointment.

She had never counted him a dear friend. Still, she
knew that he admired her, and she had enjoyed that admiration, for he was handsome and wealthy and popular. It was bitter now to think that as soon as he should
know of her changed circumstances his marked admiration would be withdrawn to a safe distance. Her pride
was touched. She wished she might do something so that
he need never know of her change of fortune, and yet
that she might always keep him at a distance. That would
be keen delight to her present excited mind.

The thought of his pity, spoken in the tone he had used
about the Van Orden girl, was hateful. His violets were
hateful. She would get rid of them. She took them from
the water, and, walking toward the window, half raised
the heavy sash to throw them out, then reflected that
some one might see them and think it strange; besides,
it would be a rude, unrefined action. She drew back, and
touched the bell instead.

"Ask Norah to come up a moment, if she is not too
busy," she said to the maid who presently appeared.
Norah was the Irish cook, and a great worshiper of her
young mistress. She came promptly, with expectant face
and willing heart, ready to perform any task asked of
her from an impromptu dinner party to a mustard
plaster.

Constance had turned the lights low and thrown herself upon the couch again, her pretty hair lying in soft
waves about her and trailing down the velvet covering.
Norah stood by the door, arms akimbo, and admired a
moment before she asked what she could do.

"Norah, how is that little brother of yours?" asked Constance. She had a way of always knowing about the inner life of her servants, and occasionally speaking with them about the things in which she knew they were interested.

Norah's lip quivered now in quick response to the sympathetic tone, and her eyes filled with tears.

"Oh, indade, Miss Constance, it's very kind of ye to ask. He's been rale bad this week. Oi can't abear to think on him when Oi'm about me work. Oi'm feared he's not long far this warld."

"Don't you want to go and see him this evening, Norah, and take him these violets from me?" said Constance.

It was better than if she had offered the girl a whole page of consolation from a book. There was quick response to the trouble in the tone of her voice, and the flowers touched a weak place in the warmhearted Irish girl's nature. She poured forth the story of her sorrow, how the doctor had said the little crippled child could not live long, and how she loved him and felt she could not live without him. Her tears flowed freely.

Constance found her own eyes wet, and felt like throwing her arms around Norah's neck and telling her own heartaches. She had a sudden wild desire for sympathy. Then she reflected that beside Norah's coming bereavement her sorrow ought not to be classed as sorrow at all. Nevertheless, it was not easy to bear.

She laid the flowers in the servant's hand, and said gently: "I wish I could help you, Norah. I am very much troubled myself about something, and it makes me long to help you."

With the quick excitability of her race Norah forgot her own sorrows, and flew to comfort her young mistress.

"Oh, Miss Constance," she cried eagerly, "is there anythin' Oi could do to help yez? Thrubble's not for the likes o' ye, Oi'm sure. Your purty oyes would be spoiled by the cryin', and then what would the young gentlemen say?"

But Norah had touched the wrong chord that time.

Constance sat up sharply on the couch where she had thrown herself again, and a red spot burned on each cheek.

"Norah, there are no young gentlemen in this whole world who have a right to care whether my eyes are spoiled by crying or not. Please don't ever say such a thing again."

"Oh, indade, Miss Constance, forgive me. Oi meant nothin' at all, sure. Oi couldn't but see how they all comes, and brings ye blossoms, and waits on ye; and wise they are, too, to pick ye out, so handsome and good and swate as ye are, and ye to stoop to care for a poor girl's little thrubbles. An' sure, Miss Constance, if yez'll only let me, Oi'll help ye in anythin' ye asks. Just thry me and see!"

The girl spoke earnestly, and just as earnestly Constance looked her in the eyes and answered:

"Perhaps the time will come, Norah, when I shall need your help, and I do not know of any one I shall turn to quicker. Yes, I mean it, Norah. You are a good girl."

The girl's face flushed with pleasure under the kind words, and she impulsively stooped and kissed the hem of the négligé that Constance wore, and then hurried out muttering blessings.

Chapter II

Two things Constance resolved upon after her night's vigil. One was that she would immediately and entirely stop all possible outgo of her finances; and the other was that she would at once go away somewhere and hide herself in the vast world, now while none but the old lawyer knew of her misfortunes. She would disappear and make a new life for herself, and none should ever know, to pity or to scorn.

Constance wondered if it were cowardly to run away. She thought not. She must at all costs keep her frail aristocratic grandmother from learning the truth. It would surely kill her. Besides Constance decided that there was no need of finding out which of her friends would fail her and which were true. Why put them to so severe a test? It would do no good to any one, and to escape it would be infinite relief to herself. She longed to begin life as if she were another girl, and to see whether she could not make of it something worth while.

Her career in this city of her birth was closed. She had been a success to a certain extent. She was popular, and was liked by many; and after all there was not much glory in it. All her laurels had been stolen ones, or, rather, reflected ones. They consisted of her grandfather's old name, her father's money, and a little personal beauty. Constance did not let that count for much. She never was a vain girl.

She understood that that, too, was a heritage left by her beautiful mother, except in so far as she might have

marred it or helped it by her own actions, thoughts, and feelings. Supposing she had been born into the Van Orden family. Would she have been a success there? Could she have carried her way through unrefined surroundings, failures, worldly pity and scorn, and come out with her face as calm and smooth as it now was? Or supposing that her life had been set so that she had been obliged to work in a mill, or clerk in a store? Would she have been a success there? Could she have gone through the endless days of such work and never have been cross like the weary-looking girl who sold her hairpins at the notion-counter the other day? Would she have kept a placid face, and left her mother's beauty unmarred by inward strife?

It was the first time in her life that Constance had ever examined herself in this way. She felt that she had to take account of stock, to find out what kind of person she had to deal with now that she was shorn of the respectable devices that the world puts around its own for the time being.

Having made these decisions, Constance, as was her wont in all things, set about carrying out her purposes.

The first thing that appeared in the morning for immediate action was a number of purchases made a day or two before. There were some books she had selected. There was a beautiful piece of embroidery she had bought for her dressing-table; there was a charming hat, a delightful forerunner of Easter millinery; and there was an evening gown.

She had congratulated herself on the choice of her purchases, and then had straightway forgotten them. Such things were too common in her life for them to matter much either way. She often ordered goods sent home on approval; and if, when they appeared, they suited her needs, she kept them. It was a common thing on her shopping-trips to pick up something pretty, and utterly unnecessary for her immediate use.

Even now, when the packages were opened by her maid, she thought little of them except for the passing curiosity to see whether the hat would be as becoming as she had thought when she bought it.

But, as she stepped in front of the glass to try on the hat, a card caught her attention. It was something new for the store where she had bought it to attach such cards to purchases sent home. Possibly good-natured forbearance was ceasing to be a virtue to them. But there hung the card reading clearly, "Not returnable if worn, or if this card has been detached." She had reached out her hand for the scissors to clip the thread, when her eye was arrested by the words and she paused. She had not expected to return the hat, for she liked it; but it occurred to her that it was unnecessary, and that this expense might be saved. She had thought the hat cheap when she bought it. Twenty-five dollars did not seem high for such a hat. She had often paid more. But four such hats represented a hundred dollars. Ten hundreds made a thousand, and only five poor little thousands between herself and poverty, and the scorn of her former world. The air seemed to swarm with dainty nothings of hats that menaced her peace, and she dropped it back into its box, and wrapped the tissue-paper folds about it hurriedly as if the sight of it troubled her.

"Tie it up, Susanne, and send it back," she said as she walked over to the gown that lay upon the foot of her couch, its sheeny folds taking delicate lights from the morning sun streaming in at the window.

"Oh, Miss Constance!" exclaimed Susanne in dismay. "Don't you like it? Just try it on; do. I'm sure it suits you nicely. It is a beautiful hat."

"Yes, Susanne, it's pretty; but I've changed my mind. They are all to go back. Tie them up, and see that they are sent back at once."

Susanne was disappointed. She delighted in assisting to robe her young mistress in these beautiful creations of dressmakers and milliners. No event of the week was pleasanter than when a delivery wagon arrived at the door with a new lot of lovely things. But she knew by the tone of Constance's voice that there was no use in arguing the matter. For some reason her young lady chose to scorn these purchases. Hers was but to obey. So with a sigh she put them all back in their wrappings.

As for Constance, she went gravely into the next room, and sat down to think. There were more things to be changed than she had reckoned upon. Every little item of her daily life must be dealt with, and that right speedily. She stepped to her desk, and glanced over the day's memoranda. There was an appointment with the dressmaker. She had put that down for the morning. The dress was to be finished in time for a dinner next week. But, if she was to make a change in her life, she would not need the dress nor the dinner. Ruthlessly the pencil crossed off that engagement. She would make no shopping-tour that morning. She reached for the telephone and called up the dressmaker. "I have changed my plans," said Constance, "and shall not need the dress at present." Then she went back to the memoranda.

Her pencil traveled down the list, crossing off everything that was not an absolute demand upon her time. She paused as she came to the last. It was the orchestra concert that evening. She always had the same pleasant seat for the season. She was a passionate lover of music. To be sure, the friends who shared the box were not those she would have chosen to be with under her present stress of mind; but that could not be helped, and if she wished to keep up appearances, it would be better to go straight ahead and appear in public as usual until she could slip out of this old world of hers altogether. That was the problem before her today—how to slip out, and where to slip to. It must be decided today. She would have no long delay. Maybe the music would help her to think, if no answer to the question came sooner.

So, leaving the evening engagement standing in her little book, she went down to breakfast.

But the answer was nearer at hand than she knew. On the breakfast table lay a pile of letters. Her grandmother was already reading the morning paper; and so Constance, looking over her mail, shoving aside society notes and bills, and recognizing at a glance the handwriting on several invitations, took up a letter in a hand that stirred her memory pleasantly. It was from a friend in Chicago, one whom she had known but a short time, and then but slightly, but one to whom she had taken a great fancy. She was surprised to get the letter as she had not expected the girl to write. She opened it with a flutter of anticipation. It was an invitation to her to visit the friend in her western home, and take part in a number of society functions that were being planned.

There was a spirit of real desire on the writer's part to have her come, and a freshness of eagerness that touched Constance. It was this in the other girl that had first drawn Constance toward her. A sudden impulse seized her to accept this invitation, and thus get away from her home, and make her plans, free from numberless little interruptions. Might she not even linger on the way in some quiet country place, and get a chance to think?

"Grandmother," she said, looking up impulsively, "I have an invitation to visit Marion Eastlake who was here last winter. Do you remember her? You said she had eyes like forget-me-nots."

"Oh, yes, I think I remember her," said grandmother, looking up with her gentle patrician smile. "Well, why don't you go, dear? It will do you good to have a bit of a change."

Constance breathed more freely when she saw how easy it was going to be to have this little thinking-time without being questioned. She wondered what her grandmother would think if she knew what was being contemplated. But now that her mind was made up she felt almost happy about it. There was an exhilaration in seeing something ahead besides the monotonous round of social functions. With a zest she had not known for a long time she set about her preparations, and all through the day her voice could be heard singing snatches of gay little songs.

She wrote her note of acceptance to Marion Eastlake and helped her maid pack. She had told her friend that she would start in a few days, naming the last of the week as the time of her arrival; but, as the trunks began to fill, and the noon mail brought in other wearisome invitations, the desire to be gone came upon her, and she resolved to leave home the next morning. There was no reason why she should not, and every reason why she should. She could take the journey slowly, stopping on the way if the fancy took her.

There was an old aunt, her father's eldest sister, who lived in a small village on the way. She told her grandmother that perhaps she would stop off and make a little visit; and the quiet old lady got into quite a flutter, preparing little messages and a delicate collar of real lace to send as a gift. Constance was almost sorry she had bound herself to this much, because, now that the desire to get away from things had come over her, she felt a great longing to go until she saw a place that attracted her, and then get off and stay there for a day or two. The thought of having a little adventure all by herself on the way excited her. She put it aside during dinner lest her face should show some sign that would betray her, but she need not have feared. Her grandmother was too much interested in telling over a time-worn tale of the Assembly ball the year she had come out and Constance had heard it too often to need to listen in order to make the right responses at the right time.

Now and then she stole a glance at the correct butler, who with impassive watchfulness stood sentinel behind her grandmother's chair. How shocked he would be, she thought, if he knew she was planning to break away from her world of dignity and tradition.

And all the while she answered her grandmother's gentle chat, and gave low orders to the butler, and wondered how it would seem to have no butler and no stately dinner served at precisely the right moment. Would she have to do the cooking herself?

She went to the concert, but she heard no symphony, for long before they had reached that part of the programme her rapid thoughts were hurrying on her journey, which she had now determined to begin on the morrow. The music became a sweet, dreamy, lulling sound that belonged to the world she was leaving. She would regret it, she knew, when it was gone; but now she felt impatient of it, of everything that kept her from taking some decided step and putting herself out of this awful dread of the future. She wanted to walk boldly up to that future and take it by the throat before it had opportunity to turn upon her and rend her.

Morris Thayer was there, of course. She had known he would be. But the chairs on either side of her were occupied. He could get no nearer than to lean across from the back of the box. She thanked him for the flowers in her usual pleasant manner; but he felt somehow that she was holding him at a distance once more. He watched her face to see whether he might read her thoughts as the grand chords of the music swept on; but he could make nothing of it. He marked her high-bred features, as he had done many times before, and each dainty and expensive detail of her toilet, and his soul rejoiced in her. There was no discount on her. Her grandfather and her bank account, as well as her taste and beauty, were all right. He would win her.

But Constance's thoughts were about the morrow and her journey.

At home again she spent half the night sitting at her desk, going over a number of little matters that had to be attended to before she went away; and, when she went to bed, everything was in readiness for her departure on the eight o'clock train in the morning.

This necessitated an unusually early breakfast; and Mrs. Wetherill did not come down, but bade her good-by in her room. Constance forced herself to swallow a few mouthfuls of breakfast, gave her orders to the dignified butler and maid, and almost gleefully drove to the station with the chauffeur. She felt that she was escaping everything—calls, flowers, parties, dinners, and all perplexing questions, albeit she was going out to face another more momentous than any of those could ever have been.

Chapter III

The train drew up with a dull "chug" of relief, like a lazy person who is thankful to lay down a burden even for a little while. It seemed to doze, and snort in its sleep.

Constance looked out from the window of the parlor car for relief from her perplexing problems.

She was almost sorry already that she had taken the journey; yet it had to be. What she had to do and decide could not be done at home, submerged as she was in an ocean of society. It was absolutely necessary for her to detach herself from the life she had been living if she hoped to accomplish the desired end of hiding the downfall of the family wealth.

She had been four hours on her way, and had reached no definite conclusions except the manner in which she would cut herself off from the world. That much she had determined. They would close the house in which they were living, indefinitely; rent it, perhaps, or sell it if the lawyer thought—ah! the lawyer had said that everything was gone except five thousand dollars! How she kept forgetting that! The house, too, was probably gone, then; sold already, or belonged to them only in name. But surely some way could be found to keep that from becoming apparent to the world. The lawyer would know how.

Yes, they would shut up the house and go away, traveling, supposedly, for grandmother's health, or her own— or both. Everybody went a-summering and often wandered away on a far western or European ramble, and no one thought it strange if they chose to stay a year. After a year was passed, who would remember to inquire more than casually, except perhaps a few personal friends who might easily be managed by evasion?

That part was plain enough. But it would be hard to make grandmother fall in with her plans.

Still, grandmother was not an overwhelming problem. She could be managed. She should be told that they were going to travel. Grandmother must know no more than that, or she would surely confide it to some of her dear old gossipy friends. It would take money to get away thus unnoticed, but they would have to invest five hundred or perhaps even a thousand of the precious five thousand dollars to get started somewhere else. Constance thought it would be well spent if it saved them from the ignominy and humiliation of being a family of fallen fortunes.

Morris Thayer's words were constantly in her mind, so that by this time the loss of her money had assumed enormous proportions. She shrank most painfully from facing it in her world. Everything must be sacrificed to escape that.

But having settled this much Constance could get no further. How were they to live elsewhere without touching their capital, after the borrowed thousand or so went? Was there any way in the wide world that she could earn money?

Her music? Horrors! No. To think of bringing down her high love for the old masters to the humdrum business of teaching stupid, unwilling little fingers to drum out exercises? Every nerve in her sensitive body quivered at the mere anticipation of the discord that would arise. She felt instantly that she was not cut out for that. No. She could never teach anything. She was certain of that.

She ran over the entire list of her accomplishments both pubic and private, and decided that they were all impossible. The life she had heretofore led would fit her to be an able assistant to some overburdened society woman, and she knew it; but her whole soul shrank pitiably from any such dependent position. She longed to be something worth while, something independent. Of course, there were typewriting and stenography, of which she knew nothing and could probably learn a little if she tried; and there was the ribbon counter in some department store; but from them all she shrank in turn, not from any contempt for the work, for she had begun in the last few hours to honor greatly the woman who earned her living in any respectable way, but somehow none of them appealed to her as being things she could do successfully. Her conservative, sheltered life had made her unfit to succeed in these ways.

So she turned with a sigh toward the window, and wondered where they were.

The place on which her eyes rested was full of greenness and beauty. There was a bit of an artificial lake, or possibly it was a natural pond, with a tiny island in the center which barely held a rustic summer house, built of the rough limbs of trees. But it was in a state of dilapidation, as if no one had cared for it in many a day, and the boys of the village had played there unmolested. Below its steps was an old boat half-filled with water, and a bird stood daintily on the bow and stooped to drink in the water below, which rippled out in a merry circle like a dimple in the laughing pond.

The grassy bank sloped up from the pond at the right toward an old house half-hidden in cedars. The house was of rough stone, and it looked as if it might have been a fine old home some time in the past. There were wide piazzas running across front and sides; but the posts of the piazzas were rotting away, and some of the shutters hung by one hinge. It had evidently been the country-place of some rich person who had been driven away by the railroad coming so near. The house stood perhaps three hundred feet away from the tracks, with a thick shelter of trees. An old broken beer sign on the way that led to the house suggested that an attempt had once been made to transform this place into a wayside inn; but for some reason it had failed, and above the beer sign there now hung one which said, "FOR SALE OR RENT CHEAP." But even this sign looked as if it had been there a good many years, and was likely to remain as many more.

Constance looked at it idly, and thought with a pang that here was another instance of the decline of fickle fortune. The old house and she were in the same case. She looked at it again half pityingly, and thought how beautiful it must have been there once, and how happy people with bright faces and gay clothing once used to go in and out and walk those piazzas and lawns. She wondered whether the young people on summer evenings used to saunter down the slope to the pond, and push the boat off in the moonlight, rowing toward the little summer-house and back again, or whether they ever skated there in winter. Constance's imagination was well developed. She would like to know the history of that house. It attracted her. Then she remembered that she had intended getting off somewhere, and she had not yet found the place that was more amusing than her own thoughts. Perhaps this would do as well as any, and it would be interesting to walk about that old place and find out all about it by questioning some one.

She glimpsed a small village where three roads met before the old house. A tiny stone church in the first fork, and in the other fork a row of dingy stores, not even a gaudy, up-to-date chain store among them. On the other side of the track were the station and a small fly-specked news-stand, with an alert little country trolley car waiting impatiently and contemptuously for the train to pass out of its way.

Finally the passengers concluded it was time to investigate, and stuck their heads out of the windows or sauntered down the aisle and stood on the platforms. Reference to the time-table gave Constance no clue to where she was. There seemed to be no such place on the schedule. Probably this train did not stop here ordinarily. Something must have happened.

The man in the chair opposite presently came in scowling and cursing all railroads for careless inefficiency. Constance gathered from his answers to excited fellow passengers that there was a double wreck a mile or so

ahead where another railroad's tracks crossed. Two
freight trains had collided and the tracks were a mass
of tangled wreckage.

The conductor came through just then announcing that
it would be an hour at least before they could get under
way again, for a derrick had to be sent from Chicago,
nearly forty miles away, before they could hope to clear
the tracks.

Constance, feeling rather blank, suddenly discovered
she was hungry. She had been too absorbed in her thoughts
at lunch time to bother to eat anything. Now would be
a good time to visit the diner. She started back through
the train, car after car. On and on she went. She had not
remembered the dining car had been so far away from her
car that morning. Suddenly she came to the last car and
looked out on the open tracks stretching away behind.

Puzzled, astonished, startled, she stood in the doorway and stared.

An interested sauntering youth, another waiting passenger, took advantage of her bewilderment.

" 'S mattah, girlie?" quoth he.

Without realizing his impudence for the moment, Constance gasped, "Why where's the diner?"

He laughed. "Dropped an hour ago, sistah. Had a hot
box. Guess they figuahed we'd be in Chi by dinnah time.
Sorry I haven't a chicken dinnah about me," he added
smartly, feeling in his pockets. "How about a cigarette?"

But Constance had fled. She made her way back to
her seat with flaming cheeks.

She began to realize that for the first time in her life
she was hungry and had nothing with which to satisfy
her hunger. She wondered vaguely whether this was an
omen of the future. Was she to know actual want?

Yet the new experience was so great a novelty, as to
be almost interesting. It pleased her to try to get out of
this situation. There must be a restaurant or a hotel in
the village. Now would be a good time to explore that
lovely estate, too. So Constance picked her way between
the train and the low picket fence surrounding the station-
house yard.

It was a most uninteresting village street upon which she presently emerged. Half a dozen loungers, black and white, stood about the station and the news-stand. As many more lounged on the steps of three uninviting stores, a cigar store and barber shop combined, a Chinese laundry, and a small general supply store. Finding no further promise in looking up the street in either direction, Constance timidly ventured into the general supply store.

A survey of the premises almost made her turn and flee. It was anything but clean, and the atmosphere was rank with tobacco smoke. But a man approached her indifferently, and asked what she would have.

"Is there any hotel or restaurant near here where I can get something to eat?" she asked.

"Not 't I know of," he responded, leaning back against a sugar barrel wearily, and pulling off a broom straw from a bundle of brooms which stood beside him. He looked his elegant visitor over carefully and critically. It was evident to the bystanders that he was in no way overawed by her. The storekeeper spoke as if the country round about were to him a vast, unexplored region which might hold many a vagrant hotel if one had but the time to look it up, but the man who half lay on the counter and the man who sat on another sugar barrel and the man behind the counter all grinned in open-mouthed amusement at the idea of a restaurant or hotel thereabouts.

"Is there no place where I can get something to eat? Not even a boarding house where they serve meals?"

"Not 't I know of," responded the astute storekeeper again.

"Well, can't I get something to eat here?" said Constance desperately, looking around in search of something promising. She was not one to be easily balked in a project.

"Well, I generally calc'late to keep a few things in that line. It's what I'm here for," he answered, biting off bits of the broom straw and keeping a sober face. "Just what was it you wanted?"

"Have you any——" Constance looked around wildly, appealing, as it were, to the cobwebby shelves, and searching her mind for any lore concerning grocery shopping. It had not been in her line. The housekeeper generally did all the ordering since grandmother gave it up.

"Have you any olives?" she said desperately.

The man settled back on the top of the sugar barrel again and folded his arms speculatively. "Olives!" he repeated meditatively; "olives!"—a long pause. "No, we don't have no call fer those. Got pickles."

"Well, perhaps pickles would do," said Constance, longing now only for an opportunity to get out of this dreadful store, and feeling somewhat under obligation to make a purchase. "What else have you?"

"Potatoes," said the resourceful storekeeper.

Constance looked puzzled. "Potatoes! Why, I couldn't cook those in a parlor car. But perhaps you mean Saratoga chips. They would be good." Her face brightened. She was getting hungrier every minute.

"No, we don't keep chips of any kind, but we got plenty of kindling wood."

Constance's face flamed. She felt sure the man was trying to insult her, and expected a loud guffaw from the back of the store; but beyond a broad grin on the face of the young clerk, who ducked down to hunt for something behind the counter, there was no sign of mirth. The other listeners did not fully comprehend the nature of the commodity discussed.

The clerk presently emerged from under the counter with a red and sober face, and suggested respectfully that they had crackers and cheese.

Constance turned to the young man hopefully and gratefully, and won his heart with a smile.

"Thank you!" she said heartily. "That is a good suggestion."

He came forward and assisted her further, until she had quite a collection of stale cakes, a glass of jelly, some baker's buns, some chipped beef, and a large red-cheeked apple. At last, with her arms full to overflowing, she stepped forth once more.

The young man held the door open for her, and watched her wistfully down the street. She was a part of the great world of better things for which he often had aspirations; the world of which his mother talked when she could take time from her hard work; the world to which she used to belong, long ago, before she was married. He recognized the indefinable stamp of culture and refinement. He watched her as she crossed the street, and noted the pretty curve of the high instep of her foot so daintily shod. Suddenly the skinny figure of a boy appeared as from nowhere. His wet sandy hair was slicked back from his freckled face.

"Kid, you run after that lady, and carry her bundles to any place she wants 'em, and I'll give you five cents and a stick of candy. Be quick, and don't you dare tell any of the kids I sent you."

The still damp swimming trunks were flung into a corner and the boy was off like a breeze. He was keen for a bargain; moreover, he scented another possible nickle from the stylish lady. He presented himself before the wondering Constance, who was already sorry that she had made so many purchases, and declared his intention of helping her.

She hesitated, not knowing whether to trust a strange boy or not; but he waited not for permission. His brother's word was law. He helped himself to the bottle of pickles that was fast finding its way from under her arm to the sidewalk; and then, as other bundles bade fair to follow, he caught at one or two. In the scramble they grew quite familiar, and she felt, when she was once more righted and ready to move onward, that she had gained a friend.

"Which way you goin'?" asked the young burden-bearer, shifting the gum in his mouth to the other cheek.

"Why, to the train, I suppose," said Constance, looking across wistfully to the old house. "There isn't any other place I could eat my lunch, is there? I hate to go back with such a lot of things. I don't know why I bought so many."

"Train!" said the boy on the alert at once for a sensation in the stupid little town. "Gosh! I did notice that train's been settin' there ever since I came up from the swimming hole! What's the big idea? Did they let you off to buy groceries for 'em all?"

Constance laughed in a carefree way as she had not laughed since her visit to the lawyer. She felt free as a bird out here in a strange village, with a strange little street child carrying her parcels and treating her with pleasant comradeship.

"I did buy enough for an army, didn't I? I didn't want any lunch but I am ravenously hungry now. When I found the dining-car had been dropped, I thought I had better stock up. I started out to find a hotel and get dinner."

"There ain't no hotel in this here town. I can tell ye that," said the boy knowingly.

As they crossed the street Constance pointed to the big stone house.

"Doesn't any one live in that old house over there?" she asked.

The boy followed her glance and his eyes grew large.

"Gosh, no!" he said.

"Why couldn't we go up there and have a picnic supper?" suggested Constance starting down the little path between the cedars. After a moment's hesitation the boy followed slowly. Constance was rather apprehensive as she thought of the strange thing she was doing. She was yet to discover how very strange it was to the mind of her escort.

Chapter IV

They reached the porch of the house in silence.

"There!" said the boy with a flourish, depositing his bundles on a wooden bench, and hastening foward to take the remainder she carried. "You sit there and eat yer grub."

He stood with folded arms, leaning against a piazza post, and Constance, a little uncertain of the situation, sat cautiously down, after wiping off the seat with a piece of paper that had wrapped the pickle-bottle. She looked furtively around, and was relieved to find that her refuge was entirely hidden from the street. Then she gave herself up to a few minutes' enjoyment of the unusual. She opened every package, and spread out everything she had bought, to the immense enjoyment of her companion, who commented upon each article.

"Say, them cakes is *dee*-lickety! Ever taste 'em before? I had a dime's worth once, and gingersnaps wasn't in it with 'em."

"Have one, do, to begin with," said Constance in childish delight, holding out the paper bag containing the delicacies. She wondered what the stately butler at home would say, could he see her now.

As they lunched together Constance began to notice the boy stealing puzzled wondering glances at her. He seemed nervous too, and would give a start at the slightest sound. She wondered at it but said nothing.

They grew quite friendly as the talk went on. He confided that his name was James Abercrombie Watts, but that she "needn't mind to use it." "Jest call me 'Kid'; it's what they all do," he added with a confiding wink that took her into the inner sanctuary of his confidence. "My brother, he works to the grocery, an' he don't never call me nothin' but 'Kid.' If it wasn't fer mother—she calls me 'Jimmy' yet—I'd forget I was anything but the Kid. 'Crazy Kid,' the fellers calls me. Say, was you ever here before?"

His mouth was full of good things, and Constance marveled at his capacity and the rapidity with which he was emptying the bench. For herself a very little of each article sufficed. The quality was not what she was accustomed to find on her home table. Nevertheless, she did quite well, considering the viands. On the other hand the boy was having the time of his life. Not even the pickles were too much for him, and he was rapidly lowering the bottle with no thought, apparently, of ceasing till he had completed his task. Constance wondered what kind of a stomach he possessed, but he seemed not in the least concerned about that.

Constance told him that she was on her way to Chicago, and had never had the pleasure of stopping in that town before.

"Then you don't know 'bout this here house." He relaxed as if that explained everything. "I thought first you did; you looked at it as if you did. This is the hanted house of Rushville."

He paused, and waited to see what effect his words would have, but Constance looked at him in bewilderment.

"What kind of a house did you say this was?" she asked.

"Hanted," he replied, "hanted. Don't you know what that means? It's a hanted house, has ghosts in it; don't you know? Didn't you never hear of a house being hanted with ghosts?"

"Oh," said Constance, trying not to laugh, "a haunted house. Yes, I know. Who haunts it?"

"Oh, a girl. And I guess she's about your size, too. My uncle seen her once when he was comin' home from work this way real late. She was down there by the pond a-rockin' in that there flat boat, an' her white lace dress an' gold hair all floatin' through the water round her, an' never gettin' wet a bit. She was singin' a pretty song, too; an' uncle said it made the tears come in his eyes, it was so sad. You see her lover, he got killed, an' she come here an' lived with her folks to try an' make her forget about it; but someway it didn't work, an' she made up her mind she'd die, too, 'cause he had, so she tried to drown herself in the pond; but that didn't work, nei- ther, 'cause the big dog they had pulled her out; and then after that she went upstairs to the attic, an' took poison. They say the dog felt so bad that he just lay round and whined till he died, too; so now she 'n' the dog, they come back and walk here every so often, and once in every little while somebody sees 'em, and it's got so that lots of folks won't come down to the station for the late train if they can help it, since M's Horner fainted away just hearin' her sing the time she come back from her daugh- ter's funeral out west."

"Oh, Jimmy, you don't believe all that stuff, now surely," said Constance when the voluble flow of words ceased for another pickle. "You're too bright a boy not to know better than to believe in ghosts in this age of the world."

Jimmy's face darkened. It was the village pet tradition. It had made his hair rise on end many a dark night. He and one or two other heroes like to tell daring tales of how they had trod the awful precincts of the haunted property alone upon occasion. It was not pleasant to have all this flouted, and by a girl with pretty clothes.

"Course I believe it," he responded darkly. "Didn't I tell you my uncle seen her once? And heaps of folks has seen her. She always comes in the dark o' the moon. Why, everybody round here knows it's true, and you can't get a soul to rent or buy this house. It's stood empty ever since she died, except when Si Barton started to keep a saloon over there; but he didn't stay but a month. One night when the men was all drinkin' hard, an' some was playin' cards in there round the tables, all of a sudden a white hand like a piece of mist off the swamp come up and turned every lamp in the room low, and then in she an' the dog come, walkin' slow's you please; an' they went all round the room, and thet there dog druv every man out'n that room; and Si Barton just stood there with his eyes bulged out, and never spoke a word till she got tired and went off, and when mornin' come he come to, an' picked up his things, and moved out, and pretty soon he up 'n' built them stores over there and now he keeps the drug store since prohibition won't let him have no saloon. Oh, there's plenty o' people seen her. This ain't no yarn I'm tellin' you, honest, 'tain't. It's *fierce,* I tell you, the way she scares folks. Lots of 'em see her every little while."

"Jimmy, did *you* ever see her?" asked Constance, laughing merrily. She was enjoying her companion immensely.

"No, ma'am, I never seen her myself; but I most did onct," and he sailed into a lengthy description of a time of which he had often boasted to the boys. The real foundation for it had been a terrible fright he had received by the vision of Mrs. Harkins's white cat from the station stealing across the sidewalk in front of him.

While this story was going on, Constance grew thoughtful. She did not give her attention quite so carefully to the details of the white lady who walked with her dog. An idea had struck her. Perhaps she had reached a partial solution of her destiny, even here in this little village.

"Jimmy," she said suddenly, rising and brushing the crumbs away, "show me the house, won't you? I'd like to go all through it. There's no danger that any one will see us and shoot me for the haunting lady, is there?"

Jimmy eyed her suspiciously. There was a hint of merriment in her voice that almost seemed as if it were directed at him. But she was smiling pleasantly at him, and her eyes looked kind. He arose and led the way to the broken shutter, and together they went through the old house. Jimmy crept in through the broken window and opened the front door on its rusty hinges, looking meanwhile fearfully behind him to be sure no haunting lady was following.

The large, old-fashioned hall opened in the center of the house. Thanks to the haunting lady, it had been kept from the marauding attacks to which most empty houses are subject. The wide, low staircase ran invitingly up to the second story, and with a square landing midway suggested a grandfather's clock. The paint was scratched, and the floor boards were warped; but the entrance was pleasant in spite of it all. On the right was the drawing-room, afterwards the barroom from all appearances, running the whole depth of the house and with windows of ample proportions on three sides. A high marble mantel and gilt-framed mirror was half-way down the side. It was the one bit of furnishing, if such it might be called, left to tell the tale of former grandeur.

"They say if you come in here with a candle at nightfall, an' look in that there lookin' glass," said Jimmy in a sepulchral whisper, "you kin always see her face lookin' over your shoulder, an' if you don't run quick away you can hear her dog barkin' an' patterin' down the stairs."

"How interesting!" said Constance. "Jimmy, did you ever try it?"

"Golly!" said Jimmy, aghast. "The' wouldn't any one dast to. You'd be paralyzed on the spot."

"Well, it's as good a spot as any to be paralyzed on, if you've got to be paralyzed, Jimmy," said Constance, laughing; "if I lived here, you and I would come in here and try it some evening, wouldn't we?"

Jimmy looked at his acquaintance with awe and admiration.

"Well, I reckon I'd try it if you would," he assented. "I ain't no coward, I ain't; you kin ask the fellers."

"Of course you're not, Jimmy. You wouldn't be afraid of a poor, sad lady who was made of nothing in the world but mist and imagination. But tell me, did you ever hear anyone say how much this house rented for?"

"No, I never," said Jimmy. "They ain't had no chance. I reckon they'd take what they could get. But you wouldn't want to rent it."

"Maybe," said Constance thoughtfully, with a little pucker of calculation on her brow. "What's on the other side of the hall? Two nice big rooms opening with double doors. That's convenient."

"Gee! but you're brave!" ejaculated Jimmy, following her through the two rooms and out into the kitchen and pantry beyond.

"Come upstairs," commanded Constance eagerly, not heeding him, for she had a purpose in view. She had beheld her vision of an angel in her block of stone.

"Yes, I'll go up ef you want to," said Jimmy, looking doubtfully up the wide stair. "My! don't your feet make a loud sound on these here steps?" but he let his lady precede him, and went up with eyes ever on the alert above him. He had never gone up these stairs before, even in daytime, in spite of his much boasted courage. It was reported to be in the attic that the lady had taken her poison. Timidly, and behind, walked Jimmy in ascending those stairs; but a few minutes after, having surveyed the four dusty, many-windowed rooms above, it was with high step and proud bearing that he descended. Had he not gone into the very heart of the haunted house, and even looked up the attic stairs, beholding nothing more formidable than a dusty sunbeam barring the way from an old oriel window above? Now he would indeed have something to boast of; and the pretty girl who had gone without shrinking through all these traditional horrors, was enshrined forever with Jimmy's list of heroes.

They skirted the house and walked down to the pond, surveying the premises thoroughly. Jimmy glanced proudly, defiantly, up at the attic windows from below, half fearful even yet lest he should see a misty form flit by and stoop to look at him.

They presently emerged from the blackness of the cedars into the sunny street; for Constance began, in spite of the conductor's assurances, to worry a little lest the train should go off and leave her. Not that it would matter so very much, for her handbag was with her, and her suit-case was in the care of the porter. Still, she did not wish to be left over night in this innless village, with nothing but the haunted house wherein to take refuge.

On the way back to the train Jimmy pointed out the church and the schoolhouse, and told her all about the church and the new minister that "preached to the kids" every other week, and was starting some kind of a society for them; and he avowed his intention of going to look on, but not to join. "No, sir-ee! You don't ketch this kid in no sech goody-goody pink-ice-cream traps as that!" he finished. "But he's a corker, that minister, he is!" he added. "Him an' you would jest about hit it. He ain't afraid o' nothin' any more'n you."

Then Jimmy's face brightened with more village gossip.

"Si Barton's talkin' about opening a restaurant next the drug store when they get the Junction here. He ain't got nothin' now but hot dogs an' sandridges and drinks— sometimes ice cream soda. You know when the Junction comes here then the trains would stop here—some of 'em most a half hour or so, and folks would get out like you today, and want a bite to eat. They say the Junction is coming real soon now."

Constance listened, smiled, and felt interested in spite of herself; why, she could not have told. Perhaps because it was so utterly new a world to her that everything seemed fresh. She remembered herself, the night before, amid the perfume and lights and dreamy music of the Symphony concert, and wondered that she could be the same. How was it that she was an interested listener to the hopes and plans and failures and successes of Rushville? She could not tell. She glanced curiously up at the dingy front of the brick building, noted its convenience to the station, and thought what a pity that an ex-saloon keeper should have the advantage of any trade that might come, when some decent person might make a good living out of a restaurant.

All at once Jimmy noticed the train still standing where it had been an hour ago.

"Gosh!" he ejaculated, "you never told me what's the matter with the train."

"Why," said Constance, "there was a big wreck of two

freight trains at the Crossing ahead. We had to wait for it to be cleared away."

"Golly! A wreck!" cried Jimmy in a stricken tone. It was the first village event of consequence he had missed in his whole life. How could he ever make up for the loss? "I gotta beat it!" he said anxiously, as if the wreck demanded his immediate attention.

"I'm sorry," said Constance sympathetically, "but I'm afraid it's too late for you to see it now. See, the passengers are boarding the train again. It must be all cleared away."

As she saw the look of real sorrow and bitter disappointment on the freckled face, she felt almost guilty.

"I'm sorry Jimmy," she said again. "I shouldn't have kept you."

With a brave effort he broke into a gallant smile. "Oh, 's' all right. I wouldn't a missed seeing you an' everything fer any old wreck."

Sudden softness came to Constance's eyes. She realized with real regret that she must bid good-by to her youthful attendant.

She had not known that there was so much of interest in just an ignorant little boy.

"Jimmy," she said, as she stood on the step of the parlor car, while he peered wonderingly into the mysterious luxury of its interior, "you're my friend now, and you must not forget me. Maybe I shall come back some day, and then I shall depend upon you to help me; may I?"

"You bet!" he responded fervently.

She gave him her address and wrote his down carefully on a card, putting it in her pocketbook and telling him that perhaps she would want to write to him sometime. "By the way, Jimmy," she added, as the conductor shouted, "All aboard," and the train gave a warning lurch, "find out for me, just for curiosity's sake, what that old haunted house rents for, or would rent for if anybody would rent it. Write and tell me all about it. Do you know where you can find out? I thought you could. Good-by."

Jimmy was left on the old station platform with a sil-

ver dollar in his hand and a dainty card bearing the name
of one of the most exclusive girls in New York society.
He gasped and swallowed a lump in his throat, as he
watched the train speed away, and caught the last flutter of the lace-bordered handkerchief. Then he turned
with the card in one hand, the dollar in the other, plunged
each in a shabby pocket as he walked off whistling down
the street trying to get his bearings. He felt that he was
not the same boy who had been playing marbles that
morning, and he was grateful beyond expression to his
brother for giving him this chance. He had had the time
of his life. Even though it had been at the awful expense
of missing a peach of a wreck. He sighed with pleasure as
he felt the smooth white card. It was almost as good as
the solid silver disk in the other hand.

Then he went off to devour what was left of excitement at the scene of the wreck and to boast to "the
fellers." His elder brother sadly lounged in the grocery
door and wondered what had become of the kid, and
why he didn't come back for his money and candy. He
wished with all his heart that something would send him
into the world where such girls lived as the one who had
visited the store that morning.

Constance leaned back in her luxurious chair, and
closed her eyes after Rushville was whirled out of her
sight. There was an undertone of eager excitement upon
her, and she wanted to cool down and settle her thoughts.
Had she, or had she not, found a clue to the solution
of the terrible problem that had troubled her ever since
her visit to the old lawyer? She hardly dared set her
thoughts in array, lest they should seem too audacious.

Mile after mile whirled by as the train rushed its mad
race to make up time, and Constance turned her new idea
upside down and inside out, and examined all the whys
and wherefores. Not all of them, either, for there were
many she did not know. There were questions that were
vital to her hopes which she did not consider at all, because she did not know enough to do so; but there were
enough things she did know to make her deeply serious.
She told herself she must go cautiously and consider each

step; but surely, surely, here in the old haunted house was a good place to hide for a season at least, with the possibility of making her grandmother comfortable without her ever discovering the change in their fortunes.

Meantime, whether it was within their means, or rather whether she could find any way of making any means for it to be within, was a question yet to be decided. The lack of any place in Rushville where a good meal could be secured had at least given Constance an idea which she would sift to the utmost before she dropped it. People had to eat. That would be one thing they would have to keep on doing as long as they lived, no matter whether their capital was five thousand or five hundred. They would have to have something to eat, and as long as that was possible they would try to have it palatable and nourishing. If they did that, why should not others share it and bring in a profit? Ah! daring thought for a girl of Constance Wetherill's traditions!

The train drew up at last at the quiet little station of the very small inland town where Aunt Susan lived; and Constance, weary, half sorry she had promised to stop, followed the porter from the train to the shackly little taxi that was to carry her to her aunt's with a wonder as to what new thing she would discover here. The taxi-driver slammed the door and started his engine. The train began slowly to puff its way from the station, the taxi gave a lurch, and racketed off over a humpy road to a little white house in a little quiet street, where most of the lights were out for the night, and no one looked out to wonder who had come.

Chapter V

It was a quaint white house, set far back from the street, with a neat brick pavement leading from the white gate. There were green blinds at every window, and they showed up dark in the night against the white of the house.

A lamp burned cheerfully in the front room, and the muslin curtains were not too thick to show the comfort of the room beyond. It was unlike anything Constance had ever come in personal contact with before, and she paused and asked the driver whether he was sure he had brought her to the right place.

"Yes, ma'am," he responded decidedly, swinging her luggage down from the front seat. "There ain't but one Miss Weth'rill in this part o' the country."

He preceded her up the walk, and knocked on the front door.

A quick shaft of light streamed out as the door opened hospitably.

It was a sweet-faced old lady with fine features and a motherly air who opened the door and stood with welcoming hands stretched out to greet her. She wore a neat brown dress with sleeves that dated back beyond Constance's memory of the fashions, and a quantity of soft white "wash illusion" in folds about her neck. Her gray hair was quaintly arranged, and she was altogether unique to her city-bred niece, though to the town in which she lived her appearance seemed not at all queer. There were many others like herself who lived and dressed as

was the fashion when they were girls, and never bothered
about the present mode. They wore a dress until it was
worn out, and when that happened, they got another one
as nearly like it as possible, even though it took more
trouble than to get a modern one, because they felt more
at ease in the plain garb. It was enough for the younger
portion of the community to trouble about the changing seasons.

Behind her aunt Constance saw another woman about
the same age, wearing a white apron.

Miss Wetherill took her niece's face between her two
transparent little hands, that made the girl think of rare,
old Dresden china, and kissed each cheek.

"Dear child, you've come at last!" she said. Then she
turned to the other woman, and said, "and this is Sarah
Ann."

Sarah Ann dropped a courtesy.

"Pleased to know you," said Sarah Ann stiffly, though
she looked kindly enough.

"Well, evenin', Mis' Weth'rill! Evenin', Sa' Ran!" said
the taxi-driver, and, slamming the front door, was off
into the night again.

Constance, bewildered, looked about her. She took it
all in, the pattern of the hall linoleum, white and gray
squares marked off with lines of black; the paper on the
wall, in imitation of granite blocks; the front room, and
its little high "center table" with spindling legs and red
cover stamped with black roses; the haircloth sofa, with
hollows where many had sat, and which yet looked so
inviting and well kept; the little haircloth rocking-chair
drawn up to the stand; the small basket with knitting-
work and the few neat books with faded covers. There
was an old steel engraving of the Last Supper hanging
over the mantelpiece. She noticed the ingrain carpet,
strong and sensible, and well preserved despite it ugli-
ness; she glimpsed the dining-room with its white cloth
and old blue and white china; caught a whiff of rasp-
berry jam and spicy gingerbread, mingled with the aroma
of coffee and perfectly fried potatoes. It seemed to her
that she was stepping into a page of a story of long ago,

when life was simple and there were no distressing problems to solve.

"Child, you look like your father when he was a boy." The old lady's voice recalled her to a very real present, and she looked down at the sweet little aunt with a pleased smile.

"Do I? I'm glad," she said, and stooped to kiss the sweet old face.

It was not till she was alone for the night in the little room upstairs, all white muslin, with the faint odor of lavender flowers, that she was able to collect her thoughts and realize that she was herself and this was a real house and a real life. It seemed so peaceful and quiet and out of the world. Her aunt had been sincerely glad to see her, all helpfulness and anxiety that her niece should be rested; but Constance felt that beneath it all there was something indefinable that was going to put her own life to the test, a new standard of living beside which she was not certain her own would shine. What was it? Aunt Susan had taken the large-print Testament from the high stand, read a short psalm, then knelt, and in her trembling sweet voice had thanked the Lord for the dear young soul that had come under their shelter for a little time, while "Sa' Ran" with dutifully folded hands listened and bowed her head over her lap.

Constance had heard of people to whom religion was a living, vital thing, influencing every action of their daily lives. She had never come into personal contact with any one who seemed to her to be moved by such springs of action. She wondered whether she were to have her first experience of this, and whether it were possible that any mere belief could make a monotonous life seem sweet and beautiful.

There was not much in the little white house to interest Constance. The mid-week prayer meeting was the one break of the quiet in which Aunt Susan lived. It was as much a duty as it was a pleasure, and severe must be the storm that would keep the old lady away. Constance was not asked whether she would go, but was taken in a quiet, matter-of-course way, just as it was announced to her that dinner was ready. It would have been no more of a surprise to Aunt Susan and Sa' Ran if she had declined to eat than it would have been for her to decline to go with them to the prayer meeting. She had opened her lips to refuse, but saw by her aunt's face that it would be a serious breach of the decorum of the house; so she was silent, and went upstairs to get ready, marveling what power it was that ruled the house. A little white satin ribbon hanging on the bureau bearing a printed Bible verse seemed to answer her as she turned on the light to adjust her hat.

"Let the peace of God rule in your hearts." She wondered vaguely whether it was this rule which made so quiet and peaceful a break in the previous hubbub and disappointing whirl of her life.

The prayer meeting was dull beyond expression. She had to stifle a yawn behind her glove. She wondered how Aunt Susan could have stood years of them when this, her first one, was so great a bore. She marveled once more when Aunt Susan in her prayer that night thanked her heavenly Father for "the precious meeting we have attended this evening," and asked that they all might make it a means of grace to them during the remainder of the week. What was it that made Aunt Susan feel so? Was it just that her life was so empty of all else that she could count a prayer meeting a pleasure? She could not be merely saying these things as a matter of form; her tones were too genuine, and the look on her face during the meeting had been too exalted, to be other than real.

There was much time for thought during the few days Constance spent with her aunt. Her whole mind and body seemed to be getting rested, and she was able to take up a question and think of it intelligently. Always the old house set among the dark cedars seemed to her a very possible refuge from her scorning world. Her imagination arrayed those large square rooms with costly rugs and bric-à-brac from the city home. She felt sure that her grandmother might be made happy there, and kept from any great knowledge of the state of their finances. The only point that troubled her was that same financial one. When the five thousand dollars should be exhausted—and she had no very definite idea how long it would last—how was she to earn more? Was that scheme of starting a tea room feasible at all? What did things cost? Would people buy in that little town? She wished she had asked more questions. Of course there were other towns where a tea room would succeed, but then there would not be such old houses everywhere with ghosts to make the rent cheap! Perhaps it was a wild scheme, but what if it was? It suited her, and she could see no possible harm in trying it.

She began to ask questions and open her eyes to little household economies. She noticed that people could dress in cotton and be just as happy as if they wore silk. At last she surprised Sa' Ran with a request that she would teach her how to make that lovely bread, and Sa' Ran, nothing loath, immediately set about her task.

If Constance had not been a most determined young woman, and also the possessor of good brains, she would not have learned so much in the few days she remained with her aunt. But she brought her modern city methods of dealing with things to bear upon bread-making, and the result was a store of knowledge that stood her in good stead later when she was ready to use it. She came to the kitchen armed with pencil and dainty tablet, and the pages that usually bore the names of society's great lights, and lists for dinners and parties, were made to tell amounts of yeast and flour and salt. Every detail Constance watched, and in her flowing hand wrote down Sa' Ran's characteristic description of the way the bread should look when it was ready to put in the pans.

The night before she started on her way once more, having prolonged her visit three days beyond what she had at first intended, she sat with her aunt Susan late into the night talking. The sweet old lady opened her heart to this niece, and told a little of her life story of love and hope and death, with its attendant loneliness and sorrow. The plain gold ring worn thin by the years, that gleamed on her tiny, satin-skinned hand, meant years of loyalty to a dead lover, and yet there were no lines of rebellion and fretfulness written on the smooth brow. There was a light of hope and heaven in the faded blue eyes, and Constance almost envied her aunt her life and its peace and surety of heaven. She lay awake long after her aunt had left her, thinking over the whole story, and wondering whether Morris Thayer would be worth being true to all those years. She decided that he would not, at least not to her.

Then step by step for the first time in her life she put plainly to herself what the future would be if spent with him. She knew that that was what he wanted. He had made it plain enough, but she had purposely been obtuse. She had not wanted to think of the matter before, and she did not wish to now, only that the sense of something lost made her wish to find out just how much it was she had lost. For she felt he was lost to her now as much as if she had announced to him that her property was gone and he had turned on his heel and told her he could then have nothing more to do with her. Perhaps she did him an injustice to feel so sure that he would turn away from her, but at least she felt certain that his talk in the car revealed more of his true character than she had hitherto allowed herself to confess. Or perhaps she had been blind in her luxury and ease.

Yes, if she should quietly let matters go their way, telling no one of the loss of her fortune, and marry him, there would be a fine wedding, quantities of presents, guests, and much society stir; and then there would be a fine establishment turned out by the hands of the latest decorators, in an unimpeachable part of the city, and a round of social engagements and dresses and trips to Europe; in fact, anything that anybody else had would be hers; all the things she had always had and the deference of her world. She would have a handsome husband who would be a credit to her wherever she went with him, and who would probably be good humored and indulgent, and bother her very little.

But her mind turned from the picture with a great weariness. There was nothing in it all to satisfy the longings that seemed to have been growing up within her during the last week. Just what those longings meant she did not understand. She only knew that life had suddenly become a more real, earnest thing to her than it had ever seemed before, and that there was a zest to each new day when she awoke, and a looking forward to new delightful sensations, which she could not remember feeling since she was a little girl.

There was something else, too. A sweet influence had touched her through Aunt Susan; a desire to have a peaceful brow, and to find out what it was that made disagreeable things bearable. When she got home—or when she got a home, she corrected herself—she would look into it. She would attend church services more regularly, and try to do good in some way, and see whether that would bring her any such halo of heavenly sweetness as seemed to rest continually upon her aunt's tranquil brow. She wondered whether all churches had prayer meetings. She felt sure they had no such service in the fashionable church which she attended, though they possibly called it something else. She would look up her prayer book and try to fasten her thoughts on religious ideas. She wished Lent were not over, that she might attend those special services, and give up something during the season of self-denial. Then she remembered again that her whole life now was to be one of self-denial, and she wondered whether possibly that would not work the desired effect upon her character. She would not even have the wherewithal to deny herself, but must do it anyway with everything possible, if she would live at all and have the bare necessities of life.

In a little book on her aunt's bureau she had read that God sometimes had to feed prosperity to some people in very small spoonfuls, because when they had everything they wanted they straightway forgot Him, and that loss and trouble were sometimes God's way of calling His own to Him. She wondered whether God could be calling her. Her aunt's gentle, wistful "God be with you, my child," when she had bade her good-night, stayed with her and strengthened this impression.

It was not Miss Wetherill's way to "talk religion" to

any one. She would not have known how, and her
quavering voice might have failed her; but she lived it
more than most people, and she had a way of taking it
for granted that every one else loved her Lord, and of
speaking to them of heavenly things in a quiet, everyday
sort of voice, as if they, too, were making heaven their
goal.

Altogether, Constance took her way into the world of
gayety again, feeling that she had had a glimpse into a
bit of heaven on earth. She almost dreaded contact with
the bright world, lest her newly awakened faculties should
be numbed. She half contemplated giving up her visit,
but thought better of it, remembering there might be letters awaiting her, and that her grandmother would be
astonished if she went home without going there at all.
She did not wish to arouse suspicion; so she went on.
Besides, there might be more to learn before her experiment was put into actual practice.

The home into which she stepped that evening was a
very different one from the quiet little white house she
had left. The building was massive and showy, a great
pile of masonry set in the midst of one of the most
fashionable semi-suburban localities. The evidences of
lavish spending of money were everywhere. There was
a daring about effects and colorings that pleased Constance's present state of mind, though she had been
brought up a conservative of the conservatives.

There was a fountain plashing in the center of the great
reception hall, and wide stairs ascended at the farther
end, turning at either side and going up to galleries
screened from below by fine Moorish carvings and lat-
ticed casement windows. The rooms opened off on either side, making the distance seem vast, and the extent
of the house almost illimitable. The thick Persian rugs,
the myriads of palms, the tinkling of the falling water,
the faint perfume of English violets from an immense
bowl of purple that stood on a pillar of the stairs, the
soft lights of stained glass from a costly window on the
first broad stair-landing, the glimpses of great paintings
and costly furnishings through the open doorways on

every hand, the vista of a great library with book-lined walls and many low, soft chairs in scarlet leather, the well-kept fire behind its bright brass fender—everything bespoke ease and luxury and lack of any need for care or thought.

The young girl who was the center of all this luxury, the one daughter and child of the house, around whom, and for whom, and by the will of whom everything moved, was a sweet, bright, gay little thing with a voice as fresh as a schoolboy's and eyes that had not yet grown weary of the world. Her face was like a wild rose, and her ways like a wild bird of the woods. She was willful and spoiled but charming. She did exactly as she pleased. It was a strange place to which to come for the purpose of studying how best to give up the world and live on the interest of five thousand dollars.

Constance looked about her, and almost shrank back; for here she recognized that which she had failed to put into her own equally luxurious life, a zest for everything. Could she go through this visit with its round of excitements, which she promptly foresaw, and not come out dispirited for the future that was so surely before her?

She had little time, however, to think about it. She was seized upon by her young hostess and carried off to the most bewildering delightful of rooms, scolded for not coming sooner, hugged and kissed for coming at all, and had poured upon her head a torrent of questions and a flood of plans for the days that were before them.

"There's a theater party, and a dance and supper tomorrow night, and a luncheon and dinner dance with a dear, stupid English lord, a real artist with a name, a cross old novelist, and three handsome men with unapproachable family trees for you to choose from. Isn't it just delightful you should be here at this time? There never were so many nice things going on at once, and all of them kind of unusual in some way, you know, not just common fun. The whole week is just full. Don't you love to have your days full? I do."

Constance sat and wondered at this girl who enjoyed everything in a fresh, frank, intense way. Did she never take anything calmly? What would she do if she were suddenly told her that she had lost everything but five thousand dollars? And then, quickly and quite at variance with her usual unimpulsive self, Constance asked her.

"You are a great child, Marion, but what would you do if you were poor?"

"Dear me!" said Marion, laughing with a ripple of dimples all round her mouth, "I would cry my eyes out for half a day, and then set to work to see what fun I could get out of it. Perhaps I'd learn typewriting, but I think that would be a bore. I'd rather be a clerk in a store. No, I think I wouldn't do anything very long at a time. I'd sell ribbons for a month, and then I'd go out to housework for another. I could be a lady's maid or a waitress beautifully; and anyway, when they discharged me, I'd try something else. I'd work in a mill awhile, and oh, I'd go to a hospital and be a nurse, too. There'd be lots of young doctors and one could have a thrill a day. And then, after I'd earned money enough to live on for a year, I'd rent a garret somewhere, and write a book about my experiences, and make my fortune. Then I'd buy this dear old house back again, and invite you to live with me, and we'd have a perfectly lovely time in it, just as we're going to have now!" and she clasped Constance in her arms, and whirled her around the room until they were both out of breath.

"You crazy child, I believe you would. I believe you'd have a good time out of anything you did," said Constance, smoothing back her rumpled hair and laughing.

That night Constance lay down to sleep with a perfect whirl of ideas in her head. Perhaps, after all, this pretty, flighty little girl would be a help to her. At least, she would have one more good time in the world before she went out of it into rural oblivion.

Chapter VI

Jimmy was writing a letter.

It was not his first letter; that had been brief and to the point, addressed to a trust company in Philadelphia. It read:

Deer Sire: Please tel me howe mutch you will reant your hanted propperty for. You ought to let it go cheep cause everyboddy is afrade to live there count uv the lady that hants it. But I aint afrade. Rite by return mail.

Goode bie.

James Abercrombie Watts.

That letter had been comparatively easy of achievement, but this second one was another matter entirely. It was to a lady, and one, he instinctively felt, of rare attainments. He wrote and rewrote, and tore up and wrote again. His fingers and face were smeared with ink, and his shocky tow hair had a long smear also where he had wiped his pen many times. But at last with a dissatisfied sigh he held the letter off complete, and scowled at it, concluding it was the best that he could do.

Not a soul had he told of his curious transaction. He had mailed his first letter the day after Constance left, having transcribed the address laboriously on the fence by the light of a street-lamp and with one eye looking up to the "For Rent" sign, while the other kept a furtive lookout for possible white ladies walking in the grass behind the house. He was afraid if he did it in the daytime he might be caught by some of "the fellers" and asked uncomfortable questions. Then he had mailed his letter and been promptly on hand at the arrival of every mail-train, not excepting one which came in an hour after his letter had started. He always put his important little freckled face and shock head before the postmaster's vision the minute the window was opened after each distribution of mail, and asked whether there was anything for James Abercrombie Watts. The postmaster got almost out of patience after the first six times, and told the boy to get out of the way, that if any letter came for him he would send him word; but Jimmy undaunted, appeared as promptly at the next mail. At last the letter came, and Jimmy retired to the sacred precincts of an old barn to read it, and then went home to write to "her."

Jimmy would have chuckled over his shrewdness, could he have looked into the Philadelphia office when his own letter was read.

"Here's somebody wants to rent that old house in Rushville," said one partner, tossing the letter over to the other. "Better let 'em have it cheap. It's some poor illiterate person; but, if you can get anybody to live there for a while till that fool notion about the house being haunted can be overcome, it may be sold to advantage. It's not worth keeping now."

The other man read the letter and tossed it back.

"All right; tell 'em they can have it for ten dollars a month if they pay in advance for a year. That'll keep 'em there, I guess. 'Tisn't likely they'll keep it after they find out the story about it, but, anyhow, that'll pay the taxes. Tell them they'll have to make their own repairs, though, if they want any."

And so the answer had come.

To Jimmy, ten dollars a month seemed a large sum. His mother, he knew, paid seven for the tiny place she lived in, and had hard work to get that paid; but that wasn't "haunted." He felt a little dubious as to whether his lady would think this cheap enough, considering the great drawback to the house; but there seemed to be nothing left to do but to report back to her. Accordingly he went to work, and in due time the letter was finished and posted, and Jimmy began once more his daily pilgrimages to the postoffice. Not that he was sure of getting another letter, for his lady had not promised to write, only asked him to do so. It might be she would never answer. It might be she had gone into the vast world again and he would never see her; but he hoped not, for he had boasted great things of her to the boys, and they had not believed. He wanted her to return and verify his statements. He wanted her, too, to come back for her own self, for there had been something about her that made him want to see her again. He did not understand it, but he felt it. He had a Sunday-school teacher once when he was a little fellow who made him feel that way, but she had died. Maybe this one would, too. Jimmy did not know, but he liked her.

So it was that one morning among other mail Constance received a funny little scrawled letter in a cheap blue envelope. It had gone to New York and had been forwarded to Chicago with others. Wondering she opened it. She had almost forgotten Jimmy, though she had by no means forgotten the old house among the cedars. But there had been so much to do since she reached Chicago that her plans had been put aside for a little. Now they all came back, and she felt that everything was being shaped for her just as she would like it.

My deer ladie: [it read]
I done what yoo tole me to. I rote the folks what owns the hanted howse and thay sed yoo cud hev it fer ten dolurs a munth an advanse. I hop yoo wunt thinck thet iss to mutch. I will sende yoo the fokes lettre soe yoo can reed it yoorselv. Ef yoo want to no ennythin alse tel me an I wil doe it for you. the wite lady aint ben seen by noe persone sence you wuz heer. I ges she wuz skerd ov yoo. I tole the felers yoo was brav. I hop yoo wil cum bak. them pise an cakes wuz delikity. Say yoo an me hed a reglar dandy piknik didunt we.

　　　　　　　　Yours truly,
　　　　　　　　James Abercrombie Watts
P.S. I lik yoo.

Over this letter Constance laughed and laughed till the tears came to her eyes. It took her some time to decipher it all; but during the reading of it the hour she had spent about the old house came back to her with renewed charm, and she felt that Jimmy had done her a service. She had found that the old house was possible even on a capital of five thousand dollars. Why, five years would cost only a few hundred dollars. Surely by that time she would have learned to earn her own living in some respectable way, and at least it was a good place in which to hide for the present distress. New York could not search her out, no, not even with the office of the agent who leased her the house in the heart of its business center. For the city trust knew no name save James Abercrombie Watts, and the idea had struck her that Jimmy should take out the lease and do all her business. There was no need that her name should be in it at all. Jimmy should be her real estate agent, as it were. Her eyes were bright with laughter and tears when Marion tapped at her door and entered.

"All the girls have fads," said Marion, fluttering a lot of letters before Constance's face. "Here's one girl that is bound we shall help her in private theatricals for her college-settlement work, and another wants me to make her a pillow for their fair, and another is bound I shall join her club. Marie Curtis goes in for golf, and there are two or three who rave over music and art, and talk a lot of stuff about the old masters that they don't understand themselves, I'm sure. They all have a fad, only just little me. What's yours, Constance?"

"Tea rooms!" responded Constance promptly, her eyes far away for the moment.

"Tea rooms!" said Marion, puzzled. "How funny! How do you do it? Are you collecting spoons or napkins from them, or what?"

"Why, I'm rather new at it," said Constance, enigmas in her eyes; "but I guess you just go around and see them, find out good ones, you know."

"Oh, I understand. You find out all the little quaint ones, and write down a description of them. I shouldn't think there would be much in it in this country. Over in Europe, now, there are plenty of them. But it's something new, at least. We've a whole afternoon to ourselves; suppose we try it. I'll order the car, and we'll go on a tour of investigation."

The idea struck Constance as a good one, and without further explanation, though with laughing eyes, she acquiesced. Thereafter it became known among Marion Eastlake's friends that Constance was making a study of Chicago tea rooms, and amid much laughter many pleasant little excursions were organized into various places where food was offered for sale in one form or another. Some of the girls were in danger of becoming sick from the number of fancy cakes, sandwiches, and sundaes they had sampled for Constance's benefit.

Through it all Constance was keeping her eyes open and really learning a few things.

But Chicago with all its attractions was no longer so full of interest for Constance as it had been. Her mind was teeming with plans, and the arrival of Jimmy's letter brought it all back again in full force that she was no longer a part of this world of fashion. So, in spite of Marion's pleadings, in spite of dinners and parties and engagements without number, Constance decided to go home.

When she had decided, it did not take her long to put her plans into operation. As suddenly as she had come she departed, leaving Marion lonely and disappointed. She was wonderfully fascinated by Constance, and had formed something more than an ordinary friendship for her. Moreover, she felt instinctively that there was something more to her than a mere society girl, and she longed to enter into the inner recesses of this choice spirit and share the fun, for fun Marion felt it would be. She was always looking out for fun. The beautiful part of it was that she generally made some fun out of everything she undertook, even though it was not planned for that purpose.

Constance had grown fond of Marion also, and it was with regret that she bade her good-by, in spite of her impatience to be again alone and perfect her plans for the future. She would have enjoyed telling all to this girl, and was sometimes tempted to do so; then, looking about on the luxurious apartments, she would remember that Marion was a part of the world she was leaving now, and not a soul of that world must know where she had gone or what had happened. For it might be that Marion, too, was influenced by wealth and station, unlikely as it seemed; and it would be better not to know it if Marion were likely to turn away from her when her money was gone.

As she left the beautiful mansion where she had spent two delightful weeks, Constance gave one glance about the lovely rooms. It was to her a farewell to all the pleasant, costly things that seem to make life one long picnic. She was going into a world of work and thought and perplexity. She went willingly enough, but she could not help a regret or two for the things of the life she was leaving.

Constance did some serious planning on the journey home. She could feel a great change in herself. The old life began to seem far away. Henceforth her sphere would be a humble one.

It was that same night after dinner that she began to set her plans in motion.

Grandmother was always in a good humor just after dinner, and nothing pleased her more than a nice long talk with Constance. She wanted to know all about Chicago, and Constance told her of the magnificence and the kindness and the largeness of everything. The old lady listened and exclaimed, and approved of some things, but thought that others showed far too much display to be in good taste, and finally Constance got around to the point toward which she had been aiming.

"Grandmother," she said in her most wheedling tone, "I want you to do something for me. I want it very much. Will you do it?"

"Why, of course, Connie; what is it?" said her grandmother, pleased as love always is to be wanted. "I always do what you ask, my dear. Do I not?"

"Of course you do, grandmother, and I know you're

going to do this. Well, I'll tell you about it. I want to close up this house and go traveling! Does that sound very dreadful?"

"Why, no, child, not the traveling part. I suppose that could be arranged all right. There are plenty of people who would be glad to have you with them, and you could go as well as not. But why close up the house, child? I'll stay right here as I always do. That'll be the best way."

"No, grandmother, that's not what I mean. I want you to go along. I don't want to be bundled off on anybody else. I want you and me to start out and have a good time together, and go just where we please without anything to hinder. Wouldn't you please go, grandmother? We could go easily, so that you wouldn't need to get tired, and I think you would enjoy it."

"Oh, child! I go traveling again at my time of life? I couldn't," said the grandmother, startled out of her usual calm decorum.

It took an hour and a half of eager argument and reasoning to convince Mrs. Wetherill that it would be good for her health to move out of her great elegant rooms, where peaceful regularity moved on money-oiled wheels. Constance almost despaired of winning the day without revealing the whole story; but at last the grandmother succumbed.

"Well, dear child, perhaps you're right. I suppose I should enjoy it some, though I've never felt any desire to go traipsing over the earth the way some people do; but I suppose you'll enjoy it, and it's very nice that you want me with you. Yes, I'll go. And now where is it you want to go? Abroad, of course. It's a number of years since I crossed the ocean. I'm not very fond of the water." Constance could see her wavering again. She flew to her side, and knelt down before her.

"No, indeed, you dear grandmother. I'm not going to drag you across the ocean. Europe's much too public for me. What I want is to find a lovely little quiet village, where, after we have traveled around some, we can take a house for a while and get away from all this rush of city life. It doesn't amount to a row of pins. I want to get rested and find out what life means."

"Dear child," said her grandmother, taking the girl's face between her fine, wrinkled hands with their rich fall of rare laces in the wrists. "Dear child," and her eyes searched Constance's face, "has something gone wrong with your heart? Has some one disappointed you? Isn't Morris Thayer—hasn't he—— I thought he was devotion itself. He kept calling after you left, and I'm sure I forwarded a letter or two in his handwriting. You haven't quarreled, have you?"

Constance was surprised that her quiet, unobserving grandmother had taken so much notice of her affairs. She had always been reticent about them, and her grandmother had never questioned nor seemed to notice. She flushed up guiltily, but laughed in answer.

"No, grandmother," she said; "that's not the matter. Morris Thayer and I do not quarrel; but yet—I don't know but I am a little disappointed in him, though it doesn't matter much, I'm sure. I want to get away from him and them all. I'm tired of the everlasting sameness of it. I want to do a lot of nice unconventional things that you can do when you're away from home, you know, grandmother."

The grandmother thought she understood that there had been a disagreement of some kind between the girl and her lover, and, deciding that perhaps the young man needed the lesson of a separation for a while, acquiesced without further comment.

At last Constance went to her room, satisfied that her grandmother suspected nothing and that she would make her no further trouble.

There was a large pile of correspondence awaiting her attention. She looked at it wearily. She had no taste now for all that had made her life heretofore. She wondered at herself that so soon she could be interested in other things. But a month before all her care had been to which dance she should go, and whom she would invite. Now she was entering with eagerness into a plan to get rid of it all. Would she be sorry by and by when it was too late and she could not come back to it?

For an instant she longed for the old, safe, easy life of gayety, with plenty of money to spend and no fear of ignominy in the future. But that could not be. She must go forward to a future with five thousand dollars as a capital, and that would be intolerable here. The precise, respectable little cousin who had stayed with her grandmother while she was away was a sample of what that would be. All her life this cousin had been hampered by too much respectability to save her from a monotony to which custom, her family, and a lack of funds had condemned her. Now, at fifty, she wore made-over dresses, and scrimped, and stayed with relatives to keep her hands white and useless as those of a member of her high-born family should be. "Poor Cousin Kate, of course she must be invited, she has so little pleasure," was what everybody said. Constance's pride never could endure a like humiliation. Her conquering courage swelled up to her aid once more, and she determined to make a new life with none to pity and none to make ashamed. She had yet to learn that there are worse things than pity, and deeper humiliations than mere lost prestige can give.

When she lay down to rest that night, her brain was swarming with plans, and there lay upon her desk a careful memorandum of things to be attended to at once. The well-ordered household slept calmly, all unknowing that the morrow was to be their undoing.

Chapter VII

She told them all in the morning, and there was deep sadness in the midst of the faithful servitors, for they loved their young mistress, and most of them had been in the family a number of years. There was no danger but that they could secure the best of positions elsewhere at what wages they desired, but there had come to be something more in their services than a mere exchange of work for wages. Norah, the cook, felt it most deeply. By night her eyes were swollen and her nose was red with weeping.

Constance was up at an early hour that morning, giving orders and writing notes. To all invitations she gave the same reply, to the effect that it would be impossible for her to accept, as she and her grandmother were going away for an extended trip. She went about the reception room, parlor, and library, pointing out pictures, bric-à-brac, and rugs to be packed, and giving directions about little details in each room that she thought the butler could look after. She had thought these things out carefully on her journey home from Chicago, else she could not have accomplished so much in one day. An experienced mover would have looked upon her planning with admiration. She directed the maid to set about packing Mrs. Wetherill's things at once, and the old lady got into a flutter of actual pleasure at the thought of going away.

Thomas was willing and handy in many ways. He was an adept in packing, as she had discovered more than

once when she sent off Christmas boxes, which always
arrived in good shape; so now she put him to work, and
saved the publicity of having professional packers. It had
been difficult to explain everything to the servants so that
they could help her properly without telling them too
much, but she had said that her grandmother and she
might be away longer than they knew, and it might be
considered advisable to let the house, in which case they
could send their goods to storage. In any event it was
as well to have valuables carefully packed. Thomas tried
to argue that they would be as safe unpacked, and the
house would thus be ready for occupancy in case they
suddenly decided to return; but he remembered he was
overstepping his bounds, and, sadly closing his mouth,
obeyed his mistress, his heart heavy that she was going
away.

Having set the ball a-rolling, Constance proceeded to
call upon the old lawyer.

It was not a protracted interview. Constance told him
briefly that she and her grandmother had decided to leave
the city almost immediately. He gathered the impression
from something she mentioned about an aunt, from
whose home she had just returned, that they were to go
on a visit. She asked him kindly to say nothing to any
who might inquire, except that they were traveling. She
mentioned that she thought her grandmother would be
better for a change of air and scene, and requested that
he breathe not a word of their change of fortune, either
to her grandmother or to any of their friends, as it was
quite unnecessary. He thought he understood that she
had other resources for money, and wished to keep this
loss quiet; so he readily promised to do as she asked, feeling thankful that this was not a case where he must have
his heart wrung with pity.

Constance arranged with him to dispose of the house,
what furniture she was leaving and several other small
effects she wished to sell, and to put two thousand dollars in the bank to her account, investing the remainder
of her small fortune to the best advantage he could.
Then, giving Aunt Susan's address as headquarters for

the near future, she bade him good morning, thanked him graciously, and departed. A great load was off her mind. He had not asked her what she was going to do, and of all the people who might find out her schemes and try to stop her she dreaded most the old lawyer who had been her father's firm friend, and was therefore not to be put aside easily.

It is marvelous what a difference a few hours' work can make in a home. When Constance returned from her ride, which had included a number of business calls—— most of them to cancel orders which had been previously given—she was surprised to find that the atmosphere of the home had departed, and that in its place was a bare expectancy of what would happen next. It made her heart sick, and she half longed to put everything back in its place again. She was only deterred by the knowledge that it could not be for long in any event as five thousand dollars could carry on that establishment only a very short time.

She noticed a furtive, frightened look on her grandmother's face all the time she was eating her dinner. The familiar pictures were gone from the dining-room walls, and the sideboard was bare of handsome silver that usually stood there. The curtains had been taken down, and only inside blinds kept out the world. Constance resolved to urge Mrs. Wetherill to remain in her own room for meals, and to keep that apartment nearly like its natural self for her as long as possible. She saw that it was hard on her grandmother, and she wished with all her soul that there might be some other way.

It was not be be expected that a girl of Constance's standing could slip out of the world in a moment and unobserved. So soon as her notes had reached their destination there began a flood of regrets. Some came in the mail, protesting against this sudden decision before the season was entirely over; others were made in person, and the street in front of the fine old brownstone mansion was hardly ever without a car standing there. There was much mourning among her intimate friends at her departure from their midst, and the genuine in-

terest manifested roused in Constance a doubt as to
whether she had been altogether right in supposing most
of her friends would have deserted her, or relegated her
to the place in their affections belonging to cast-off articles that had been prized in their time, but were out of
date. It was quite possible that a few of them would have
retained the same feling for her, although she knew that
with their standards that feeling must of necessity be mingled somewhat with pity, and from pity she recoiled as
from a serpent. It is only the meek spirit that has been
through chastening that can receive pity graciously.

She felt it a fortunate thing that just at this time Morris
Thayer should have accompanied his mother and sister
to Palm Beach for a few games of spring golf in the
balmy atmosphere of the South. It is quite possible that,
if he had not been made to understand that Constance
intended remaining in Chicago for at least a fortnight
longer, he would not have taken himself so far away from
New York. But, interrupted in his courtship, he was
doing his best to pass away the time until her return, feeling sure that he would have even better chances when
he came back. He had begun to feel that he had shown
his deep interest in Constance altogether too soon, and
it would be as well for her to see less of him and to feel
that she was not so sure of him. She would then, he ar-
gued, be wondering where he was, and be glad to see him
when he came.

Constance felt slightly piqued when she discovered that
he had gone so far away, though much relieved that she
would not have him to face and answer. All the more
she set herself to get away quickly out of his reach. He
should find her irrevocably gone when he returned. To
this end she hired extra helpers, and pushed her preparations with a vigor that her friends considered wholly
unnecessary. One of those friends was also a friend of
Sarah Thayer, and happened to mention in writing to
her the intended departure of the Wetherills on an extended trip.

It came to the ears of Morris Thayer in a short space
of time; and, much annoyed that a slight illness and a

determined stubbornness on the part of his mother made an immediate return to New York an impossibility, he set himself down and framed an expensive telegram suggesting that, as he heard she was contemplating a trip of some sort, Palm Beach was the very place, and they were all eager for her coming.

Her response to this was a polite note thanking him for his interest, and stating that it was quite possible that they might travel south before they had finished their wanderings, but that for the present they were going west to the home of a relative. This note was adapted to keep Morris Thayer in a more or less restless state of expectation and to prolong his stay in the land of flowers, which was exactly what the writer had intended.

His telegram had come to her at a moment when her heart had been experiencing a sudden wrench over the giving up of certain things in her life, which, though comparatively small, were hard to relinquish. There came to her a temptation to take the attentions he was offering for what they seemed to be worth, and accept the life of ease he would give her. The attention of the telegram and the evident desire for her company had touched her. It was hard to give up old companions, old ways, old delights, and start out into the world again as if she had just been born into it. Therefore she hastened to be gone, that she should have no further temptation to remain where she was.

In these days a vigorous correspondence with Jimmy was kept up. He was instructed to write at once to the trust company who owned the haunted property and to say that he would take the house. He was by no means to mention Constance's name in the matter, and he was to promise to pay a year's rent in advance at the beginning of next month. She told Jimmy that hereafter he was to be her agent, and that she intended rewarding him for his services in the matter when she came, which would be shortly before the time when the money would need to be paid. She would then give him the money and instruct him how to forward it to the trust company.

Jimmy, vastly important in his new office, went about

with frowning brows, and would not be gainsaid by any of the other "fellers." He intimated that he was growing up and had important business when asked about his inky fingers, and he frequently took walks in the neighborhood of the haunted house, and looked toward its cedar-surrounded piazzas with almost the satisfaction of an owner.

In due time Jimmy was instructed to select a painter, and ask him to go through the old house and make an estimate for painting and papering. Meantime Constance was hard at work with the help of her faithful servitors.

The day after her return from Chicago Norah had presented herself to Constance, her eyes red with weeping.

"He's dead," she sobbed, "me darlint is dead. No ma'am, Oi didn't sind ye no word, ma'am, 'cause I knew ye was busy, an' Oi wouldn't throuble yez. But Oi want ye to know what a coomfort he took wid the floo'ers, an' th' ooranges. He called yez 'the purty leddy.' An' now, Miss Constance, he's gone, an' Oi've no call to stay home. Oi come to say as how, ef ye'd hev me fer a maid, Oi'd come wid yez meself. Oi don't know nothin' yit but the cookin', but Oi'll learn, Miss Connie, Oi will fer sure, joost to stay by yez."

Constance smiled. She wondered whether this were another link that seemed to be arranged for her new life. Some thought of this very thing had come to her, for Norah was the only one of the old servants who seemed in the least suited to life in Rushville. And yet it had only been a passing thought.

She told Norah she would see, that they were going to the home of a relative for a few weeks, and she would think about it while there, and perhaps send for her. She gladdened the heart of the sorrowful girl by whispering just as she left: "I have a scheme, Norah, and I may want you to help me carry it out. I think I shall send for you pretty soon; as soon as I get grandmother quietly settled somewhere for a few days. Will you help me, Norah, if I need you? Promise me."

Most willingly the girl promised, and looked after the

departing train with a lighter heart and a more hopeful countenance.

Then Constance set to work to make her grandmother have a good time. She pointed out places of interest on the way and talked in her most winning manner, until the old lady fell into a delightful nap. She suggested lunch, and had it brought in just at the right minute; and in short the day moved so delightfully that the old lady did not feel weary nor look back longingly to her home.

Constance had arranged to stop about five o'clock that evening at a hotel in the mountains which in summer time was usually filled with guests, but at this season of the year was almost empty. She had thought the quiet would be restful for her grandmother, and would be not too severe a change from the monotonous days in her own luxurious rooms in the city. And so it proved. Mrs. Wetherill sat for a little while on the lonely piazza with Constance and the maid, and looked out over the mountain where soft greens were beginning to show. She watched the sun slip away across the valleys and dip behind another mountain, and declared she would like to stay there awhile, and was glad she had come. Chill though the evening mountain air was, she was well wrapped, and it seemed to do her great good.

They stayed there a day and Constance tried to get better acquainted with her grandmother, and find out if possible how best to save her from the trouble which might come to her with any possible knowledge of their losses. She sat a long time one day, and told of everything that had occurred during her brief visit to her Aunt Susan, even speaking of the evening worship and the regular prayer meeting. The old lady's face was soft and sweet. She made not much comment as she heard the details of this other woman's life, so different from hers, but Constance could see that she was interested in it all; and, when she had finished about the prayer meeting, and the last little talk with her aunt the night before she left, her grandmother said:

"Susan always was a good woman. She had a sad life, but it does not seem to have hurt her."

And so Constance dared to suggest that her grandmother should visit there, and, contrary to her fears, Mrs.
Wetherill appeared much pleased with the idea. Everything seemed working out in the way she had hoped, and
the next day they took up their journey again, this time
with Aunt Susan's little white house in view. Constance
had prepared the way for this by a letter and a telegram
to her aunt, which had been cordially responded to; for
Aunt Susan had begged them to come to her many times
before.

Constance found awaiting her there a number of letters, some of which pleased her and some of which she
frowned upon. It would seem that her world was not
going to drop her so suddenly after all. There were even
a few invitations begging her to join certain parties who
were starting off hither and thither. It was not so easy
to get out of the world as she had thought. But after two
or three days spent at Aunt Susan's, Constance was able
to slip away on the pretext of visiting for a short time
a friend whom she had promised not to pass by, leaving
her grandmother happily ensconced on the other side
of Aunt Susan's red felt table-cover, the glass lamp casting its impartial light alike upon the plain knitting of
Aunt Susan and the fine embroidery of Grandmother
Wetherill.

The friend she was going to see was Jimmy, and her
destination was Rushville. Moreover, she had written to
Norah, and expected her to arrive in Rushville an hour
after her own train reached there.

Chapter VIII

Constance felt as if she were going to a picnic on the sly as the train drew near Rushville. Many times had she gone over the details of what she would do when she reached there once more, and now everything was planned as carefully as could be. She watched the names of the stations on her time-table, and thought the train dragged slowly along. What if Norah should fail to get off at the right place, or Jimmy should go off to a game of marbles and forget her? How should she ever get things into shape by night without these two, especially if the rest of the inhabitants of that peculiar town proved to be as stupid as the ones she had found in the grocery?

But Jimmy was not playing marbles. No, indeed! He had been at the station for an hour when the train finally drew in. He had scowled at the old clock, which did not go, upon the waiting-room wall, a dozen times, and had asked the station-agent and his assistant three times whether they were sure the western train was on time, and then had marched importantly up and down the platform again.

They went into the station, Jimmy and Constance, and sat down to have a brief interview. Jimmy showed her the letter he had prepared according to her instructions to accompany the money which she had brought with her. Then they called at the post office and astonished the postmaster by sending so large a money order, for of course he knew nothing about the house being taken in Jimmy's name. This business finished, Constance went with Jimmy to see the house. He exhibited it to her with the air of a caretaker, and took pride in showing her the new greenness that had come upon everything about the grounds.

He had, through much maneuvering, brought the painter there to meet her, and the man stood in the front hall, squinting up at the ceiling, occasionally measuring a window frame, and figuring on an old envelope. He turned and gave Constance a comprehensive stare; but, when he saw that she could talk business, he felt that she was all right, and let her understand that he did not always charge such low prices; but, "seeing it's you," he would be reasonable.

He was a paperhanger as well as a painter, and the business of renovating the old house went forward briskly. The paper bought in New York had been sent on some days before and Jimmy had proudly received it and deposited it by installments in one of the closets that would lock. Somehow, the ghostly lady had ceased to frighten Jimmy since he had a sort of partnership in the house. It is true he usually made his visits there in broad daylight, and was careful never to go upstairs; but he did not dread the first glance about in the still, empty rooms as he used to before his lady's coming.

Constance opened her bundles of paper, and exhibited them to Jimmy and the painter. The painter looked at them critically, but finally expressed grim approval. The patterns, he said, were not altogether what he would have chosen, not all of them; but they would do very well, and some might look better than he thought when they were put on. But Jimmy opened his eyes wide, and whistled, and expressed unalloyed approval. He looked about on the scarred walls almost reverently to think they were to be so decked out, and swelled his chest proudly as he walked back to the station, the arrangements with the painter having been completed.

They went back to meet Norah, and Norah arrived according to promise, her arms laden with bundles and her face shining with expectation above the cheap black clothes she wore.

Jimmy took several of her packages, and went ahead; and they all went to the house. The painter soon after departed, promising to return and begin work in the morning.

Jimmy put down the bundles on the piazza, and, giving an extra brush to the already well-dusted bench, seated his ladies, and retired to a little distance until further orders. He felt instinctively that they would wish to consult alone.

"Norah," Constance began, "I am going to take you into my confidence, and tell you something that I have not told another person in the world. Nobody knows anything about it except our old lawyer."

Norah's face beamed with expectation, and she sat back prepared for an elopement at least, and at once saw herself chief assistant. It was therefore somewhat of a disappointment to her sentimental nature to find that the story ran in more prosaic lines. She listened with dismay to the few brief sentences that told of the change in the Wetherill wealth, and then her quick Irish sympathy came to the front.

"Och, an' you a sendin' me brither the grapes an' the flo'ers an' thim good things, an' spendin' the money you should have ben savin' fer yersilf, Miss Constance! Oi'll niver forgit it, niver! Oi'll work for ye all the days of me loife widout a cint's worth of wages, an' coont it a plizure, that Oi will!"

Norah spoke with fervor, while the tears rolled down her cheeks, and Constance knew that she was a staunch friend.

"I believe it," she said, laying her hand kindly on the rough one, "and that is why I sent for you. I'm going into business, Norah, and I want you for a partner. But you're not to work without wages, not a bit of it. I'm not sure but they will have to be small for a while till I get started; but you shall have all I can give you, and if I succeed—and I believe I shall—I'll make sure that they are good wages. And now listen, for there is a great deal to be done this afternoon, and we must not waste time. Nobody else knows anything about this, remem-

ber, and I don't intend they shall; so you must not tell
a soul about it in your letters. Don't say anything about
our change of fortune, or what we are doing. I do not
want one of my old friends to suspect it, or even to know
where I am. You and I must even keep grandmother from
finding out, if possible. I'm not sure whether we can, but
we'll try. And now, Norah, I've rented this house, and
I'm going to keep a tea room. Will you do the cooking?"

"Shure!" said Norah, delighted to find her part so easy.

Norah was one of the sort of whom it is said,

> Theirs not to reason why,
> Theirs not to make reply,
> Theirs but to do and die;

and so, when Constance added:

"That's right! I knew you would stand by me, Norah.
Now come and I'll show you the house." She arose with
shining eyes and followed, asking no questions. They
would come later, perhaps, but for the present she knew
only this, that she was with her young mistress in all she
cared to do.

When they were through with the survey, and Constance stood talking with Jimmy about arranging to have
some of the furniture from the carload which had arrived brought up to the house that afternoon, Norah retired to the seclusion of the kitchen, which was her
rightful sphere, and wept into her handkerchief. For,
while she was with her mistress in all she might choose
to do, her heart ached at the thought of the beautiful
girl brought low amid surroundings that ill befitted her;
for the smeared walls and cracked plaster of the old house
seemed to her unredeemable. However, she rallied and
wiped her eyes in time to answer her mistress's call.

"Of course we can sleep here tonight; can't we Norah?"

"Shure!" said Norah, hastily mopping up and taking
a quick survey of her premises. "Oi've brought the clean-
in' rags an' things yez wrote me aboot. That range looks
as though it was a sulky thing, but Oi'll deal wid it.
Jimmy, me bye, thur's a store here, ain't thur? Well, hus-

tle yoursilf, an' git me some wood an' coal! That's a dear!
Oi'll dance at yer weddin', Oi will. An' mind ye hurry!
Oi'll nade hut water an' a bucket; git a bucket, bye, an'
a brum, don't forgit."

Jimmy nodded from far down the walk to the gate,
going on fleet feet to do her bidding, but his soul was
marveling over two women who were not afraid to sleep
in that haunted empty house on that first night. He must
not permit it, of course, as he was their rightful protector, but how was he to help it? That was the question.

Meantime, Norah had quickly doffed her black garments, and arrayed herself in gingham, covered by a big
apron. Fortunately there was running water in the house.
The two women did not know, when they fretted over
the poor, old-fashioned plumbing, how much better it
was than an old reluctant pump, which might have been
their lot.

Jimmy was back in a short time with the broom and
bucket, followed by a boy with a load of kindling wood
and a bushel of coal. Jimmy had confided somewhat in
his brother, though he had not revealed his own intimate
connection with the matter. The brother knew only that
there were some new folks moving into the old haunted
house, and that they had asked Jimmy to run errands
for them. He was curious, of course, to see what kind
of people would take the haunted house, and every one
in the sleepy little store was on the alert to serve; for there
was a rival store at the other end of town. Therefore the
young clerk came himself with his orderbook, and went
away in a tumult of pleasure that the pretty girl had come
back to town, but he sealed his lips close about the matter. He had no mind to have her first visit to the store
recalled by any of the old loungers.

Constance, mindful of her first difficulties in finding
anything to eat in Rushville, had allowed Sa' Ran to put
up for her a bountiful lunch, and Sa' Ran always put up
about five times as much for a lunch as any reasonable
being could possibly eat; so there was plenty for Norah,
as well as a goodly share for Jimmy, who didn't go home
the rest of that day. It was two o'clock when Norah ar-

rived, and by three the fire was under way and the three sat down on the bench on the piazza for a hasty lunch. Like magic did Sa' Ran's puffy raised biscuit, pressed chicken, damson plum preserves, and doughnuts disappear; and yet there was enough left for supper, besides fruit cake and gingerbread. The air, though decidedly springy, was still chilly, and they found it necessary to stir about if they would not take cold; so as soon as the lunch-box was closed again they all set to work. Norah would not permit Constance to soil her white hands by putting them into the water.

"There's no sinse in it at all," she said. "Oi'm able to do all as is necessary this night, an' there's plenty fer the loikes av yez. Just ye git down to the railroad, an' till that man to brang up the foorniture. We'll be all clane fer tonight. Oi'll just wash aff the sink here, an' a bit about the floor, an' then Oi'll make ye a bedroom fit fer a quane, ef soap an' water kin do it." And she went vigorously to work.

So Constance and Jimmy went to find the inert drayman, who was not intending to get any of the goods from the freight car moved that afternoon, in spite of his many promises to Jimmy. He had other things which pleased him more to attend to; and, if he moved the furniture this afternoon, it would be necessary for himself to put a shoulder to the work. This he did not like, preferring rather to sit in his office with his feet high above his head and converse with whoever might drop in, while he steadily chewed tobacco.

But the sight of Constance, and her insistence, finally moved him to bestir himself; and a little before six o'clock a meager one-horse load struggled through the gateway into the yard, and wound its way to the back door. It was not to be expected that affairs would go just as they ought, and it was like the perversity of such things that some of the articles which were brought in this first load should be a box of bric-à-brac, and several fine old paintings in their crates.

"Now how convanient!" said Norah, peering between the slats of a picture-crate, and discovering two large lazy cows grazing on a meadow bank. "It was noice av the man to brang thot. We can't ate it, nor slape it, but we moight milk the cows."

Constance sat down on a packing-box, and laughed until she cried. There were phases about this new life that were refreshing. She could not remember laughing like that since she was a little girl in school. There was a pleasant comradeship in these two, this uncultured girl and wild little boy, that made her forget all she had left behind her. With that laugh she seemed to drop her old life and throw herself with zest into the new one.

The load was not all painted cows. There were a kitchen table and a box of bedclothing, a barrel of dishes, a leather couch, three or four chairs, and a mattress.

Norah scrubbed, and kept up a stream of Irish wit, and Jimmy was everywhere with eyes and hands and feet alert. Constance sat down upon the leather couch, which Norah had elected should be her bed for that night, and which was placed in the center of an island of cleanliness where Norah had scrubbed carefully. A piece of carpet which Constance recognized as belonging to the back upper hall in the old home was spread out in front of the couch, and a chair was drawn conveniently near for a dressing-table. It was all exceedingly primitive and inconvenient, and the girl wondered, as she looked upon it, why she felt such intense satisfaction in it all when it was so marked a contrast to her old luxurious room with its elegant appointments.

She unpacked her little hand-bag, laid brushes and combs upon the chair, threw her kimono over the back of it, then lay back for one moment upon the couch and closed her eyes. She felt thankful to somebody or something, she did not quite know what.

Then she bestirred herself once more. There must be a carpenter brought to fix the window so it would lock. Jimmy must get one. She went downstairs to call him, and to tell Norah to bring her own mattress, upon which she was to sleep, up into her room, so that they might be company for each other. Everything seemed to be going delightfully. Jimmy ran off for the carpenter, and

Constance opened a trunk that had just been brought
from the station. She was searching for one or two things
that she wanted to use, and in doing so came across a
little white dress, an old one, but a favorite of hers, a
soft white flannel simply made. It struck her that it would
be a relief to get off her traveling dress and get into this.
If she had had more practical training, a white flannel
would hardly have seemed to her the correct thing to don
on the night of her arrival in an old dusty house which
called for much work. But to her, used to dressing for
dinner, the little white flannel was as plain as plain could
be. So, hastily pulling it out, she put it on, and went
down to spread out the remainder of the contents of the
lunch-box.

Norah smiled when she entered the kitchen, where
everything was now in good order. This was not saying
much, for there was very little to put in order; but the
room itself was clean; so were the table and the old range,
though lack of stove polish sorely tried Norah's sense of
the fitness of things. She had unearthed a pan, and a
teakettle, and was attacking the head of the barrel of
dishes when Constance came in. Norah laid down the
hatchet, and clapped her hands with pleasure.

"That's just right, Miss Connie; ye dressed up fer dinner, now, didn't ye? We'll soon be in order, my dear;
so don't yez worry. Och! but ye looks swate in thet little
white dress!"

Jimmy appeared at the back door at that moment with
a carpenter in his wake, but stopped short when he saw
Constance, and for a moment his eyes bulged with terror.
He almost turned to flee away. He thought the white lady
had appeared at last, and was about to vent her wrath
upon him at the goings on which he had been instigating.

But the new white flannel ghost smiled so sweetly at
him, and said so pleasantly, "Oh, Jimmy, you found the
carpenter, didn't you?" that he subsided, and never told
any one, save Miss Constance herself, a long time afterward, how much he had been frightened. And with that
smile of Constance's, Jimmy's last personal dread of the
white lady faded away.

They ate their supper, Norah, Jimmy and Constance, and finished the last crumb of Sa' Ran's bountiful supply, for they were very hungry. Then Constance, thanking Jimmy, and receiving his promise to be on hand early in the morning to do whatever she wanted, laughingly refusing his earnest offers to sleep there as her protector, or to get her some one else, sent him to his home. She never knew how many times during the evening he went to where he could see whether the candlelight was still flickering in the upper window, or whether there were signs of alarm about the old place. And, as he stood there watching, he wished within his soul that he were a man, and brave; for he somehow felt that he could grow braver if he were given time, though he realized that he was at heart a coward at present, a great thing for a boy to realize. He knew that if he were truly brave like the boys in the story books, he would go and throw himself across the door of the old house, and sleep there to protect the lady inside; and *that* Jimmy knew he was not willing to do.

The moon was full that night; and, as they had realized at the last minute before Jimmy left them that candles were their only chance for light, Constance wandered outside for a few minutes in the brilliant moonlight. The kitchen with its weird, flickering candlelight was not a pleasant place to sit, and, besides Norah was making a clatter with the dishes from the barrel, which she insisted upon washing that night, and which she would not allow her young mistress to touch; so Constance felt that a breath of the evening would do her good. Her soul longed to get near the loveliness of the night, and to see what she had in this queer old place that had been rented for a year. She walked slowly down the grass-grown path that led to the pond noticing the trees and shrubs on either side, and now and then pausing to look up at the round, full brightness of the moon. How still and beautiful it was here! she thought. No whirring trolleys, no rumble of city life, no dust, no murmur of the thousand voices that fill the air of a city at night. Only the quiet stars like polished diamonds, and the great full moon looking at her. A lovely place in which to walk if a spirit could walk this earth again. She wondered how much truth there might be as a foundation for Jimmy's story about the lady who had killed herself. She hoped no one would tell Norah, for perhaps she might be superstitious and unhappy there. She must warn Jimmy about it. Dear, faithful, funny little Jimmy! How he seemed to have fitted right into her plans, like a little urchin angel dropped down from heaven just when she needed him! She must try to make his life happier in some way for the help he had been to her.

Down by the water's edge a pathway of silver stretched out before her into the soft deep darkness. It made the night look wide. She stood a long time watching the play of the ripples in the water, noticing the dark penciling of the rustic summerhouse on the little island, against the moonlit sky, trying to realize that it was her new home, and wondering whether she would ever get accustomed to the change.

Then she turned in the dewy path, her ears filled with the music of the frogs that made the summer seem near at hand, and suddenly before her in the way, but a few feet in front of her, stood a man!

Chapter IX

John Endicott's train was nearing the station, and familiar objects presented themselves. He could see the old lumber yard, the ice-house off at the side, and one corner of the supply-store steps, but a freight car hid the rest. He turned to the other side of the track, marveling at the advance of spring during his absence. It was growing dusk, but the moon had risen and was shining in glory over everything. It bathed the little pond and island behind the old haunted house, and made the dark cedars stand out primly like sentinels set to guard the place. He placed his face close to the window pane and peered out to see whether he could tell whether the grass was green. He lifted his suit-case ready to get out. He had no need for such haste, save that he wished to get away from his loneliness that seemed to be threatening to overwhelm him. To come back to Rushville, and to know that there would be no mother a hundred miles away praying for him, to whom he could write and who would write him long, cheering letters, asking about his work and planning for the time that would never come now, when she could be spared to leave her daughter and the baby, and would come to make a real home for him, it was all hard. It was no wonder that John Endicott looked out of the window, and tried to take an interest in the spring growth of grass. But now, as he looked, a strange object met his gaze. Out on the moonlit slope of grass, glistening with diamond drops there appeared a patch of light. It seemed a kind of focusing of the white mist

that was rising from the silvery pond, and it took the
form of a girl, slender and white-robed.

For just an instant his heart stood still, and his mind
experienced great wonder and doubt. It seemed, in very
truth, that he must be looking upon a disembodied
spirit, the spirit of the woman who had lived in the old
house and was walking the earth again. Then his strong
New England common sense, sturdy through the years
of poverty and hardship, rose. At once he rejected the
feeling. There was some explanation, of course, and he
would find it out. He would sift this superstition to its
depth, and rid the village of a troublesome tradition.

The train had already started to move, and in a moment more would be past these grounds and on its way
to the station. There was no time to be lost. Gripping
the suit-case, he strode from the car, his eyes fixed
upon the white object still visible through the car-
windows. The train was moving faster when he swung
himself from the back platform, and without waiting to
pick his way he set out at once for the object of his coming. Over the fence, suit-case and all, he went, and
through the dewy grass, silently and swiftly he moved,
lest he should disturb this seeming wraith, if living it was,
and not some odd arrangement of tangible things upon
which the moon brought a peculiar light. His specula-
tion was at work, but he could suggest nothing that
should give such lifelike form to the old story of the village. He was conscious of a satisfaction that there was
something real to lay a foundation for so ridiculous a
story which held a whole village in fear. Then he came
nearer, his eyes still fixed upon the luminous white object, and out of the evening the form grew more distinct
as he drew nearer, until a girl, fair and lovely, stood before him in the moonlight. He could see the perfect pro-
file now with a dark cedar for background, a wave of
hair outlining one delicate ear, the exquisitely molded
hand holding back the soft white drapery, and over all
the unearthly light.

He paused and caught his breath. Almost he could believe she was a spirit, so ethereal did she seem, so mo-

tionless and beautiful, as she stood looking out over that silver sheet of water with dewy sparkles all about her feet and an early firefly over her head, matching its little light against the moon. It did not seem as if she could be ordinary flesh and blood.

Then he came a step nearer, and she turned and faced him.

He looked at her, and saw that she was a real woman, alive, and lovely. What could it mean? Did some insane person secretly live in the old house, and come out at night haunting the place? Or was she a poor creature that had fled from something terrible in her life and was taking refuge here from the world? Not from sin she had committed, surely, for the face into which he was looking was pure and true. But he must know what it meant.

His voice was stern and commanding when he spoke at last.

"Who are you? What are you doing here?" he asked, and to himself it seemed that he had spoken almost harshly.

But the girl was not frightened, apparently, nor did she scream and turn to run away, nor fade like a wraith. Instead she turned quickly and faced him.

"I might ask the same of you," she said coolly, "I happen to be on my own premises."

Puzzled, wondering, half abashed by her manner, John Endicott paused. Actually she had made him feel that he was the intruder, not she. And yet what had he gained, and how could he go away without sifting the mystery futher? What had she said that would not make matters more sure to the believers in the walking lady? Nothing. She talked as any reasonable ghost might be expected to talk, provided she had killed herself in this house and had chosen to return and walk within its grounds.

No, if he went away now, it would have been better that he had not come. He would not dare mention the occurrence; for it would only confirm the stories that had been going about, and the fear of the poor old house would grow. He must find out what this meant. She was a woman, of course, as real and alive as himself, and she did not look like a maniac. She must be made to explain herself, and make it plain why she chose to walk in these lonely grounds alone at night, and frighten a whole village of harmless people. If she had a secret, he would guard it, but she must explain.

"I beg your pardon," he said courteously but firmly, "I must understand your presence here. You have asked me who I am. I am the minister of the church, and for the good of this community I have come here to find out this mystery. Why do you walk about in this strange way and frighten a whole community?"

"You may be a minister," she laughed, "but I fail to understand why that gives you a right to question me on my own premises. I walk here because I choose to do so. As for frightening a whole community, there does not seem to be anybody frightened but yourself."

She turned toward the house.

"But—" he said, "I——"

She was gone. A slight rustle, a breath of faint, almost imperceptible, perfume, a bending of the grasses; that was all. He stood dismayed, worsted, humiliated, out there in the moonlight. He watched her as she went up the path and into the house. As she stood on the low porch for an instant, her hand on the door latch, he caught the gleam of a diamond flashing on her finger.

He stood still, too dazed to move for a moment. Then he looked up at the old house, and saw a candlelight flicker through the windows. Was he perhaps "seeing things" too, like the rest of the village? Had his recent sorrow and loss of sleep unstrung his nerves?

But he could not stand there, a tall shadow in the moonlight, for some passer-by to see and construct another ghostly story about. He must go home. It went strongly against the grain to leave, however, without knowing more about the matter. He was half inclined to walk boldly up to the door, and knock.

He had never been in quite such a situation before, chasing ghosts through property that did not belong to him, merely for the sake of proving to the community that there were no ghosts. He told himself that he should

have minded his own affairs, and then there would have
been no trouble.

Altogether, his spirits were much depressed as he
wended his way to Mrs. Bartlett's little brown house, and
a sharp pang of sorrow went through him as he thought
that the person to whom he would like to have told this
strange adventure was gone from the earth.

Mrs. Bartlett laid down the paper she was reading, and
opened the door, looking over her glasses at him speculatively. She would have liked to ask him the particulars
of his mother's death and the funeral, but he was always
so brief about such things. She would rather he were a
little more of a gossip. The next morning she told her
neighbor that the minister looked "kind of peaked" when
he came home; she "guessed he felt his ma's death,"
though she "couldn't see why he should; he had been
away from her a good many years."

There was not much comfort for John Endicott in Mrs.
Bartlett's home. Her house was clean, however, and she
gave him plenty to eat. He never complained even when
the meat was warmed over three times, nor said how tired
he was of stewed prunes. She thought that what was good
enough for Mr. Bartlett was good enough for the minister; "he didn't hev to work near's hard's Hiram, anyway—
just make a few calls, and talk a little while on Sunday."
That was Mrs. Bartlett's estimate of a minister's labors.

Mrs. Bartlett set forth for her boarder, sour bread,
weak tea, strong butter, tough meat, heavy gingerbread
and sloppy prunes, remarking significantly as she did so,
that the train must have been late. He made no attempt
to satisfy her curiosity however, and betook himself to
his room as soon as possible.

His room was small and overcrowded with his books
and papers. Mrs. Bartlett never meddled with his things,
she told her neighbors with pride; so dust and papers and
missionary circulars lay in undisturbed confusion over
table and floor and window-seats, wherever he chose to
lay them down. They lay so now, just as he had left them
two weeks ago when he hurried off in response to the
terrible telegram that lay on the top of all, there on his

table. He caught sight of it and groaned as he flung himself into the cane-seat chair before the pine table that
served as a study-desk. The whole dreadful two weeks
passed before his mind in a flash. The confusion in the
room served to deepen the feeling of desolation.

He seemed to see everything in it with his eyes shut,
and knew just how dismal it all looked. The red and green
carpet carefully darned in places, and a great patch wrong
side out just in front of the door; the rows of dusty books
on the unpainted pine shelves along the wall; the hard
little lounge, that was a foot too short for him; the
framed picture of his theological professors, and another
of his seminary class; the cracked blue paper window-
shades, were all as plain to him as if his eyes were open;
and the yellow telegram focused itself as the center of
all this desolation, even though his face was buried in
his folded arms upon the table.

He went over it all again, the journey, the death-bed,
the funeral, and his heart grew sick within him.

He rose quickly, and went over to the cheap oak bureau. There was a white towel on the bureau for a cover;
and his mother's picture stood there, the only ornament
in the room. A neat and ugly strip of rag carpet lay in
front of the bed. On this rag rug beside the patch-work-
covered bed the minister knelt.

He had been wont on cheery days to call his quarters
pleasant ones, and himself fortunate to have got them
at such a possible price, this when he wrote to his mother
and made as bright a picture of his life as he could find
it in his conscience to do; but on this sad night of his
return the whole place looked bare and desolate.

He buried his face in the small, lumpy pillow, and cried
to God for help. He felt so alone, and so suddenly weak,
and unable to cope with the world that seemed against
him sorely.

Long he knelt there and brought every burden, for he
was accustomed to talking with his Lord "face to face
as a man speaketh unto his friend." Then, comforted,
he lay down to rest.

Chapter X

When Constance reached the house, she was trembling from head to foot, whether from fright or from anger she scarcely knew. At first, when she turned around and faced the strange man in the moonlight, she was frightened, and expected to be seized by the throat and choked, perhaps, or gagged and robbed; but, when she saw his suit-case, and noticed that he was respectable looking, her fears were quieted. When he spoke, she recognized the tones of a gentleman, and then she began to be angry.

It was ridiculous of him to think a woman could do any harm, even if she were walking at night on land that did not belong to her near an old deserted house. So she had passed by him with a grand air, and entered the kitchen.

Norah was flying around, putting away dishes on a shelf which she had washed to receive them, and Constance felt that she must either laugh or cry at once; so she lighted another candle, and went swiftly upstairs. It had suddenly come over her what the man must have meant as she remembered the story Jimmy had told her of the white lady. She had entirely forgotten it and thought the stranger most officious.

But now she saw it all. The man had thought her the ghost who haunted the house, and the whole thing took on a funny aspect. She wanted to laugh aloud. But it might frighten Norah so she must not tell her.

She stole to the window, and looked out into the moonlit world. The man was just striding away through the darkness of the cedars, his head bent down, his whole tall form drooping. Something familiar in the form hovered about her memory. What was it? Where had she seen some one like this man? She turned from the window, and threw herself upon the couch; and before she knew it she was fast asleep. Norah, coming up a little later, shaded the candle, threw a light shawl over her, and left her so.

It was broad daylight when they both awoke to the thundering noise of the men banging on the door below. The first load of furniture had arrived. The painter came also and said his paper hangers would soon be there, as they had gone after their paste and tools. Constance went about directing, too busy to stop for breakfast, though Norah made her a cup of coffee, and sent Jimmy, who soon appeared, to the store for supplies. It was a busy day, and by night confusion seemed to reign everywhere, save in the room that Constance had chosen for her own. That Norah had attacked and made shiningly clean the first thing, and had seen to it that her young mistress's furniture was duly set up. She meant that Constance should have a quiet resting place as soon as possible. It was her loving instinct to care for one who had been good to her.

By night everybody in Rushville knew that some one was moving into the old haunted house, and many were the speculations concerning the people who would be willing to live there.

The owner of the drug store made an errand over to see whether he had left a shovel in the house, which had been missing ever since he moved. His coarse, red face and hard blue eyes appeared at the door during the morning, while Constance was alone for a moment in the kitchen, and made her start unpleasantly. She answered his questions coldly, gave him permission to search for his shovel, and withdrew at once; but the man went back to give a report of her that would have made her writhe if she could have heard it. He was much struck by her beauty, and boasted of her friendliness. And so the knowledge of her coming spread in ways of which she little dreamed.

Constance had selected for the long, high room on the
right of the hall a creamy paper covered with wide-
spreading palm branches that seemed to be alive in their
feathery greenness. The native paper hangers shook their
heads over this design, sighed, and said of course they
would put it on if she said so, but they wouldn't be
responsible for the way it would look: and then stood
back in amazement at the effect they had produced when
their work was done. It required a wider opening of the
artistic in their souls to appreciate it; yet they could but
confess that the whole room was lovely. The palms
spread like a grove all about. It did not seem like paper;
it was like great trees growing all about the room.

The men turned to Constance, who stood looking the
room over critically, well pleased with the outcome of her
experiment, and with one accord they gave her their hom-
age. Thenceforth during the rest of their work she was "the
missis," and they spoke it proudly, as if they had found
their fit leader. They asked her advice instead of taking
their own way, and they praised her at the fire house in
the evening when they lounged to smoke and talk.

"I bet you anything, now," one man said, slapping his
thigh with his hand, "that her folks has been paper
hangers. She comes by it natural; anybody can see that
with half an eye."

Constance came to this room after the men were gone,
and looked it over again with satisfaction. This was to
be the tea room and in her mind's eye she could see that
it was a success so far as beauty was concerned. The paint
had been enameled white and the floor was stained dark
walnut. It was not a fine floor, to be sure, but the stain
hid some of the defects. Constance with Norah's as-
sistance untied bundles of rugs, and dragged them out,
until she had made a selection; and the lovely room took
on a new air of elegance when a number of antique
Kazak, Beloochistan and Daghestan rugs were strewn
about over the bad places in the flooring.

They brought little tables of solid mahogany and rosewood, highly polished and of beautiful grain, and put
them about the room at pleasant distances. Constance

thought with a pang of the tremendous price she was going to have to pay for plate glass to cover their polished tops, but she shut her lips firmly and went on. The great painting of the cows grazing was hung at the lower end of the room; and above the mantel, opposite the wide hall door, hung a canvas of the ocean, its liquid green depths and foamy curling waves so lifelike that one felt about to step out upon the sands. It was a large, fine painting, and one that Constance prized. It had cost much money. It had not occurred to her that she might have sold these beautiful and costly belongings, and had more money to live upon. They were a part of herself—the rare old rugs, the fine paintings, the rich mahogany furniture.

In the evening when the men were all gone, Constance and Norah shoved the mahogany buffet in from the hall where it had been put when unloaded. This they placed where its mirror would reflect the palms well and give distance to the room when one entered. After they had brought in a few chairs Constance went to the sideboard drawers, and began to take out fine linen embroidered and lace-in-wrought cloths, and spread them upon the little tables. Norah was as eager as her mistress.

"Thur's just wan thing more ye nade," said Norah, standing in the doorway, her arms akimbo, surveying their work.

"Yez better sind fer thim pams ye used to hev in th' porler."

"Why, they're here, Norah; they came in the last load. They're out on the side piazza. You thought I sent them to the florists, I suppose, but I didn't. Come! Let's get them. Can you get the crate open?"

They dragged the great palms into the room and set them about where their greenness mingled with that of the pictured ones, and made the illusion more perfect. On the whole, they went to bed that night satisfied.

"We'll soon be ready for guests, Norah," said Constance, laughing as she bade Norah good night.

When Jimmy came in the morning as usual, he was taken to look at the new room. He stood in the hall door,

his little bare, dusty toes keeping reverently back from
the rich rug in the doorway, and looked in. Never before had a sight of anything like this appeared to Jimmy's
dazzled vision. He was used to a dingy little kitchen and
a still dingier attic bedroom. He had seldom been in other
people's houses, and then not further than the kitchen
or a long, dark hall, when he was sent on errands.

"Gee whiz!" he said at last, after a prolonged gaze.
"Ain't you a clipper? Say, that's great! My! I wisht the
fellers could see them green trees a-growin' right up in
the room. Make pictures ov 'umselves on the wall, too!
Say, thet's great!"

But the tea room was not the only room in which
changes had been going on. Up on the second floor three
lovely rooms had been in preparation, a bedroom, a
sitting-room, and a dainty dining-room. It was the nest
that Constance was preparing for her grandmother. Into
these rooms were put all Mrs. Wetherill's fine old furniture, her rugs and pictures and books, arranged as nearly
as possible in the way in which they had been arranged
in her home in New York.

The bedroom and dining-room were the two back
rooms; and the sitting-room, though on the front, had
its windows so sheltered by large trees that it was impossible to see the front door or the path leading to the gate.
The outlook was lovely at this time of year, into greenness everywhere, with a nestling church spire and a few
dormer windows of houses in the distance. In winter the
cedars would still stand guard over the front door. There
would be no need for the old lady to learn the secret of
their maintenance from her windows, at least.

And now letters from her grandmother, though not
saying so in so many words, showed Constance that she
was feeling homesick, and that it was fully time to go
after her. Constance had been in Rushville two weeks
and two days, and there was much yet to be done, but
she felt that Norah might be able to do it with some help;
so, securing Jimmy's mother to stay nights in the house
and to help Norah, Constance went after her grandmother. She felt that the hardest part of her task was

now before her, to get rid of the maid and to induce her grandmother to be happy for the summer in Rushville.

One fear she had, and that was that Norah would in some way hear about the ghost who was supposed to haunt the house, and that her Irish superstition would take alarm. Constance decided that she must say something to her before she left, lest Norah should be frightened and desert her post. But, when she broached the subject, the girl only laughed.

"Bless me sowl, Miss Connie! Did yez think I was feerd o' ghosts? The painter man, the rid-haired wan, he towld me all about the lady wot wahks; but Oi sez, sez Oi, 'Oi'll not be a-carin' fer any speerits. Oi've two good han's an' two feets, an' Oi'll resk meself wid any trailin' gentle leddy thet only wahks. Whot horm cud she do?' Na, Miss Connie, yez no need to be feerd fer me."

Jimmy was established as regular right-hand man for Norah until Constance should return.

"I'm going to pay you a dollar a week, Jimmy, while I'm away; and you will do all you can to make things easy for Norah, won't you? Then, when I come back, we'll have a talk together and make some permanent arrangements. You are my partner, you know, and I must pay you something for the use of your name in renting the house."

Jimmy smiled at her confidently. He thought there never was anybody in the world like his new friend. He swelled with pride daily as he walked through the streets, for was not he an established friend of the house that was haunted, and did he not walk in and out familiarly where even yet the village boys would not have dared tread except in broad daylight? It was not that Jimmy did not believe the stories about the ghost, but that he felt that this new and lovely spirit that had come to inherit the place would drive out the other. At least, he had lost the dread of the house he had once felt, and so he enjoyed the prestige of courage among his comrades, who often watched from afar to see whether he really did go into the house as he said.

John Endicott had found much for his hands and brain

to do the morning after his return. He had no idle moments to mope over mistakes he had made, or sorrows that had come into his life. There were letters to be answered; there was a promised article, already overdue, which he must write; there were sermons to be written; and there were many calls to be made. It seemed as if everybody in the parish had been ill since he went away, and he must visit and comfort them all; and each one watched the street with jealous eye lest he should go to the other one first. It required untiring energy and a heart full of love to do all that fell to his lot.

Whenever he sat down for a moment alone, however, the annoyance he felt over the little incident that occurred near the old house troubled him.

It had not taken him long, of course, to discover that some one had really taken the old house. Mrs. Bartlett was informed of it early, and duly reported it to him with Bartlett notes thereon. She expressed her hearty disapproval, in advance, of any one who was fool enough to rent that house. If they were ignorant of its history, then they showed shiftlessness in not inquiring. They couldn't be a respectable family, or they never would take up with a place that had once been a tavern, and had so bad a reputation. Besides, there was something wrong about that house. Not ghosts, of course; she didn't believe in them; but something went on at that house in the dead of night, she felt sure; and the evil ones who carried it on covered their tracks by these stories of ghosts. These people would leave, as all others had done, just as soon as they found out; that is, if they were worth anything, she finished with an air that said it was extremely doubtful whether they were.

It was the morning when Constance left that he met his friend Jimmy returning from escorting her to the station. Jimmy was feeling a trifle sad over her departure; for she had said it might be two or three weeks before she would be able to return, though she hoped to come back sooner. He brightened up when he saw the minister. Mr. Endicott always had a pleasant word for boys, and never forgot names.

Grace Livingston Hill

"Well, Jimmy," said the minister, "I missed you last Sunday." Jimmy grinned.

"What was the matter that you were not at church?"

"Been busy," said Jimmy mysteriously, in a tone that invited further inquiry.

"Busy? Gone into business, have you?"

Jimmy grinned wider, and looked important.

"Had to stick around, fear Miss Constance would want something. She's a friend o' mine; been movin' into the big house here," and he jerked his thumb over toward the cedars.

"Oh!" said the minister, showing unusual interest. "A friend of *yours*? Well, can't you bring her to church?"

"Mebbe!" said Jimmy with a confident wink. "She's an awful nice singer. She play on the pianner, too."

"Indeed!" said John Endicott. "Well, Jimmy, if she's a friend of yours, perhaps you can persuade her to come." John Endicott was puzzled.

He could not make the beautiful sight of the girl he had seen, full of refinement, grace, and loveliness, accord with Jimmy's statement that she was his friend. She did not look to him like one who would be a boon companion of the Wattses.

"She's just gone away fer a while," volunteered the boy. "I took her down to the station. She's gone after her grandmother."

"Ah!" said the minister interestedly.

"You'll hafta come ta the tea room when it's ready," volunteered Jimmy with an air of proprietorship. "Thur's goin' to be eyes cream. Don't you like eyes cream?"

"Ice cream? Why, of course, Jimmy," said the minister, smiling with kindred boyishness; "but what's this about a tea room? Are these new people really going to keep a tea room?"

"Sure thing! She told me this mornin', an' she said I might tell folks ef I was a mind to. It's a-goin' to be peachy. Thur's pams all round the room."

By this John Endicott expected to find it thoroughly furnished with palm-leaf fans.

"You jest wait till you see her," boasted Jimmy. "She's

a peach! Good-by. I'm goin' in here now to help Norah. Don't you forget the eyes cream when the tea room opens."

"All right," said the minister; "I'll remember. And don't you forget church next Sunday."

"I'll come, an' I'll bring *her* soon 's she gits home, ef I can; an' I guess I can."

Jimmy waved his hand and disappeared behind the cedars. The minister walked on, pondering what kind of family could have moved into the old house.

Chapter XI

Constance found that getting rid of the maid was rendered easy for her by the maid herself. She showed strong signs of homesickness; and, when she received a letter saying that her mother was ill, she came to Constance declaring that she would have to give up her position and go.

Mrs. Wetherill looked as if the foundations of the earth were being shaken when this announcement was made to her, and Constance was not a little troubled lest all the changes that were coming would be very hard upon her grandmother's health; but she saw no other way, and she thought she knew her grandmother well enough to be sure that the changes would be less hard upon her than the knowledge of the true state of their circumstances.

"Never mind, grandmother," said Constance cheerily, "I'll be your maid. Don't you think I could for a little while at least? I think you might teach me how, and I'm sure it will be much less trouble when we're traveling to have just us, and not always be having to look out for the maid."

It was a new way of looking at things. Mrs. Wetherill had been used to having all tasks performed for her. She could not remember the time when a maid had not made the way smooth, before her gentle feet, carried her bundles, arranged her chair, and laid out the clothes she was to wear. She was as helpless as a baby as far as looking after herself was concerned, and it took much argument

from Constance to overcome her dismay; but she finally
agreed to try it.

The next morning, accordingly, the maid departed, and
Constance and her grandmother, a day or two later,
started in another direction. Constance had suggested
that perhaps Norah would train into a good maid, and
she would write and find out whether the girl would meet
them somewhere on their journey. So the old lady went
quite contentedly with Constance, finding, after all, that
the young girl was as quick in anticipating her needs as
the departed maid had been.

They started on their journeyings once more, for it was
no part of Constance's plan to bring her grandmother
to Rushville at once, or to let her see the place until all
things were in order. From one hotel to another they
went, staying a day here and a day there, never going
a great journey from Rushville, and yet visiting many
pretty places, often driving about and drinking in the
beauties of spring.

The old lady enjoyed it all in a way, but Constance
could see that she was growing weary and restless for a
quiet room and her own things about her. This was the
time that she had been waiting for, and gently, little by
little, she suggested the idea of taking permanent quarters
for the summer in some quiet little country village.

About this time a letter reached her from Norah,
reporting progress in the house, and she told her grandmother that Norah had consented to meet them and do
the best she could at anything they wished of her. The
old lady brightened perceptibly at this prospect, and readily agreed that it would be good to settle down and have
some of their own things sent for. She expressed a desire for her favorite rocking-chair and books, and to have
the New York papers reach her regularly each morning.

With a sigh of relief Constance sat down and wrote
to Norah that she might expect them within a few days
now. That afternoon, when her grandmother's nap was
finished, she got her out upon a quiet side piazza of the
hotel, where she might look into lovely green woods, and
began to describe the house in Rushville, which truly

enough she said she had seen and fallen in love with on
her way out to Chicago the first time. She said that there
were pretty apartments where they might use their own
furniture if they chose, and that there was a lovely tea
room downstairs which would send up their meals to their
own apartments. She felt sure that it would be a pleasant place in which to spend the summer, and if her grandmother approved she would send word at once to have
their furniture, at least a part of it, sent on and put in
place. Norah would see that things were in order for
them, and she thought it all might be arranged very soon.

Mrs. Wetherill, having for so many years lived her
peaceful life, saw no inconsistency in the idea of having
their furniture brought and arranged within a few days,
and readily gave her consent. Indeed, she was almost a
child in matters that pertained to the world, and her mind
had partially gone to sleep in many ways.

Jimmy was waiting at the station with shining eyes full
of expectation. If he had worn the full regalia of a
liveried porter, he could not have swelled with more importance as he strutted up and down the platform. Constance had planned that they should arrive in the early
evening, for she did not care to have her grandmother
get a view of the forlorn little village which surrounded
this new home of theirs. The worst part of Rushville, as
of all small towns, was down by the station, of course.
So Jimmy had been instructed to secure a closed car, and
have it in readiness to convey them to their new abode.

Jimmy had wheedled a friend of his brother's into
meeting the train with his neat sedan. He had roared with
laughter over Jimmy's offer of pay and had consented
to go merely out of curiosity.

Jimmy, with the éclat of having ordered the car, held
his head high, jingled a silver quarter and two nickels
in his pockets, and felt large.

"Oh, I say," he called, hailing the minister who passed
on his way from the bedside of a sick person to the prayer
meeting, "she's a-comin' home tonight, an' I'll bring her
next Sunday ef I kin work it."

"Is she?" said the minister. "Do," he added fervently.

At last Jimmy's patience was rewarded, and the train rounded the curve and drew up to the station. Jimmy devoted himself vigilantly to the sweet-faced old lady, picking up her handkerchief when it fell, hovering round her, and in every way making himself the wheel on which all moved. He slammed the door shut with importance, and slid into the front seat in spite of the driver's protest that there was no call for an able-bodied boy to ride across the road. Jimmy held his seat, and bounced to the ground to open the door for the ladies. He received as a reward a kindly smile of gracious acceptance from Madame Wetherill, and a silver half-dollar, for in such wise had she always been wont to pave her way.

They passed into the wide hall, and the old lady glanced with mild eyes into the long palm dining-room, and told Constance it seemed "very nice." Norah appeared with voluble welcome at the top of the stairs, and fairly lifted Mrs. Wetherill up. But, when she came into the sitting-room, and looked about, and saw everything arranged just as it had been in her sitting-room at home, a room of very much this same shape and size, she dropped into her easy-chair by the low stand where stood her own reading-light, and Constance saw almost with fear how great had been the strain of the time spent out in the world. She said only, "Oh, this is good!" but there were tears of gratitude in her eyes, and she seemed entirely satisfied.

Had Constance known that the old lady had undertaken this hard journey for the sake of her beloved grandchild because she fancied she was running away from an affair of the heart with Morris Thayer, who somehow needed a severe lesson, she might not have been so thoroughly satisfied with the easy way in which she had carried out her plans.

It was as well, however, for Constance that she had no further burdens upon her; for there were enough with all the strange things she had undertaken, and all the mistakes she must inevitably make and the disappointments she must meet. She had been counting up that day. The thousand dollars she had nominally set aside to use for

traveling expenses and in getting started had melted away
like dew. There was none of it left, and she had even
encroached upon the next thousand she had told the lawyer to put into the bank for her. Money must begin to
come in at once, or they would soon have to spend some
of their capital; and that, she knew, was swift and certain ruin.

She lay awake most of that first night planning and
worrying, and on the next morning called a conference
with Norah and Jimmy, as the result of which it was
decided that the tea room should be opened at once.

The room that was to be the scene of action was in
immaculate order; the porch and front hall were neat-
ness itself. Nothing could have been more attractive, even
if large sums of money had been spent. Constance surveyed it, and was satisfied. Moreover, she knew that
Norah's cooking would be as irreproachable as the room.
Now if people could be made to believe and come and
see! And if a demand could only be created!

Work had begun on the tracks for the new Junction
and that made the outlook more hopeful, but it might
be months before any business could come from that
quarter.

Now that she had spent so much time and thought and
money, the awful thought kept crowding upon Constance
that perhaps there were not people enough in this town
who would want to eat outside of their own homes to
make it pay. However, she had tried, and she could but
fail. She must wait and see.

It so happened that all these fears had come to Jimmy
also. He was young; but he was wise, and he wanted with
his whole soul to have his beautiful lady succeed.

Jimmy was no fool. He knew that the greatest obsta-
cle in the way of the success of her new enterprise was
the ghost story attached to the old house. He had done
his best during the last few days to make "the fellers"
see how harmless the place was; but they seemed to suspect some trap, for they were exceedingly wary about going with him inside the gate. But he determined to begin

to work upon their feelings and create custom for the
new tea room.

He was on hand bright and early the next morning for
a game of marbles. He had not condescended to marbles much of late, he had been so busy in other directions. Marbles were a trifle out of season, but Rushville
did not keep quite so closely to the fashions in games
or anything as they do in many places; so marbles were
still in vogue. He played abstractedly, and did not seem
to mind when two of his best marbles were won from
him. He did not mind, because he saw it put the boys
in good humor.

The new tea room was open that day. A notice had
been put into the village paper, and notices printed on
thick white cards in Constance's own lettering were
posted in prominent places about the town. Jimmy had
put them up the night before. They read:

THE CEDARS
Meals at all hours
Table d'hôte or à la carte
Home-made Ice Cream   Cakes   Candy

Jimmy had read it over carefully every time he had
tacked it up, standing back after the last tack was set,
until he knew it by heart. He had learned what the mysterious foreign phrases meant, and felt he could explain
to any inquiring citizen, though he was a trifle uncertain
yet as to his pronunciation.

At right angles to a post of the great wooden gate of
the old house hung a neat white sign with dark green lettering "The Cedars." The fence and gate had both been
mended and painted a rich, dark green.

About half past ten on that first morning of the opening Jimmy stood among a crowd of boys.

"Say, ain't any you fellers got fifteen cents, hev ye?"
he asked disinterestedly, looking round upon the ring of
boys. One boy said he had, and another, and another,
and a fourth said he had twenty-five at home in his bank.

Whereupon there arose a cry of scorn. What good was twenty-five cents at home in a bank? They demanded to see it before they would believe, and the urchin sped home to pry open the mouth and extract the money, but was discovered by his mother in the act, and returned crestfallen with a boxed ear instead. Meantime Jimmy had proceeded.

"I know a place where there's eyes cream!" remarked Jimmy with his eyes half closed, taking a sly squint at each boy in turn to try the effect of his words.

"Where?" demanded seven eager voices.

"Come with me, an' I'll show ye," said Jimmy slowly, drawing a grass-blade between his lips, not, however, rising to go; for well he knew his case was not half won as yet.

"Can't git no eyes cream better'n the drug store nowheres," asserted one boy loftily.

"Aw, you don't know everythin', Lanky. Shut up!" said Jimmy shortly. He had no mind to be interrupted in the flow of his argument.

"Well, show us where you mean," said one eager fellow with his mouth watering for the treat. He had no money but it might be possible to get some if he once saw the place and were sure of it.

"Don't fool yerself, kid," said the tall boy who had disputed the quality of the cream. "Jimmy here, he's jest talkin' to hear hisself talk. He don't know 'bout no eyes cream. He jest wants to get you green little kids down there to the hanted house, an' git the ghost after yer; thet's wot he's after, kid. Don't you let him put anything over on you."

The blood flamed into Jimmy's cheek and the fire into his eye. He clutched the silver half-dollar that Mrs. Wetherill had given him, and resolved to vindicate himself or die in the attempt. But first he must settle with his adversary.

"Come on!" he cried, doubling up his fists; and, leaving no choice for the other boy, he lowered his head and flew at him.

The tall boy sidled away from the fence, and prepared

to return fight. The small ring of onlookers formed about
the two, ready to follow the victor, whichever he might
be. Then followed a confusion of arms and bare legs,
the sound of ripping garments, and the quick revolution
of two sturdy bodies this way and that. The tall boy was
agile, but he was also lazy; and, besides, he had not the
incentive to fight that Jimmy had. Jimmy fought with
a great purpose, and he was as determined to win as any
knight fighting for the honor of a fair lady would be.
He had all he could do, for the bigger boy gave him a
tremendous pommeling; his nose was bleeding, his shirt
minus one sleeve and his hair, which for a wonder had
been nicely combed that morning, stood up fiercely all
over his round, belligerent head.

But when the fight had gone on for some minutes and
the revolutions of the pair had become so rapid as to
make it impossible to distinguish the legs of the tall boy
from the legs of Jimmy, there was a sudden murmur of
admiration from the ring of observers which had increased in numbers as the fight went on, and the ani-
mated bundle in the center suddenly became quiet. When
the dust subsided, Jimmy could be seen red and triumphant, sitting upon his prostrate opponent, his knee upon
the insulting breast, one eye rather the worse for wear,
and a stream of blood running down his face and across
his faded little blouse.

"Now," said the victor, when he could get his breath
again, "you stays there till you owns up I ain't no liar,
and promises you'll go an' git some eyes cream an' see
fer yourself; an' I'll tell you what you does. These here
little kids," motioning to the two smaller boys who had
owned to having no money, "is a goin' with me to have
eyes cream"—he looked at them with a fatherly wink,
wherat the two small boys huddled together pleased and
frightened, and looked upon one another with awe, for
they had great fear of that ghost, and yet great curiosity
to see her—"an' they don't have nothin' to pay, fer I'll
stand 'em treat; but the rest of you fellers pays yer own
way, an', ef ye don't come 'tall, it's cause yer 'fraid cats,
so there! Now Lanky Jones, do you choose to git up an'

walk over to thet there tea room peaceable, an' pay fer yer own eyes cream, er hev I got ter lick yer some more?"

He punctuated these sentences by punches in the ribs of his victim, and Lanky was glad enough to promise all that was asked of him.

"Ye hear wot he says?" said Jimmy, his bloody little face looking solemnly about the company; "an' you all stands by me an' makes him do it?"

There was loud assent. The rest were with Jimmy unanimously. They wished to see this thing carried to a close now, and began to believe in the ice cream. Besides, what ghost would walk amid such numbers? Their courage was up, and they would be glad of the adventure. It would be something of which to boast during all their future lives.

So the band retired to the spigot at the garage and made their several toilets, and then started on their way. Jimmy, his wet hair licked down as smoothly as two hands could pat it, led the way with his tall prisoner walking crestfallen by his side, thus by might, if not by right, the first guests entered "The Cedars," braved the mahogany furniture and Oriental rugs and sat down to partake of a ghostly dish of cream.

Jimmy gave the orders, but first he made each boy lay down his money on the table before him, and he himself gathered the whole collection, and swept it with his own fifty cents into Norah's hand. The four older boys who had confessed to having money, cast a lingering farewell look after it, half regretfully.

But, when Norah appeared in the doorway a few minutes thereafter, a huge tray in her hands, upon which stood seven immense saucers of delectable ice cream, then their eyes bulged, their mouths watered, they smacked their lips, and prepared to enjoy themselves as they had never enjoyed themselves before. They cast no more furtive glances back of them for ghosts. They applied themselves to their several dishes of unadulterated bliss. Seven pairs of bare legs swung contentedly, or braced seven sets of toes whose owners dared not move lest the wondrous dainty should disappear before their gaze. There was content, and there was a great silence in the new tea room until every dish had been scraped, and in some cases licked. Then those seven boys arose, silently stole forth over the Persian rugs and filed down the path till they reached safely the other side of the gate, whereat they with one accord threw up their caps and raised a great shout. Jimmy was declared victor.

Chapter XII

Holly Beech stood with his feet wide apart, his rough, freckled hands on the hips of his jean overalls, his red shock hair ruffled in its usual carroty mist over his large head, his shaggy yellow eyebrows drawn into a good-natured frown, as he studied the neat white card which Jimmy had tacked up at the station. Holly was truck-driver for the freight station. If any one moved into Rushville, Holly handled all their goods, and his broad shoulders upheld cherished pianos and heavy old lounges and desks.

His usual haunts were the station and the drug store, but he was attracted by the new tea room. He had noted Norah's clean capability when he moved the furniture.

Jimmy sidled up behind Holly. Jimmy wished to promote custom. He had just seen his six associates march homeward with six large tales of the new tea room and the ice cream, and he felt that the ball had commenced to roll. But he had passed through the kitchen not three minutes ago, and the odors that greeted his nostrils had been comparable to none that had ever entered his experience, not excepting the time when he went with his brother to the town twenty miles away and passed by a candy kichen where molasses candy was being made.

Jimmy felt that it would be an everlasting pity if that delicious dinner should be allowed to go uneaten and unknown in the village of Rushville. He determined this should not be, not if he had to go out into the highways and hedges and compel them to come in, as it were. No drummer could have been more enthusiastic than Jimmy.

"Ever ben thur to dinner?" he ventured to ask Holly, which, considering it was the first opportunity that any one had had to go there to dinner, was a rather daring question for such as Jimmy to ask of such as Holly.

"You speak 's if you had, youngster," said Holly shortly, half ashamed to be caught reading the advertisement.

"Wal, not 'xactly to dinner sence the openin'," said Jimmy knowingly, "but I ben over fer a lunch this mornin' already. They hev the best eyes cream I've ever et. Most enny kind you care to call for."

"You don't say," said Holly, looking at the boy with some interest. "Well, wot do you make of all this stuff? T-a-b——"

"Oh, tab doat!" said Jimmy gleefully. "That means the hull shootin' match at one settin'. Dinner all the way through, you know, soup an' pie an' eyes cream the same day, an' pay fer 't all 't oncet."

"H'm! Sounds good! 'Spensive?"

"Dollar fer the round trip!" said Jimmy indifferently, as if dollars grew on blackberry bushes along the road. He had neglected to ask the exact price, but he thought it would be well to put it high. Holly drew a whistle.

"Must be good!" he said, sarcastically.

" 'Tis!" responded Jimmy, growing warm. " 'Tis worth it, every cent. You jest ought to smelt the things I smelt over there in the kitchen a while back. You'd think you never seen a dinner before."

"You don't say!" said Holly, studying the boy's face intently. "But what's this other kind? A lay carty! What does thet mean?"

"Thet there? Ah lah card. It's when you picks out what you want on a card she has, and takes your chances what you gets."

"Wal, I suspicion I better go the whole figger. I'm purty hungry, an' don't want to run no chances. What time does they hev dinner, son? Run over an' tell 'em I'm com-

in', and see if they'se ready fer me. Then when you call
I'll come."

Jimmy obediently went; and, though he walked in staid
manner until he was out of sight behind the cedars, he
arrived in the kitchen breathless.

"Got one man to dinner," he announced to Norah. "He
wants a dollar's worth. Give him three helpin's, ef he asks
fer it, of everything. He'll send some other fellers, mebbe.
He wants to know how soon it's ready."

"Luncheon is served from twelve till it's gone," said
Norah with a wink, and Jimmy was off again.

Jimmy had the commercial instinct strong. His ways
might not have been the ways of the young proprietor
of the tea room, perhaps; but they worked well in Rushville. He was a self-constituted salesman for the new place
of business, and he worked hard that first day. After that
he made himself so indispensable to the place that he was
regularly engaged, and did not have to depend upon stray
dimes to get his ice cream.

The next three hours, Jimmy hung about the station
and did good service. He sent over a salesman from the
noon train, and a woman agent for a new kind of hose
supporter, and last, but by no means least according to
his own estimate of people and things, he accosted the
minister who was driving home in a borrowed car about
three o'clock in the afternoon, from a funeral far in the
country.

Endicott had no very hopeful prospect that Mrs. Bartlett would have saved lunch for him till that time of day.
He would have to wait till evening prune-time for something, very likely. Jimmy's announcement about the tea
room gave him an idea. He returned the borrowed car
and promptly walked into the gate of "The Cedars."

Constance, meanwhile, was having an exciting day.
She felt as if she must go down to the gate and watch
the road each way to see whether her venture was to be
a success, and it was hard to restrain herself from at least
going to the front window every five minutes to see
whether any one was coming up the walk. She was glad
that her grandmother was comfortably and happily

seated in her favorite rocking-chair with a book, and would not be likely to want any attention until dinner-time.

Constance was free to give her attention to business. Norah, of course, had the eatables well in hand. She was a marvelous cook, and had been baking, boiling, and brewing for two days. Early as the morning light two large ice-cream freezers had ground their steady way, and there was as much food prepared as the highest hopes of the trio could expect would be needed the first day. The house was well stocked with all kinds of material for preparing any dish that was ever heard of, and there was not much likelihood that they would be sold out immediately. Rushville was much too conservative for that in spite of its name.

Constance happened to be standing at the front hall window when Jimmy came through the gate and up the path heading the file of his six "fellers," and her eyes danced with merriment at her first customers. She could not forbear stealing downstairs and peeping through the crack of the great doors at them as they sat wholly engrossed in ice cream. She wondered whether this was a sample of what her custom was to be.

Promptly at twelve o'clock Holly appeared, ushered by Jimmy. Holly had felt shy at the last minute, and told Jimmy he had better show him the way in; he might "get mixed on the doors."

Norah was arrayed in the trim cap, cuffs, and apron of a waitress; and Constance, having received thorough instructions, was to stay in the kitchen "dish up," and keep things from burning. With many an anxious injunction to Constance "not to bourn thim purty fingers o' yourn," Norah took her tray, and departed to serve.

Holly stood with his feet squarely planted on a Kermanshah rug, his hands behind him, holding his old straw hat, his head tipped back, surveying the great ocean painting that hung over the mantel.

"Wal, I swow!" he ejaculated, turning to Norah with a grin. "Thet there's right naterul, ain't it? I thought when I fust seen it I was lookin' through some sort of a spyglass down to the Atlantic coast. Wal, where shell I set? I want one o' them there tab dinners you advertise fer a dollar. Fetch it on quick, fer I'm mighty hungry."

The tables were set in New York's best style, the only style about which Constance knew anything. The linen was of the finest, and the silver was of the heaviest and solidest. It is safe to say that Holly had never in all his life before sat down to a table so spread.

Constance need not have had a troubled conscience over charging him a dollar for his dinner. He got his money's worth and he enjoyed himself. From the soup, of which he ordered three portions, and of which he partook with long swishing inhalations of enjoyment, down to the dessert, consisting of pie, pudding, or ice cream with cakes, his pleasure showed no abatement. He promptly ordered all three, cheerfully assenting to the extra charge. He looked with satisfaction upon the three dishes of dessert, put them in a row in front of him, and went straight through them, first pudding, then pie, then ice cream. When the tiny cup of black coffee was brought him, he looked puzzled for a moment, and then made a triumphant dive after the little after-dinner coffee-spoon, exclaiming:

"Wal, I swow! Thet's what the little feller was for, ain't it?" For he had been much bewildered by the array of silver, being accustomed to a steel knife and tined fork and a single tin spoon.

Constance, hovering in the hall to see that all was going right, fled precipitately into the room on the other side of the house, and sat down to laugh.

In spite of herself Constance was interested by the small boys and the uncouth man who were her first patrons. There was something pleasant, too, about seeing that each one had good things to eat, and enjoyed what he got. It was to her more like an amusement than a business, for sometimes it went sorely against the grain to think of having to get her livelihood from such people as these.

John Endicott was weary in body and soul when he entered the long dining-room. The funeral had been a particularly trying one, for it reminded him so keenly of his own recent loss. His very flesh seemed sore, and even a deep breath was a weariness. He sank into a chair at a table near the back of the room, and dropped his head into his hands for a moment, rumpling back his curly chestnut hair.

Norah entered quietly, handed him a menu card, and went deftly about waiting upon him, filling the delicate cut glass with ice water, getting him a large, fine napkin; and as she worked she cast furtive glances toward the first customer in whom she had taken the slightest interest. All the others had been beneath her notice. It humiliated her to think of her dear young mistress serving people so much beneath her in every way. But this man bore a look of refinement and ease which came only with contact with the outside world in some way. Norah knew that he was, as she termed it, "edoocated." That term included all culture to her way of thinking.

John Endicott took the bill of fare, and studied it with interest, the letters, fine and clear and delicate, every one the same height, every line showing a careful, skillful hand. Fried potatoes never seemed so attractive before as when their name gleamed from this card. He studied the card thoughtfully, and at last looked up to Norah with a smile of almost boyish pleasure.

"You may give me a beefsteak if you please, and some fried potatoes."

Norah went into the kitchen and remarked to Constance as she prepared to broil a tender bit of sirloin steak:

"There's a man in there now, Miss Connie, as looks like he had been starved fer foive year. He's ordered a beefsteak, an' he's expectin' to enj'y it, an' I'm goin' to see as he gits a good un. He's edoocated, too, an' Oi b'leeve he knows a good un when he sees it. He looks loike he'd seen a soight o' thrubble. Beats awl how you find the thrubble in folks whin you've hed it yersel'."

Constance, her warm heart touched at once, set about helping Norah. She took a dainty china dish, and put two or three olives in it. Olives did not go with beefsteaks on the bill of fare, but what of that? They were her olives, and the man might like them. Then with a bright thought she slipped out the back door and down between the nodding grasses to the little brook which trailed away from the pond, where grew water cresses. She had discoverd them growing luxuriantly there a few days before on one of her walks, and she hastily picked a handful now, and came back in time to wash them and fringe the little platter for the beefsteak. On the whole, the dinner that Norah brought to the minister a few minutes later was enough to make a weary, hungry man revive. The beefsteak was done to that perfect, exquisite brown on both sides, with just the right shade of juicy pink in the middle. The fried potatoes were like unto none that John Endicott had ever eaten in a restaurant before, and they made him think of those his mother used to cook when he was a little boy and came home winter afternoons cold and hungry to find a nice supper all ready for him.

John Endicott ate that meal with a zest he had not known for years. Every shred of beefsteak, every morsel of the sweet, white bread. He enjoyed it fully as much as Holly enjoyed his dinner, if not more, and that is saying a great deal.

He did not order ice cream or pudding. The state of his pocketbook did not admit of such delicacies. But the memory of that beefsteak lingered with him for many a day. Its juiciness and tenderness put to shame all such humble imitations of its kind as had ever appeared upon Mrs. Bartlett's table.

But he had to pay for it with a glum supper. Mrs. Bartlett pursed her thin lips together shortly after they sat down to their evening repast, and remarked with an alacrity that showed she had been preparing the remark for at least two hours:

"I hear you've been tryin' the new tea room. Ain't our things good enough fer you any more?"

Her next door neighbor's niece, who was visiting in the village for a month, had happened to be passing "The Cedars" as he came out. She kindly ran in to tell Mrs. Bartlett of the offense.

"Why, Mrs. Bartlett, I came home so late from the funeral I knew lunch would all be cleared away; and, as I was very hungry, I just ran in there to get a bite to stay me till supper-time."

"I could have given you a piece, if you had asked me," she answered in an injured tone; "but it makes no difference. I s'pose there are attractions there that we haven't got." After that she closed her lips, and for the remainder of the meal no remarks from the boarder could coax to her face any relaxation, nor draw from her lips other than monosyllables with regard to the tea and gingerbread. The minister was in ill favor, and he knew by former experience that he would be punished for several days before he would feel that his old place was his own again. He sighed as he went up to his lonely room that night to hard work, but his thoughts during the evening were not of Sister Bartlett, nor of her whims and moods, but of a slender, white-robed girl, who sat in a large leather chair by a low table in the room across from the dining-room as he came out from his afternoon repast.

The next-door neighbor's niece had not been the only one who had known of his being at "The Cedars" that afternoon. Holly had stood across the road, and by his side Silas Barton, one-time saloon keeper, now a bootlegger masquerading as a druggist.

Holly had just been boasting to Silas of his dinner. Here was opposition springing under Silas' very nose! He had intended opening a sort of restaurant soon himself; and now he was taken unawares, and would not have the advantage of the first trade in that line. Silas was angry: His face took on an ugly sneer.

"It won't last," he growled. "No one could do anything in that house. It's been tried and failed."

Holly declared that the good looks of the present innkeeper would keep up trade, if nothing else. Holly had had the advantage of seeing the young proprietor a good deal when he helped them to move in.

"Ef she's such a beaut," boasted Barton, "I'll *marry* her and take over the business myself!"

Holly laughed loud and long. Holly was not too dull

to see how far apart these two would be. The laugh, for some reason, angered Barton beyond his usual control, and he turned an ugly face toward Holly.

Holly just then spied the minister, and, thinking to have a little more fun, for he meant no harm to any one, answered the minister's bow with a familiar greeting. "Ben to try the new eatin'-shop, parson? Purty good, ain't it?"

John Endicott smiled pleasantly, and agreed heartily that everything was very nice, adding a commonplace remark about the desirability of having such a convenience in the town. Si Barton turned his evil eyes on the minister with a leer and spoke in a loud voice that all in the vicinity could hear:

"So you've fell for her too, have ya? A painted face and a wicked smile'll get um every time. I thought you wasn't so doggone holy as you try to make out!"

A loud guffaw from a few loungers around the drug store followed this insinuation, and John Endicott, his face white with righteous anger, wheeled and faced the ugly bully.

Chapter XIII

By this time Jimmy had arrived. Jimmy was never known to have missed anything that happened in Rushville since he was old enough to toddle except the wreck the day that Constance arrived and he never quite forgave himself for having missed that.

A crowd gathered instantly from nobody knew where. For a moment it looked as if there was going to be a fight. The bootlegger's face was red with challenge. He was almost twice the size of his adversary. But there was something about John Endicott's attitude that made one think he could fight, and the sudden quick lifting of his arm gave the impression of not only strength but skill.

The crowd flashed a mute admiration at their minister, and stood back respectfully.

Then, suddenly, it was as if something unseen had restrained him. As if he had been denied permission to do this thing, the hand that had been lifted was slowly lowered to his side, though his eyes still held Barton in a stern look of rebuke, contempt flamed high in the red face of Barton and a laugh that was not good to hear rang out, feebly echoed by two or three bystanders.

Some would be glad to see the minister downed. They had a contempt for all ministers in general, and this one in particular, because his preaching had aroused the interest of the girls they went with; but they were too cowardly themselves to utter it.

With an oath the bootlegger, as if to draw his adversary on, brought out a sentence about Constance that was enough to make the blood of any good man boil. For a second again John Endicott's eyes and arm moved; but still the restraining power was upon him, and an exalted look of submission seemed flung over his face like a light from above. He stepped back suddenly as if a serpent had been in the way.

"Barton!" said he, a contempt now in his own voice, "you dishonor yourself by such words more than you could possibly dishonor me or any woman, good or bad; and this one is a stranger to us both."

He turned after his rebuke, and walked away amid a silence that was unbroken until he reached the corner, and was just about to pass out of sight. Then a single word was hurled at him by a boy on the edge of the crowd, a thin boy with hay-colored hair, light eyes, and a weak, contemptible mouth.

"Coward!" he yelled, loud and distinct. He would not have dared do it with the minister's eye upon him. It reached the minister's ears, and the crowd knew it must have done so, but he did not swerve a hair's breadth from his course, and was gone from their sight. The word seemed to rebound from him as if it had struck a wall of adamant.

Instantly, Jimmy dived under the arm of the man who stood between him and the tall boy. It was Lanky, whom he had whipped once that day. Jimmy gave him no time to prepare this time. Without warning he bounced, head down, straight into the stomach of the boy who had dishonored the minister, and, taking him thus unexpectedly, upset him into the road.

Jimmy was upon him before the boy fairly knew he was landed, and once more he recoiled under the iron grip of the wiry little fingers. Sitting astride of him, his seat well chosen for distance, his small bare legs encircling his victim's arms, pinioning them to his sides, Jimmy rained the blows thick and fast upon him.

The crowd stood back well pleased, not interfering, though a passing woman protested, "Some one ought to separate them kids." The crowd was being amused, and now that the fight between the minister and Barton was off they were willing to have a substitute.

Lanky, a coward himself by nature, cried out for mercy, and Jimmy paused in his work of retribution.

"You gotta say thet you know the minister ain't no coward," said Jimmy calmly, holding a threatening fist aloft ready to strike again.

Lanky, looking eagerly among the crowd for a friend, and meeting the wavering laugh of the bystanders, shut his mouth sullenly. He had not much choice. If he obeyed Jimmy, he would be the laughing-stock of the town, and, of all things, Lanky hated to be laughed at.

But he had not long to wait. The blows descended upon him once more with redoubled force and energy. There was determination in Jimmy's red, mad little face, and his grip was that of a bulldog. Lanky tried to unseat him, but in vain. At last he cried out,

"All right; have it yer own way!"

"Well, say it then, good an' loud," and the blows continued, though lighter.

"I say it," said Lanky at the top of his voice.

"No, that ain't what I mean. Yer to say the words *'The minister ain't no coward,'* just like that, only louder."

"The minister—aint—no—boo—ow!—ow!—ow! you stop! I can't talk when you hit me like thet."

"Well, then, say it good an' loud, loud enough fer the minister to hear. I'll wait till you get it said."

Jimmy paused threateningly.

"The—minister—ain't no—*coward*!" gasped Lanky shamedly.

"No, that ain't loud 'nough. The minister's clear to Mis' Bartlett's gate by this time. You *holler* it! Holler it loud 'nough fer him to hear!" And this time Lanky "hollered," and the word "*coward*" came sounding through the air, alone, to the minister's ear, making him long to turn and face them all. He looked down the street, half expecting to see a mob of small boys after him.

"Now," said Jimmy, looking down into his victim's face, "you ken git up. An', ef I ever catch you at anythin' like thet again, I won't let you off so easy."

Lightly he sprang up from his work, and, turning toward the crowd, who had of course sided with the victor, he cast one glance of scorn at them all as if he had but been doing what they should have done. The red face of Barton leered in the center, and Jimmy's eyes fixed themselves upon it for an instant, recognizing some subtle enmity between them; then he said, as he stuck his hands unconcernedly in his pockets, and turned to swagger away,

"Fer half a cent I'd lick *you*, too!"

The ready guffaw of the listeners followed him down the street, and he knew that he had the laugh on the bootlegger, whose angry, menacing glance he did not see. Straight into the gate of "The Cedars" he marched, and shut it slowly after him as if he were Constance's natural protector, and whistled as he walked up the path, reflecting on all that had happened.

"Thet's a great kid, thet is," reflected Holly aloud as he turned to leave the audience after the play was over. "He'll make his way in the world, I'll bet—an' some other folks's too, mebbe!" and he walked away pondering on chivalry. Later he took his way to the side door of the drug store and asked Jennie if she would go with him to have a dish of ice cream.

Jennie was a pretty girl though she was Si Barton's sister. Her chin tilted slightly, she had synthetic pink cheeks, large blue eyes that were not shy, and wore cheap, abnormally brief silk frocks, gaudy beads, and her hair in a bushy bob, which she constantly patted and smoothed. Jennie took a fashion magazine, and aimed to keep up with the times.

Commonly, Jennie looked with contempt upon Holly's advances, but this time Jennie was bored and besides she had another admirer whom she felt needed a little punishment. Therefore Jennie accepted the invitation.

She had on her pink sweater that night and a pink-and-white pleated skirt. Holly thought she looked unusually pretty. He decided that she was really prettier than the new lady who kept the tea room, though there was something stately and far away about *her* that made

her seem like a picture that one ought not to touch. Holly
was a thinker, in his way.

Jennie, half fearful of the twilight as she passed the
cedar trees, clung to Holly's great arm, and giggled a
good deal. She looked around the palm room with open
admiration, and declared it would make a lovely ball-
room. She wondered whether the new lady would have
a dance sometimes, and invite them all. Then she
remarked upon the missing mirror that was supposed to
exercise such strong ghostly power, and wondered what
the new lady had done with it. Holly called her attention to the great painting of the sea. Jennie said: "Yes,
it is pretty. Gosh! What a frame! It must have cost a
pile!" Holly saw she did not feel as he did about the
water, nor seem to imagine ships coming by in the misty
horizon. Holly was greatly struck by that picture.

Norah was very tired, though she would not admit it,
and Constance had sent her upstairs to rest, telling her
she was sure there would be no one else there that evening. Norah, saying she would just lie down a bit if Miss
Constance would call her when any one came, had finally submitted.

Constance sat in the sweet spring darkness of the piazza in her white flannel dress when Holly and Jennie
arrived. The room was lit up behind her, making a halo
of light. Her grandmother had retired for the night, and
there was nothing for Constance to do but wait to see
whether other customers would come. She did not expect any, or she would perhaps have kept Norah, for she
shrank from coming into contact with people; yet she
was trying to make up her mind to it, for she knew it
would have to be done sooner or later.

So it was Constance who took the order, and went in
her unaccustomed, awkward way to the freezer for the
cream. It was a wonder she did not flavor the cream with
salt, but good fortune attended her efforts; and, when
she had placed it before her customers, she felt that she
had accomplished a Herculean task. She was pleased as
a child being allowed to try some new duty. She sat in
the library across the hall, waiting to see whether there

was anything else needed while Holly and Jennie ate their cream and cake, and talked in low, half-shy tones.

"My! ain't she handsome?" exclaimed Jennie under her breath, following Constance with her eyes as she went out of the room. "She looks for all the world like one of the ladies in my fashion paper, and I don't see what makes it! She hasn't got much jewelry and no make-up at all. Her clothes look as if they grew on her and didn't bother her a bit."

"I don't see's they look's purty's yourn," said Holly gallantly. "Thet there bias pink rosette you've got slung on your shoulder, ef that's what you call it, 's mighty becomin'."

Jennie giggled and flushed a pretty pink over the compliment to the artificial rose she wore, but she could not get done with the appearance of Constance.

"Wisht I knew how she waves her hair," she murmured.

"Why don't you ast her?" said Holly. He always went straight to the point.

"Would you?" said Jennie, pleased with the thought. "Mebbe I will when I get to know her better."

"Seems to me your hair's purty enough as 'tis," said Holly with a clumsy wink that was meant to show appreciation.

Jennie felt a glow of pleasure over his gentle tone. She looked her rough admirer over critically. He wouldn't be so bad-looking, she thought, if he could be dressed up like a real gentleman. A white shirt and a stylish necktie was the making of a man in Jennie's opinion.

When they had finished, Jennie lingered in the hall, casting a wistful eye into the open library that had a look about it of a world Jennie did not know. It invited her, and she longed to go in and investigate. But Holly had in view a walk in the moonlight and he hurried her out.

It was late the next afternoon, when Constance sat down in the library to answer some letters and put a few old friends off their trail, that Jennie made her first venture.

She came stealing to the front door, half afraid. Tiptoeing into the hall, and finding no one about, she ventured to knock on the library door, then, half abashed, drew back to the shelter of the front entrance.

Constance, surprised, opened the door, and there stood the girl, in all her bravery of best clothes. She had chosen a new, cheap, bright blue silk for the occasion, and she looked shy and uncomfortable.

"I thought I'd come over to call," said Jennie shyly, as she found Constance expected her to speak first, evidently thinking she had come to order somthing in the tea room. "I thought mebbe you'd be lonesome in a new place, and would like another girl to come in and be friendly."

"Why, certainly," said Constance, bewildered. It occurred to her that this was kindness. "Won't you come in and sit down? Come right in here," she said on second thought, pushing back the heavy portières of her own inner sanctum, the room back of the library, where stood her beautiful piano, her favorite books, and all the prettiest of her own particular things. It was her spot where she could come and feel at home when the new life grew hard and unbearable, if it ever did. Just now it was interesting, though she saw possibilities in the future which made this room seem like a citof refuge. What impulse seized her to bring this girl into her inner sanctum she did not know.

"My! ain't this pretty!" said Jennie, looking around with satisfaction. "This looks egzactly like a room in my fashion paper. They tell how you can make rooms real pretty. I been thinking of trying, but I was afraid. Mebbe I'll try, now I've seen a real one to pattern after. Oh, do you play the py-ano? Won't you please play for me? Oh, I'd just love to have a py-ano. I've got a norgan, cab-'net, you know, and I took a whole term of lessons on it. I love to play hymns. I can play 'Jesus, Lover of my soul,' and 'Way down on the S'wanee River,' and 'All by yourself in the moonlight.' Can you play that? I've always wanted to see if I got it right. Sarah Briskit sent it to me from Philadelphia. She's moved there. She was my girl friend. I haven't had any since she went away.

Mebbe you 'n' I'll get to be intimate friends. I think I'd like you real well."

Constance smiled, though she was conscious of a chilly feeling about her heart. This was not exactly the kind of intimate friend she would have chosen. Nevertheless, it might be that this was all that was left to her. Well, a friend was not to be despised. She would find out what kind of a girl this was.

Jennie rattled on.

"We haven't been introduced, have we? I'm Jennie Barton. My brother owns the stores across the road. I keep house for him. No, we haven't anybody else in the family. Pa and ma died a long while ago. I lived with my aunt in Cross Crick till Si came here and wanted me to keep house for him, but I don't like it much. I hate to live over a store. I tried to get Si to rent our rooms to another party, and get us a house down the street; but he won't do it. He's awfully set in his ways. What's your name? Yes, I know the last part, Weth'rell. Jimmy Watts told me. But I mean your first name. If we're going to be intimate, we'll have to know each other's names. Constance? My! What a funny name! I don't know but it's kind of pretty and high-sounding, though. But do folks call you that? What do your girl friends where you come from call you?"

Constance thought quickly. She certaintly did not care to have this girl flinging her first name about familiarly in the drug store. But neither did she care to hurt her feelings.

Constance hesitated:

"Well, you know," she said pleasantly, "in a city people are a little more formal than in small places, I guess——"

"Well, what do you like to be called?"

Here was the question. Constance must face it; and in her answer she showed the delicate tact of her high breeding.

"I think I like to be called 'Miss Wetherill' usually. That is what I am accustomed to, you know. Except, perhaps, here in this room when we are all alone. You might call me 'Constance' then, if you wanted to. When other people are by, 'Miss Wetherill' would be much more suitable."

Jennie looked at her in undisguised admiration. Already the subtle something in Constance, which made the difference between them, had impressed her. She was half-ashamed that she had presumed.

"My!" she said at last, " 'Constance!' I don't know's I'd dare! I think I'll call you just 'Dear' if you don't mind. You look like 'Dear'; do you know it?"

Constance's heart melted at this sincere admiration. Jennie was crude but she had possibilities.

The call lasted some time. Constance played for her caller. She explained that "All by yourself in the moonlight" was not in her répertoire, but she would play some of her favorites. She tried a bright waltz or two just to test the taste of her guest. Jennie's eyes shone, and she came and stood beside the piano with great delight in her face, her cheap little high-heeled shoes tapping the floor in time to the music. Then Constance, just out of curiosity, opened a volume of Chopin's Nocturnes and Preludes.

"Now I'm going to play you something that I love myself. I want to see what you think about it."

Jennie's face flashed a smile.

She began to play, and the girl stood in a strange fascination. The music no longer claimed her attention. She was watching the white fingers gliding over the keys, the gleam of the rings, the pretty turn of the wrist; admiring and envying. Oh, to be like this!

She drew a long sigh when the music was over, and sank down in the easy-chair near the piano. "I like the other best," she confessed frankly. "This one makes me feel kind of sad. Do you like to be sad?"

"Why, no," said Constance, wheeling about to her guest. "It isn't all sad. Next time you come over I'll play it again, and explain it to you. There's a meaning to it, you know."

"There *is*?" said the girl wonderingly. "Is there a meaning to all music? Well, now that's queer. You know a whole lot of things, don't you? My! I wish I was like you.

I never had much chance. But I take a fashion paper, and I'm trying to do all I can. I reckon you'll be a help to me, too. Say, do you mind telling me how you wave your hair? Holly said he thought 'twould be all right for me to ask."

"Not at all," said Constance, laughing good-naturedly; "I never wave it at all. It waves itself. It was made that way. But who is Holly?"

"My!" said Jennie. "How nice! Natural curly! I'd just give anything if mine was. Why, Holly? He's a friend of mine's [Holly had made some progress with Jennie during his walk the night before], the one I was with for ice cream last night."

Jennie left soon after that, leaving Constance somewhat shaken in her ideas of things. This was an entirely new type but amazingly interesting. Yet she could not help wondering what Morris Thayer would say it he could see her playing Chopin to this crude girl.

Chapter XIV

Jimmy had preferred his request about churchgoing early in the week. Constance was somewhat dismayed at the idea at first, and told him she would see; but Jimmy was not easily balked in a desire, and he talked so much about the church, the minister, the singing, and the service that Constance, laughing, promised to go with him the following Sabbath evening.

Jimmy appeared with his hair slicked smoothly back, and a collar several sizes too large surrounding his thin little neck like a high board fence. It was, in fact, one which had belonged to his elder brother. He put it on for this occasion because it seemed more grown up. He looked very happy and uncomfortable, if those two things can go hand in hand.

Constance in quiet city Sunday garb walked by his side, looked at him surreptitiously several times, and tried to keep from smiling. She decided she liked the Jimmy of every day better than this young country coxcomb, and wondered whether it would not be possible for her to induce him to send for a nice dark blue serge suit from the city, and let him pay for it in installments. She did not wish to make him conscious of his attire that evening; so she forbore to suggest it then, and Jimmy swaggered along by her side, calmly unconscious of the impression he was making upon her. He looked at each one who passed to see whether they saw with whom he was walking. Jimmy was exceedingly proud of his lady.

Constance noticed as they passed into the church how

near the drug store seemed to it. The loungers by the
drug-store door could easily hear the singing and preaching when the windows were open. The store was brightly
lighted, and business seemed to be going on as briskly
as on any other day in the week.

Some of the church windows were open a foot from
the bottom, and the heads and shoulders of people could
be seen from the street. The church looked pleasant and
very bright inside. There was a warmth of spirit in the
very atmosphere that made Constance think of her aunt
Susan's home. That was it, it was homelike.

There was only a much-worn red and black carpet on
the floor reënforced by coarse cocoa matting in the aisles,
and the walls were white plaster, much cracked, with no
attempt at decoration. The windows had a border of colored paper in imitation of stained glass, and the rest of
the panes were coated with something white which looked
like whitewash. The pulpit was plain and "grained." The
two chairs behind it were covered with haircloth, the do-
nation of an old elder, long since departed from this life.
It was plain and dingy and unassuming in the extreme,
nothing beautiful nor churchlike about it; yet the moment Constance entered, she felt a pleasant sense of cheer
and hopefulness.

They sat about half-way up the side, and Constance
looked about her in wonder. The church was filling
rapidly. It was evident there would be no empty seats.
Two old ladies in front nodded their black bonnets together, whispering loudly about some sick one in their
family. They took an eager interest in all the newcomers
who walked up the aisles, keeping up a running comment
on them. Constance quite enjoyed it. Her eyes danced
in spite of her, though the rest of her face was demure.
She kept reminding herself that this was church service,
though it was so unlike any she had ever attended before that it was hard to realize it.

She compared it to the deeply carpeted aisles and dim
arches of the stately edifice in which she had been accustomed to worship on Sundays, and a sense of the vast
difference made her wonder whether this church were not

a sort of travesty on the sacred temple of the living God. Yet she knew that in her own church there was probably, that evening, no such crowd gathered to worship, for the home church was not well attended in the evening. She had been once at night with a relative who was visiting with them, and there were no more than forty people in the great church. She had heard it said that that was the usual evening attendance except upon special occasions. She had always supposed that most people were weary in the evening, and did not care to go to church; for her own part, she had never felt a desire to go again.

The minister came up the aisle just a moment later. The people at the door seemed to flock about him and be anxious each to have a word with him, and many followed in at once as if his coming was what they had been waiting for. The old sexton, a little man with grizzly hair and a roughly shaven face, went over to the front door, and took hold of the bell-rope. With a pause, as if he would give the boys about the steps a warning, he held his hands high for an instant and then threw his weight upon the rope, and the old bell turned and gave forth a doleful utterance, loud, penetrating, wailing, yet solemn as a warning from the grave. The whole church shook with the fervor of its utterance. Constance started and looked around to see what could possibly be happening. But all the people sat still, and no one seemed to think there was anything unusual going on. Gradually it dawned upon her that the hour for evening service was being rung, and that this ceremony had been waited for by that line of boys outside the door, who now were slipping in and filling the back seats decorously enough. An elderly woman with tired eyes and hair sprinkled with gray took her place at the cabinet organ, and as soon as the last reverberation of the bell died away the organ began.

To Constance's ear, trained to enjoy a symphony orchestra, the whole thing was awful. The bell seemed like the falling of tin pans and pots and kettles in one awful clanging crash; the organ reminded her of an asthmatic cat, as it drawled out a gospel hymn.

To Jimmy, whose soul rejoiced in both bell and organ, the sounds were solemn and awe-inspiring. Whenever he sat in church—and particularly since this new minister had come—and the old bell began its work, little tingling thrills of mingled joy and awesomeness would go through him. He felt it tonight in double force, because, in a sense, the church was his, and he was displaying it. He glanced at his companion a number of times to see whether she was properly impressed, and was well pleased to see her turn to watch the bell-ringer an instant.

Jimmy took delight in song, and he was glad for the tune that had been selected for an opening that evening, "There is life for a look at the crucified One." It was a favorite one since Mr. Endicott came there. He had them sing it a great deal. Jimmy liked it. He knew all the words and even growled it out to himself sometimes when he was dressing in the mornings. He found the place in the book, and held it out to his companion. Constance took it, her eyes dancing with the merriment she felt over the organ prelude.

But now the people began to sing, and Jimmy was singing. His little colorless brows were drawn together in an earnest frown, and he was putting his whole soul into the words. So were all the people. They dragged horribly, it is true, and their voices were untrained and nasal; but they were singing from the heart, and they were *all* singing. Their minister had trained them to that. He had impressed it upon them that the music was a part of the service as much as the prayer or the sermon, and it was their part. He had told them that he could not do his part well without their incense of prayer and praise, for which God listened and waited. So they sang.

Presently the spirit in the room came over Constance, too, and she sang. The words were impressive. Constance could not help wondering whether the men around the store heard, and whether the words meant anything to them. Was there life for such men as that at this moment if they chose to take it? Could they turn around by simply believing in a system of religion and be different? Did the crucified One have a real power in the world, or not?

Constance was unconsciously dealing with deep theological subjects, but ever since the change had come into her life she had been more or less filled with the thought of God; how and why He let certain things happen to certain people; whether He really did take any personal interest in individuals as the Bible stated. She would have been incredulous if she had been told that she might as well have been an out-and-out infidel all her life as the kind of negative, indifferent Christian she had been, a Christian only because she had been confirmed when a child, and because it belonged to the traditions of her house to be trained that way. It had given her no peace or comfort, nor had it been in any way a part of her daily thought or life. Not until she spent those days with her aunt Susan had it come to her to wonder whether there was anything else in religion for her than the mere going to church once on Sunday and giving to charitable causes when asked.

The people bowed their heads with a slight rustle, and Constance bowed her head also. The minister prayed briefly:

"Jesus Christ, Thou who hast promised that where two or three are gathered together in Thy name there Thou wilt be in the midst of them, help us to feel Thy presence here tonight in this room. Let Thy Spirit brood over each heart, and impress us with Thy life that is freely given to us. Help us to take it. Help us to know if we are not taking it."

During the rest of the opening exercises Constance watched the minister. She made up her mind that he was an interesting man.

And this was the man who had patronized her tea room the first day of its opening. She had caught one glimpse of his face as she passed into the library through the hall. She had not connected him then with the man who had addressed her in the moonlight, and indeed had almost forgotten about that little adventure, for John Endicott had never yet made up his mind to say anything

more to her about the matter. His little experience with
Silas Barton on the day when he had been to the tea
room, and Mrs. Bartlett's after-comments with pursed
lips and offended air, had made him cautious of the new
family. He did not care to become town talk. He would
bide his time.

So Constance was having her first view of him in full
bright light. She decided at once there was something fine
about him that held attention. He looked like a man who
would be true no matter what came.

He divided his subject that evening into three heads,
with a text for each. The first was, "Ye will not come
to me that ye might have life." He spoke very simply and
searchingly about the indifference of the world to Jesus
Christ, and the general apathy concerning eternal life,
while yet life was the thing that all were reaching after.
As he talked, Constance felt that he was looking straight
at her, and searching into her life. She knew suddenly
that hers was an empty life, an indifferent life, just the
kind of life he had been describing. She listened intently
to all that he said. His directness appealed to her. She
was ready for the next heading.

"I am come that they might have life, and that they
might have it more abundantly." The common idea that
Christianity was a wearisome business was combated by
the words of Jesus himself. He was come that every one
might have life in abundance, full, free, delightful, not
a poor groveling for existence. He spoke just a word on
what life should be, life at its fullest, and compared it
to the life that many led. Then he told of a poor, hungry wanderer whom some one brought into his house,
and put down to a table abundantly supplied with all the
good things of the season, plenty, more than could be
eaten, and in richness and variety. He showed them how
that was what Jesus would do for the soul that would
come to Him.

Jimmy sat there, his eyes big and round, drinking it
all in, thinking of the fine meals he had had lately of
Norah's cooking, and comparing them to the scanty ones
which were sometimes served in his own home, where

his mother could barely get bread enough to go around. Jimmy was not quite sure what part of him his soul was, but he felt that he would like to have his soul as well supplied as his hungry little stomach had been lately. A dim idea of what more abundant life might mean was dawning upon his young animal senses, and it was appealing to him through the new experiences that had been his since Constance came.

Constance looked about the room. Every eye was upon the minister. People had forgotten about everything but what he was saying. In some faces there was a wistful longing for a fuller life. Constance suddenly knew that her own heart felt a great need.

She turned back, wondering whether in this little country church, with its outlandish furnishings, atrocious music, and uncultivated people, she was to find anything that would satisfy her.

The sermon had reached the third head.

"And this is life eternal, that they might know Thee, the only true God, and Jesus Christ, whom Thou hast sent."

The minister pictured a life that not even death could cause to tremble and fear, because Jesus had conquered all things, even death.

The speaker's voice changed slightly, as one will change tone to speak to another person who stands close by, and he said:

"O Jesus Christ, wilt Thou show this roomful of people how much joy and comfort and *life* they might find in Thee if they will come and get acquainted with Thee, as a man talks with his friend face to face? Go with us this week and help us to get hold of a different kind of life, the kind of life Thou canst give us if we know Thee. We ask it because Thou hast promised, and we trust in Thee. Amen."

There was a solemnity that pervaded the audience even after the hymn was given out. No one looked at his neighbor, or stirred to gather up wraps. All were intent upon the hymn, which seemed to be looked for as a kind of climax to the sermon. And Constance found herself look-

ing curiously at the words to see what the preacher had
selected to finish his discourse.

> I sighed for rest and happiness;
> I yearned for them, not Thee;
> But, while I passed my Saviour by,
> His love laid hold on me.

As she read the words, Constance felt as if they were
written for her, and she longed to be able to sing the
chorus with the heartiness of the old man who sat across
the aisle:

> Now none but Christ can satisfy;
> No other name for me;
> There's love, and life, and lasting joy,
> Lord Jesus, found in Thee.

As Constance followed Jimmy down the aisle after the
benediction, she was conscious of having been a part of
that service more than of any service she had ever attended before in her life.

"We are glad to see you here tonight," said the minister
at the door as he reached out a welcoming hand.

"Thank you," said Constance simply. "I have enjoyed
the service."

It was merely a pleasant thing to say, but in spite of
herself Constance put more meaning into the tone than
she wished to do. She did not care to have that minister
see how deeply into self he had searched for her. But
there came a sudden lighting of his eyes as if he had met
a kindred spirit.

"Then you know Him," he said in a low tone, for the
groups about them were talking to one another at that
moment, and did not seem to notice. They were almost
at the steps.

He looked at her almost eagerly. It seemed as if he
longed to have her understand.

Constance was embarrassed. She did not know how
to reply. Her face flushed.

"I am afraid not, in the way you have been describing," she answered half shyly. Then the crowd surged between them, and she passed out.

Jimmy was very quiet on the way home. He seemed thoughtful. At last he said: "Thet there dinner he told 'bout was like some o' yours. Say, I guess you're one o' them kind of folks, ain't you?"

Constance started in the darkness. The same question, with the same taking-for-granted tone that the minister had used. Only the phraseology differed. She had been honest with herself and the minister, and confessed that she was not what she had been supposed, but now with Jimmy she shrank from saying "No." She recognized a something in his voice like inquiry. She knew instantly, though she had had no experience in such things, that this little soul was reaching out after some kind of newness of life. He was as ready to take it from Jesus Christ as he had been to take if from Constance Wetherill. Her instinct told her that it might be disastrous to him to be turned aside from his search for better things. Strange to say, though she was not fully impressed that Constance Wetherill needed newness of life, she fully realized that Jimmy Watts did. Therefore she hesitated for an answer, and found herself turning the question upon her interrogator.

"Are you, Jimmy?"

Jimmy kicked a stone out of his path, and dug his hands deeper into his Sunday pockets in search of something familiar to help him out.

"Never knowed much 'bout sech things. I might try ef I thought I could be like him. He's great, he is. Mebbe I'll try," said Jimmy. "Good night!" and he sped away into the darkness.

Chapter XV

The next afternoon Jennie made her second call. "I saw you at church last night. I meant to speak to you, but you got out so quick I couldn't. I sing in the choir. Didn't you see me? I nodded to you twice, but you just looked straight ahead. I s'pose you didn't expect to see me up there, did you? Yes, I sing. I've sung ever since I was a little mite of a thing. They used to have me sing at all the children's concerts when I was little. They asked me to sing, and I don't mind. It makes something goin' on. Si didn't like it very well when he found out I'd promised, 'cause, you see, he don't like the minister. He says he meddles with what don't concern him, and tries to make trouble about his selling sodas on Sunday. Well, I don't know but I 'gree with him. I've got a boy friend that drives a truck. He goes all over the country, and has real nice times; and he makes a whole lot of money. I wish Si had some business like that. But there's no use talkin', Si is awfully set. Say, why don't you bob your hair?"

Constance hesitated. She could not tell this bobbed head that she hated it.

"I never saw any hair look prettier than yours," went on her admirer, "and yet it isn't like that in the fashion-book. It doesn't look quite fashionable to me."

Constance smiled pleasantly; "Don't you think it is better for people to have a little individuality in the way they dress? They can conform, of course, to the general mode of the prevailing style; but, when it comes to every woman in the world cutting her hair just because some one else does, it seems ridiculous. I think it is so much better to wear things that are becoming."

"I never thought about it that way," said Jennie thoughtfully.

Constance ventured a little further.

"Did you ever try your hair in that new way that so many girls use now, parted and waved and done in a soft knot behind? I think that would be becoming to you, and your hair seems quite long enough to do that way."

Jennie arose, and walked solemnly to a mirror that hung at one end of the room, where she surveyed herself with dissatisfaction.

Constance went on, "You should study the lines of your head and face, and try to follow them. See, you have put your head all out of proportion letting your hair bush out that way."

Jennie blushed uncomfortably. She had been very proud of her hair, but she admired her new friend exceedingly and she now perceived that one or the other must go. Which should it be? She looked at the clear reflection of herself in the glass, and then back to the cultured, lovely face of her friend, crowned by the soft golden-brown hair, then again to herself in the glass; and behold, she was no longer pleased with her pretty little self.

"Fix it!" she demanded, tears springing into her eyes. "Put it up like yours."

Constance sat in dismay before her, her hands shrinking from the task put upon them. Her influence had worked with a vengeance. Arrange human hair on another head than her own! Horrible! Her flesh shrank back from the thought. She, who had always from her very babyhood had some one to arrange her own hair whenever she chose, to be asked to arrange the hair of this coarse, possibly unclean girl! How could she?

"Won't it fix like yours?" demanded Jennie, anxiously peering through her bushy locks, a kind of fierce desperation in her eyes. Constance was touched. She had undone this girl's self-satisfaction and given her nothing in its place. She must help her out.

It is strange how interested Constance was in that hair after she had once conquered her aversion to touching it. The skillful fingers went to work swiftly subduing the wiry locks to comeliness. In a few minutes Jennie stood before the glass staring in amazement. She did not know herself.

"My land! I never knew I could look like that!" she ejaculated. "Why I look almost as good as you do. I don't believe folks will know me. If I can only keep it like that I'll be satisfied. I know there's something about you that's all right and I haven't got it! Say!" she said suddenly, whirling around and facing Constance, "You're a Christian, aren't you? I knew you must be the minute I laid eyes on you. You make me think of the minister every time I see you. There's something about you both that there isn't many in this town has."

Here was the same question again, and this time it was embarrassing. Without her own desire she had come to stand in the attitude of helper to this girl. She had seen Jennie in church, and had watched her changing face as she listened to the sermon. It had been swept by many emotions, and Constance felt that here was another who needed the help of that Helper of whom the minister had spoken. Jennie had paused, and was waiting for an answer, her eyes upon Constance's face searchingly. Constance had always considered herself a Christian. Why should she not say, "Yes"? And yet she felt in her heart that she was not the kind of Christian the minister had meant when he spoke of that "fulness of life."

"Why, yes," said she hesitatingly, "I'm—a church-member."

"There, I knew you were! Say, then, you'll take our Sunday-school class, won't you?"

"Take your Sunday-school class? Oh, I couldn't!" said Constance, aghast. This was worse than doing up hair. Was this what her new life was leading her into?

"Oh, yes, you must. I thought of it myself, and asked Mr. Endycut if he wouldn't give you to us. I told all the girls in our class, and they're just wild about you."

"But you'll have to excuse me," said Constance in consternation. "I've never taught a Sunday-school class in my life. I couldn't think of it."

"Well, but you see we all want you, and we won't have anybody else. Old Mis' Bartlett tried us; but she got mad the second Sunday, and said we tried to insult her because we laughed when she got somebody's name mixed up. I said I knew a teacher we could get and the girls were so pleased, and said they'd all keep on coming if you'd take the class. Jimmy said he thought you ought to have a class of boys and he'd be one if you'd come teach, but I thought we'd get ahead of him asking you."

"It will be impossible at present," said Constance a trifle stiffly. She longed to flee back to her old home and its safe shelter, where no young urchins nor impossible girls would trouble her with their hair and their morals. Jimmy was all right. Jimmy she was fond of, but a whole class of boys! Horrible!

It was almost nine o'clock that evening when the minister made his first call. Perhaps he purposely made his visit late, that there might not be a number of loungers in the vicinity to witness his entrance to the house. He was not anxious to have any more scenes such as had occurred in front of the drug store, but he was determined to find out this newcomer, and if possible explain his abrupt appearance in her back yard that first evening.

Constance had spent a weary two hours listening to her grandmother's stories of the past; for somehow, now that she had left that old life of society, it was not pleasant to her to hear much about it. Those old scenes and people belonged to another girl, a girl with money and social prestige. She was just a plain, every-day girl earning her own living, no better than any one else. Her friends back there in her past would want nothing to do with her here.

She almost felt like crying that night, for she had worked hard all day. There had been an unusual number of people in for meals, and Norah had to have help. She had been learning a lot about cooking; and, though she was interested in it and wanted to do it, it wearied her as any new work will. Norah would not let her wash the dishes nor do anything that would soil her hands; neither would she let her appear to wait upon people in the dining-room. She felt that she was the only one in the wide world now to take care of her young lady, and she meant to do it to the best of her ability. Waiting upon common people was no work for a lady, and she would prevent it as long as possible.

But neither Norah nor Constance had been brought up under circumstances calculated to teach them economy, and the first week's receipts had not been enormously satisfactory. On the whole, Constance was weary and discouraged, and longed for her old life more than she had done since she had first left it. There was, too, an undertone of a new want, a want which had been growing upon her ever since she visited her aunt Susan, a want which the Sunday's sermon had deepened, and made more insistent. Then, too, that girl Jennie, with all her queer requests and impertinent questions, was a problem yet unsolved. Constance half wished that she might run away from it all.

Her grandmother had been asking some troublesome questions about this house, and who owned it, and why there were not more boarders; and, though she expressed herself as very happy so long as her granddaughter cared to remain, Constance could see that she was feeling that it was only a temporary residence, and was looking forward to a return to New York in the near future. She was not sinking into that blissful oblivion to the outside world and its happenings that Constance had hoped for. For instance, she had been very curious to know when Constance had heard last from Morris Thayer, and why he did not come to see them. It seemed queer to her, she said, that he should forget them so utterly; of course Constance had kept him posted as to their whereabouts. And Constance had not dared to tell her that she had not, lest the dear old lady should immediately write to some friend and send Morris Thayer the information Constance most earnestly desired he should not have.

It was, therefore, trying, to have Norah come to her

and announce that there was a man downstairs who wanted to see her.

"But I'm tired tonight, Norah; I don't want to see any one," she said irritably. "Who it it? What is his name?"

"Indade he niver guv it me, ma'am, an' me bein' so onused to door-tendin' niver thunk to ast. He's a gintlemon, though, ivery bit, an' it'll mebbe do ye a bit gude to tahk wid him."

Constance turned on her with sudden suspicion.

"What do you mean, Norah? It's no one from home, surely? It's not Mr. Thayer?"

"No, indade, Miss Connie. Sure, did yez thank I'd be afther a kapin' me muth shet ef 'twas the loikes ov anny of them? It's sumbuddy as lives in the toiwne, an' he axes right p'lite, cud he see Miss Wetherill."

Constance unconsciously gave a glance in the glass as she passed, and a touch to her hair. She was curious to know who would call. Perhaps some one wished to engage regular board. That might be a help. She swept down the stairs with her regal manner and the minister, waiting for her in the library, for Norah had not dared admit him to the inner room without her mistress's permission, looked up to wonder and admire.

There was something winning in his smile, and his eyes had a way of lighting up that made them handsome. Constance could not help answering with another smile.

"Will you ask me again, Miss Wetherill, what I am doing here, and give me a chance to explain myself?" he asked; and Constance, knowing at once what he meant, laughed merrily.

"I understand," she said; "you need not explain. You took me for the white lady who lived in this 'haunted' house. Jimmy has told me all about her, and I have quite enjoyed the joke."

He watched her face as she spoke; noting the pretty curves of lip and cheek and chin, the ease of her pose, the perfect grace of every line in her slight figure, the soft, well-modulated voice, and wondered where she dropped from, and what good fortune, or ill, sent her to Rushville to keep a tea room.

"Won't you sit down?" she said. "No, not in here; we are liable to interruption," and she pushed back the curtains, and led him into the room beyond.

Instantly his faced changed. Delight, appreciation, spoke in every feature. Ah! here was a room that spoke forth the character of its occupant. His mental vision compared it to his own suite of apartments at Mrs. Bartlett's. Here were luxury and ease and all the beautiful things to which he had never been accustomed, and yet which his soul naturally recognized and appreciated.

"Oh, this is a good place to rest and talk," he said as he settled into the great easy-chair to which Constance motioned him. Everything there was a delight to his beauty-starved eyes. Constance looking at him saw the sharp outline of his face in the soft lamplight, and thought he looked tired. She touched a little bell, and, when Norah appeared, told her to bring them some tea; and presently Norah, acting on her own advice, set before them a tray containing tea, dainty sandwiches, and little cakes, and the coziness seemed complete.

Doubtfully had the minister entered the haunted house; well had he drilled himself in the thought that it was late and he must not stay long; and many times had he told himself that he must go cautiously, because he really knew nothing about this strange girl; nevertheless, he stayed a whole hour and a half. After they had finished the tea and cakes, and had talked about a number of books that lay upon the table, some of which he had read, and all of which he had read about, and longed to read, but had neither the time nor the books, he turned toward the piano lovingly as to an old friend, and said, almost pleadingly:

"You will play me something, Miss Wetherill? I have had no music since I left college, and I long to hear some again. My chum was quite a musician, and had a piano in his room, and many's the hour I have lain and listened to him play."

She sat down at the piano, and then of course the time flew by on wings. He closed his eyes, and reveled in the sound, then opened them to steal glances at the player.

He could scarcely believe his senses that he sat here amid those sounds, with this lovely woman playing for him. He must be mistaken. Was he not back in Mrs. Bartlett's second-story back room with the red and green ingrain carpet, dreaming wild dreams that would never be realities?

But suddenly the music ceased; and he knew it had been real, and that it must be late. Mrs. Bartlett would be on the watch, and if it were a possible thing would discover where he had been, by the law of elimination if by no other method. She would begin on Lamper's baby, and inquire whether it were dying, or whether old Deacon Trumpet had had another bad spell; and she would find out every place where he had been or had not been that day. He must hurry away. Besides, what did Miss Wetherill think of his staying so long this first time? He had enjoyed himself so much that he had forgotten everything else. He had even forgotten to find out what kind of a person she was, and whether she would take a Sunday-school class. They would have to wait until another time now, and he sadly reflected that the other times must be few and far between if he would not have Mrs. Bartlett and all the other good ladies of his congregation after him with their sharp tongues.

He stood, hat in hand, preparatory to going, when he remembered some of his reasons for coming. It would have been easier to ask her certain questions before he had listened to her music, for now he felt she was so far above him in many ways that it seemed presumptuous to think of helping her. He looked at her hesitatingly, and then said:

"You have given me a great deal of pleasure this evening, and your music has almost made me forget to ask you what you meant last evening. I hope you know the Lord, Miss Wetherill."

Constance felt a sudden chilly breath sweep over her with a realization of something which troubled her. She had not known before that this subject had become a vital one to her, but now it seemed like something she could not get away from. It pursued her everywhere in this new home. The minister's call, the first touch with her own native world of culture that she had had since coming to Rushville, had made her forget the new life with all its perplexities for a little while. She had heartily enjoyed talking about her favorite books and music with one who knew and loved them, and she had found many a gleam of appreciation in the dark eyes that met hers as they were talking, or as she looked up from her playing. She had a pleasant sense of companionship with one who would understand her mood. But now with his few quiet words all was changed, and a cloud settled upon her sweet brow.

"I do not know," she answered simply after a pause. "I have always supposed I was; that is, in a way; but a number of things lately have made me feel that I am not. Your sermon made me feel so. I never heard a sermon just like that, or perhaps I never listened to one before. I do not understand the kind of life you spoke of. I wish I did. It seems ideal and impossible.

"It is not impossible," he said earnestly. "I should like to tell you all that Christ has been to me."

Constance, watching him, could not but compare this man with Morris Thayer. She felt that he had something of which she was not possessed.

"I should like to hear it," she answered gravely.

He did not linger much longer and when he was gone Constance went to her room thoughtfully. She had enjoyed this evening. The young minister was interesting, and had a keen sense of humor. She smiled as she recalled several witty stories he had told. How different he was from Morris Thayer!

He could not be a great man probably, else he would not be preaching in this out-of-the-way place, but he had fine traits, and it was easy to see that his tastes and instincts were right. Then, too, he was not lacking in education. He could appreciate Chopin and Beethoven.

Altogether she was glad he had called. It had made a pleasant break in the secluded life she led.

She went to sleep with a dreamy satisfaction in the finding of one congenial friend in her exile.

Chapter XVI

The minister knelt long beside his study chair that night. How soon might he go and tell her more about his Lord? It must not be at once, for he must go cautiously. There were many tongues to wag in Rushville, and they made as loud a clamor as the katydids when they began. He did not wish to have them turned upon him. He could almost imagine it. "Mr. Endicott did! Yes, he did! I know he did!" and few would be the voices on the other side to say: "No, he didn't! I say he didn't!" He must just put that matter into the hands of the Lord, and ask Him when to go. There would be some guidance, he felt sure. With all his heart he wished a way might open for him to visit Miss Wetherill frequently for the music and the talk had put into his life an element which had been lacking since he had left college, and for which he often felt a great longing. There were few people of culture in Rushville, there were many quiet homes of true refinement, where the opportunities for culture had been lacking. In these he was a welcome visitor, and enjoyed many restful hours. Nevertheless, there were not many where music in its highest forms was even understood, much less was a part of the daily life, and where the latest books were read and discussed; neither was there a single home where art and luxury united to make beautiful surroundings. This plain man, born in a plain home, surrounded all his life with the simplest of this world's goods, seeing luxury only occasionally and from afar, yet loved beautiful surroundings, and was rested by them.

It came about through old Mrs. Wetherill.

She had declared a wish, one day, to take a drive. She seemed to forget that they had moved, and that the car had been left in New York. For a moment Constance thought she would leave her undeceived; but then she reflected that it would be impossible, for her grandmother would at once notice that the car was not their own; so she said gently:

"Well, grandmother, you know we didn't have the car sent down. But I think I can get one here. You lie down and rest a bit while I go out to see."

"Send a servant, child. Don't go yourself. It isn't becoming even in the country," said the old lady. "It's likely they have a garage here, or a telephone, at least."

"All right, grandmother," said Constance, slipping away quickly as she always did when her grandmother began to ask troublesome questions. There were a great many of these, and Constance sometimes felt as if she were living in a web of deception, and was half-tempted to tell the old lady the whole truth now that they were established here, and her grandmother seemed tolerably comfortable; only some little sentence would so often reveal how utterly shaken to its foundations her grandmother's life would be if she should discover the true state of their finances, how perfectly crushed and humiliated to know her granddaughter was earning her living by keeping a tea room. Why disturb her last days by so great a revolution? It was too late to change her ideas and show her that a girl who earned her living by making toast and coffee for Holly Beech was just as good as when she made chocolate and served it with expensive wafers to Morris Thayer in her New York reception room.

She pondered these things as she ran downstairs to tell Norah she would have to get along with the tea room as best she could until their return. She would try to be back in time to help at noontime. For the new business had received not a little patronage, first from curiosity and then from real liking, and was growing in favor with the few in town who were without a home table. A few housewives had slipped in curiously to get a dish of ice

cream and wonder why the sponge cake was so much
more delectable than their own.

The doctor's wife, who aspired to set the social pace of
the town, had given a select dinner and ordered her ice
cream and cakes and salad from "The Cedars," which
had given considerable prestige to Constance's enterprise.
The other wives were envious, and stepped in to get a
dish of salad when they thought no other woman would
be there, and then went home to try to imitate or excel
it. Only Mrs. Bartlett held her head high, and went on
her culinary way with set lips and a firm adherence to
her old ways, not deigning to notice the innovations that
had come to town, except for an occasional sniff at people who would be led about by every new-fangled notion.

Among the new tea room firm adherents was Holly
Beech. He did not always get dollar dinners, for his trea-
sury was often depleted by the steady stream that flowed
from his pocket into the pocket of Si Barton, the bootlegger; but he came almost every day to get something,
and he had not been slow to learn the prices and the
differences between "tab dinners" and "by the cart," as
he called them.

It chanced that Holly Beech had that morning just
finished the loading of a huge wagon with goods which
were to go to a farmhouse at some distance in the country over a rough and hilly road. He was to start with them
almost immediately, and there would be little or no time
to get dinner. His usual habit on like occasions was to
get a sandwich or two at the drug store and stock up well
with something stronger; but this morning he left his team
hitched by the station, and slipped over to the tea room.
He threw down a silver half-dollar, and said to Norah:

"I want a good big dish o' soup in a hurry. Kin you
git it? An' I want you should fix up some o' thet thar
bread an' butter, an' hard-biled eggs, and pie, an' stuff
in a box. I'm goin' out a good piece in the kentry, an'
it'll be a while afore I git ennythin'."

Norah had obeyed his orders in a very short space of
time, had set the soup before him, and was preparing
a tempting lunch with all possible expedition. Holly was

swooping in the hot soup with audible satisfaction, his broad back to the wide hall doorway, his coat off, slung over the back of his chair, his shirt sleeves rolled high, showing his freckled, hairy arms, his whole appearance extremely négligé, when Mrs. Wetherill appeared in the doorway.

She had lain down obediently, as her granddaughter bade her do, but her mind had been by no means at ease. A number of things had troubled her of late, and she was puzzled beyond anything over some strange sounds and sights. She listened with her hearing made keen by suspicion, and distinctly heard Constance's steps go to the kitchen, then back to the hall and out the front door. Going with unusual haste to the window in Constance's front bedroom, a room which she seldom entered, she caught a glimpse of the girl as she hurried out between the cedars, putting on hat and gloves as she went—a very strange proceeding for the carefully bred Constance Wetherill, to put on gloves after leaving the house. It was extremely countrified, and she felt she must speak to her about it.

And why did Constance run around town in that strange way, and not send a servant? Were there no servants? Perhaps the proprietor was disagreeable, and Constance did not like to say anything because they seemed so nicely settled. But that must not be. She would speak to the manager herself, and see that he understood who they were, and that they must have proper service. It they wanted more pay, why, of course they should have it.

She had not been downstairs since arriving, for Constance had impressed it upon her that the dining-room downstairs was for the public. But now it seemed necessary for her to descend if she would follow this thing up at once and find out. So, putting on her hat and wrap herself, and carefully buttoning her gloves, a thing she had not done for herself for years, she set out to find the manager. She felt, it is true, somewhat like Columbus discovering America, for she had been so carefully kept that this seemed quite like an adventure to her; but she

summoned all her stateliness of bearing, for which she
had been noted in former years, and slowly descended
the stairs.

Elegant and lovely as a rare old withered rose, in her
rich silks and foamy laces, with her crown of fluffy silver hair, she dawned upon the astounded Holly. She had
been beautiful as a young woman, and she had lost little
of her beauty as an old one. With the haughty manner
of her time she raised her gold-rimmed glasses to her
sweet, dim eyes, and gazed at the rough man who sat
eating soup as if he were sucking it out of a trough.

By some subtle law not understood by Holly he became aware that a presence was near him, though he had
been making a sound with his lips so near akin to the
rustle of her skirts that he had not heard her approach.
Slowly he turned around and met her gaze, and for one
full, long minute they looked at each other. Then Holly
recovered his speech, and ejaculated.

"Wall, I swow! Ef 'tain't the old un'!"

"Sir!" said Mrs. Wetherill, in gentle, stately tone.

And then the front door opened, and Constance came
in. She stood aghast for just an instant, taking in the situation, and then swept down upon her little silken grandmother, and almost carried her out into the sunshine.

"Grandmother!" she said. "What a start you gave me!
Why did you come down before the car came? Did Norah
put your things on? What a hurry you were in! but the
car is coming now; here, let us go around to the side
where they can drive in."

"But, Constance," protested her grandmother as she
was hurried along, "I don't understand. What kind of
place is this in which we are living? Do they allow their
help to eat in the dining-room at the public table?"

"Oh, no, grandmother!" said Constance feverishly,
anxious only to get her grandmother around the corner
of the piazza before Holly should come out or any other
guests enter. She had seen Jimmy in the distance as she
came in at the gate, heading a band of urchins, who
looked as if they were coming on ice cream intent. Mrs.
Wetherill must not see them. But the old lady stopped

short in her progress when she heard her granddaughter's answer.

"Well, then, Connie, that man ought to be reported at once. Go in and tell them. I will not go a step until it is done. Such insolence ought not to be allowed. I saw him myself, a great, big, ugly creature that looked like a stable boy, and *in his shirt sleeves*! Think of it! And he was making a dreadful sound with his lips when he ate. It was disgusting."

Constance was divided between her desire to laugh and cry, but she knew neither would do any good at this critical moment; so she put her hand gently on the old lady's arm, and drew her along.

"Grandmother, he is not a servant. Come on, and I will tell you about it. Here is the car. Do you think you can step in? It is not high. Put your hand so on my arm. Are you comfortable? Drive down that pretty woodsy street beside the church, please. Now, grandmother, let me tell you. You know this is a quiet little village, and there are a good many plain people, farmers and that kind, who do not pay much attention to city ways. Sometimes they come into town, and I suppose they get hungry. I know there are a number of people who dress very curiously, and have queer manners, but I am told they are very respectable people. I suppose perhaps that is why we have a separate dining-room. Some of the people here are shy, and like to take off their coats without being looked at."

It was a lame story, and did not quite ease the old lady's perplexity. "But, my dear, are you quite certain that this is a perfectly respectable house where we are? You know it is inexcusable to come to the table with one's coat off. Every one knows that. Not even a respectable servant would do it."

It was a trying drive. Constance was glad when a diversion occurred as they passed the minister. He bowed to them with a pleasant lighting of his eyes, and the old lady asked who he was. Constance explained; but, when Mrs. Wetherill heard he was of another denomination than her own, she had little further interest in him, except to say that he looked a trifle shabby, and suggest that Constance send a contribution to his church, that probably they needed help. Constance turned her head away to hide a tear that crept into her eyes as she thought how they almost needed help themselves. She wondered how things were to go on if her grandmother became troublesome, and whether she would have to tell her after all. Two or three times she almost tried to frame the words to let her know the truth; but somehow she could not bear to do it, and they drove back home without its having been revealed. It was a nervous strain to get the old lady into the house, for she seemed determined to see the manager and report about the strange man in the dining-room before she went upstairs; but at last she was persuaded that the proprietor was busy and could not be seen, and she agreed to leave it to Constance to report the case.

Much troubled, Constance at last left her grandmother comfortably ensconced upon her couch with three or four letters from home bearing the familiar handwriting of old friends. She stole to her room, and lay down with closed eyes, feeling keenly the weariness of what she had been through that morning, wondering whether there were anything in religion to help in such a time as this. How she wished she could talk with the minister, and get a hold upon something which would calm her spirit! How was it she had never known before how little real foundation she had for contentment in her life? Had money given her all that trust and light-heartedness, that freedom from care and fear, that she had always had till now?

Then, suddenly, in the midst of her troubled thoughts, she heard a slight sound. It was not much, but it was startling, the click of breaking glass, the gentle thud of something falling, the uneven shoving of a chair, that bespoke the unusual, and gave the indefinable alarm.

Constance sprang from her bed, and flew into her grandmother's room. She could not tell why, but she felt that something had happened. It might be nothing, but she must see.

The old lady lay on the couch as she had left her; only
the chair was shoved away as if in a sudden effort to rise;
it had been grasped, and a small glass of water had fallen
on the rug. Coming closer, Constance saw that her grandmother's eyeglasses lay splintered on the bare floor beside the rug. But the old lady lay very still and rigid, one
hand grasping the letter she had been reading.

Constance knelt down beside her, and spoke to her,
and took her cold hands in her own; but the rigid hands
did not relax, and the drawn, agonized expression remained fixed upon her face. With a cry the girl sprang
to the bell, and rang for Norah, and then went back to
the couch. She had no experience whatever with illness,
and did not know what to do.

She rang the bell so violently that Norah came rushing up at once, with Jimmy at her heels. Jimmy always
knew instinctively when there was anything happening,
and in his boldness was somewhat like those people
described as rushing in where angels fear to tread. He
saw no reason why he should not follow, and see whether
he was needed; and it happened that this time he was
very much needed.

For Jimmy was a person of experience. He had seen
a man that was taken off a train in an apoplectic fit, and
he had been with his grandmother when she had her last
stroke of paralysis. Such things were too common among
the common people for Jimmy not to know what was
the matter. With one lightning glance of pity toward his
friend and patroness he turned, and, yelling out as he
went, "I'll bring the doctor," he sped down the pebbly
path and out the gate, nearly knocking over Mrs. Bartlett who was passing by, thereby adding one more to her
list of reasons why the new tea room was not needed in
the town.

Chapter XVII

Now there were a number of physicians in Rushville, and they lived in various directions in the town; but there was no hesitation in Jimmy's flying feet as they reached the street. Straight as an arrow to its mark went Jimmy to the house of the doctor he had decided should be the man of his choice if ever any of his friends or acquaintances were sick.

His choice was based upon two incidents in the worthy doctor's career. Jimmy had once seen him pick up a stray kitten with a broken leg, and care for it tenderly, carrying it away with him in his car. The doctor had also allowed Jimmy to "hitch on" behind sometimes in winter when the sleighing was good. There might be other good qualities in the other doctors of the town, but these were enough for Jimmy. Therefore to Dr. Randall he sped with all promptness, and it was Dr. Randall himself who presently came driving back with him at lightning speed, for Jimmy had represented the call as urgent.

The doctor entered the old lady's room, gruff, gray, grizzled, silent; and Jimmy lingered long enough to notice with satisfaction that he handled the old lady as gently as he had handled the kitten in the road. Then, as if he had known it would be so, he turned contented, and sped away on another self-imposed errand.

Jimmy had his eyes wide open always. He had noticed the look of fright and anguish on his dear lady's face. He felt that she needed a friend and supporter in this trying hour; and, looking about quickly in his untaught

little mind for such a one to call, he could think of none
more fitting than the minister.

John Endicott was in his study, trying his best to ban-
ish the vision of Constance as he had seen her in the car
that morning, and bring his mind to bear upon his next
Sunday's sermon. Try as he would, the sermon framed
itself all for her, and it was her wistful eyes that looked
up to him from each line that he wrote.

Mrs. Bartlett was out. She was sitting at that moment,
much shaken, detailing to a friend on the other side of
time the account of how Jimmy nearly knocked her over
in front of the new tea room. She did not often take the
long walk over there, and it was likely she would stay
until she was obliged to come home and get supper. The
minister was conscious of satisfaction in her absence.

Then Jimmy arrived with his imperative summons.

"Come 'crost this here way," said Jimmy doggedly as
they passed a field on the other side of the street from
the Bartlett house. "Thur's a short cut through the orchard. It'll save a lot." Jimmy in his secret soul wished
to save the minister from the gaze of the street loungers.
He had not fought his battle for his minister for nothing. He was learning how to protect him. This was not
an occasion when there was time for fighting.

The minister, nothing loath, followed Jimmy through
the meadow and down the orchard path.

"What did you say was the matter, Jimmy?" asked the
minister, taking long strides beside Jimmy's running trot.
"Did you say they sent for me?"

"Guess she's got a stroke," said Jimmy wisely. "Looked
like it to me. No, they didn't send fer nobody; I just come
myself. Thur ain't nobody thur to hep 'cept Norah; an'
Miss Constance, she oughter have some one ter kind of
hep her out. I went fer the doctor, but he has to 'tend
to Mis' Weth'rill. I thought they oughter have you."

Silently and gravely, like two engaged in the same
important business, they walked across the orchard, and
skirted the pond, and so up to the house by the back
path where John Endicott had first seen Constance in
the moonlight. He looked kindly down on Jimmy's ear-

nest little freckled face, and felt a warmth of kinship.

"Good work, old scout!" he said gravely, looking down into the troubled young face.

Jimmy flushed under his tan and plodded along with only a flashing glance of gratitude toward the minister. But they walked together now as fellow laborers in one cause.

Confusion still reigned in Mrs. Wetherill's apartments. The doctor had issued his orders, and Norah and Constance were doing their best to obey him; but they were both untrained in nursing, and were so nervous that they could not accomplish things as rapidly as a stranger might have done. Jimmy, after a bit of reconnoitering, led the minister straight upstairs, where Mr. Endicott found he needed no announcement. Quietly, as if he had been told, he slipped into line, and did the next things that nobody else knew how to do. He helped the doctor to lift the old lady into the next room to her own bed, where she could be made more comfortable at once; he arranged window-shades to make the light just right, and took the doctor's orders for some things to be brought from the drug store, with merely a grave bow of recognition toward Constance when he entered the room. It was as if he had come in answer to her summons, and somehow there came to her a strong sense of security in having him near.

It was the minister who volunteered to go for Miss Stokes, the village dependence for nursing. She was a plain-faced, amply-proportioned woman with a kindly way and much experience; and, when, a couple of hours later, Endicott drove up to "The Cedars" in an old Ford he had hired and helped Miss Stokes out, Constance felt a relief that almost brought the tears. She felt so inexperienced and so troubled and alone!

When Miss Stokes was established under the doctor's orders, Constance took time to speak to the minister and explain. Norah made them sit down in the stately dining-room which had been fitted out for Mrs. Wetherill with all the old furnishings from home. There she brought them a most delicious supper. It was all very pleasant to the weary man, who fairly hungered for a bit of companionship; and to Constance it was like having a strong new friend. She wished she might keep him there till the time of stress was over, but she knew she could not do that.

"No, nothing happened that we know of to excite her, except the letter she was reading. It contained the news of the sudden death of an old friend of grandmother's. Yes, they were deeply attached, and I suppose it startled her a good deal. It was careless of me to leave her with letters. I shall always blame myself. But I had been having a good many perplexities myself; you see grandmother knew nothing of my enterprise here. I think I shall have to tell you all about it. No one else in the world knows but Norah and my lawyer."

Constance told her simple tale in few words; and John Endicott, listening, watching her changing face, marveled that she could speak so composedly of the great change that had come into her life. A tragedy it seemed to him, for he who had never known luxury had been wont to pity those who had and were suddenly called upon to give it up. His heart longed more and more to help her. He must have shown this longing in his face, for Constance felt the sympathy and was comforted by it. He spoke but few words of comfort, it is true; but he showed by a number of small acts that he felt deep sympathy, and would do anything in his power to help her.

And after he had eaten the tender chops that Norah had broiled, the delicious salad, flaky bread and butter, and fragrant coffee, ending with some frozen dainty and delicate spongecake, he went home to Mrs. Bartlett's meager supper, well knowing that if he did not he would have to give account of himself. The meagerness of it did not trouble him that night, and she wondered that he took but one slice of bread, and ate but half of that. It was unaccountable. And he actually refused a second piece of gingerbread, a thing she had never known him to do since he boarded with her. She set her lips grimly, and reported to Ellen Sauters, her next-door confidante, that he must be sick, that her gingerbread was "as good as anybody ever made—the sour milk was extra nice this time."

For, although Mr. Endicott had promised to go back to "The Cedars" that evening to see whether there was anything further he could do to help, he yet saw no reason why Mrs. Bartlett should learn of Mrs. Wetherill's condition until the next day; so he went out without saying anything about it. But he had reckoned without knowledge of his landlady's resources. He had not been gone from the house more than ten minutes when Ellen Sauters entered the kitchen door with a quick glance, without the ceremony of a knock, and sat down to tell all about it.

"Say, what did Jimmy Watts come here for this afternoon when you was out?" she began.

"Was Jimmy Watts here? Nobody told *me*," said Mrs. Bartlett, sitting down with the butter plate in her hand.

"Yes, I was lookin' out the kitchen winder, an' I see Jimmy scootin' in the side way, an' knockin', and presently the minister come down to the door, an' he never went back in, only just reached up to the hall rack an' took down his hat, an' he went off with Jimmy. They must 'uv ben in a nawful hurry, fer they jumped the fence, both of 'em, and went 'crost lots, down by the old pond. I couldn't make out where they was goin' till George cum home fer his supper. Then I put two an' two together. He said Mr. Endycut came over there to the garage, an' hired a car an' was gone two hours; an', when he cum back, he seen Miss Stokes settin' beside him, an' they druv in to the hanted house; an' then Jimmy Watts brought the car back an' the money fer it. I told George he didn't know much that he didn't ast Jimmy what was the matter; but he said he never thought till after he was gone, an' then he happened to remember he'd seen Dr. Randall's car standin' in front of the station; so es soon's I got George's supper on I hurried an' run over to Mis' Randall's to borrow her sleeve-pattern, an' ast her ef anybody was sick to the hanted house; and she said the old lady hed hed a stroke."

Mrs. Bartlett set her lips firmly. Undoubtedly the min-

ister had known all about it, and had told her nothing.
This was treason. When he first came to board with her,
she had told him she would be a mother to him, and she
had made a great deal of studying his tastes; but he had
not rewarded her properly. People came to her expecting to find out all about every marriage and death and
birth and church quarrel; and she never knew as much
as they, headquarters of the minister though this was.
It was mortifying in the extreme to be considered the
source of all church information, and yet have none to
give. She decided not to have custard pie next day as she
had planned. She would give the minister what was left
of today's bread pudding.

Constance was glad to have Mr. Endicott return that
evening; for the doctor was there, and his grave face troubled her. She dared not ask him again what he thought,
for he had told her that it was impossible to say posi-
tively what would be the outcome. It might be that her
grandmother would recover and be herself again to a certain extent, and it might be that she would slip away without ever coming back to the use of her faculties.

When Constance heard this, she was in despair. If her
grandmother should die now, she would feel that she had
killed her by bringing her away from home and allow-
ing her to be so excited. She wanted to ask some one
about this doctor. Was he skillful? And ought she not
to send for a physician from home? Or perhaps some
noted man in Chicago, if she only knew for whom to
send. Then she remembered that she no longer had an
unlimited bank account and she must go cautiously in
the matter of expensive doctors' fees and traveling expenses, unless it was a matter of life and death, though
she resolved that every cent she had should be spent to
save her grandmother's life, even though it were but a
possibility.

When Mr. Endicott came, she put her trouble before
him.

"I do not believe," said he, "that you need send for
any other physician. It is not as if it were an obscure case
requiring great skill or surgery. Dr. Randall is an old

man, and has had a good many years' experience. He
may not be up in the latest methods, but I sometimes
think that experience counts for more than new theories
in any line. For years he has devoted his life to saving
life, and he has succeeded, too. He does not spare himself. I have seen him sit up all night holding a dying baby
for a mother who was near to death's door herself, and
had no way of ever hoping to pay him for his services;
and in the end he brought them both through, and they
are living yet. I have seen him do the work of a physician and nurse for hours under the most trying circumstances, and I have seen him happy as a child when the
crisis was past in some trying case, or broken utterly in
spirit when some one died. He does not often lose a case.
He is as much like the old doctor of 'Bonnie-Brier-Bush'
renown as any you will find today. He tells me there is
great hope, and he would not say so if he did not feel
sure. I will speak to him about a consultation; and, if
it is necessary in the least, he will be the first to suggest
it, I am sure."

They went together into the sick-room, and the minister talked with the physician in low tones. Constance
stood at the foot of the bed; the drawn, agonized expression of her grandmother's face was heart-breaking. Instinctively she stooped over, and spoke in gentle tones.

"Dear grandmother," she said, as if talking to a little
child, "don't be troubled. You will be better soon."

Did she fancy it, or was it true that one side of the
face seemed to soften and relax at her words? She felt
she could not bear it. It seemed as if her grandmother
were standing on the dark brink of the river of death and
reaching to her to take her hand, to help her in some
way. What could they do for her? Suppose she were
dying? Suppose it were her own case? What would she
want done? Some one to speak to her, some one to pray
for her? Ah! that was it. But could she hear? Well, at
least God would hear; and a sudden conviction came to
the girl that God would take hold of the hand of this,
His aged servant, and lead her gently.

She turned to the minister.

"I think I would like you to pray if you will," she said in a low tone; "that is, if the doctor thinks it wise."

"There is no objection," the doctor said.

"Can she hear me, doctor?" inquired Mr. Endicott.

"It is quite possible, though not probable," responded the man of few words. He was working with an electric battery as he spoke, and Constance watched his hands as they moved skillfully and surely through their work, and felt a confidence in him which made her thankful.

And so, going near the bed where his words could reach the ears that might be deaf, but yet might hear, John Endicott prayed. The doctor went steadily forward with his work, and in her slow way Miss Stokes helped him; but they both held their heads reverently lowered, as if their hearts joined in with the prayer.

Constance, her face hidden in her handkerchief, stood a little to one side and listened; but, as the words went on, like a great wave of comfort that bore them all into the presence of the Almighty, and surrounded them with His mercy and loving-kindness, she leaned forward where she could look into her grandmother's face. The troubled look had gone, and there was dawning a look of peace there. Words of Jesus, the minister was repeating, words from the Psalms, and yet petitions that seemed to reach the very throne of God with their earnestness, for they were strong with the promises which belong to God's children. Was it possible that the dim ears could hear the prayer and feel the comfort?

The doctor presently tiptoed over softly, and looked at his patient, and then stepped deferentially back, and waited. He, too, had seen the change in the face, and hoped.

They went out presently at the doctor's word, and Constance promised to lie down if they would call her at the slightest sign of change in her grandmother. When the minister bade her good night, she thanked him for the prayer, and told him it had helped her, too.

John Endicott reached out his hand and took hers in an earnest, quick grasp as he said, "Oh, I wish you knew how to go to my Lord for comfort!"

It was only an instant that her hand lay in his strong grasp; but Constance felt that she had received help from that quick, friendly touch. He had come to her in her trouble; he was strong; he had not turned away. Where was Morris Thayer now, who ought to have been by her side in this distress? To be sure, it was her own act that had put herself out of his reach; but womanlike she blamed him that he had not found her in spite of it.

Her courage almost failed her that night. She dozed, and then awoke to a realization of the suspense in the house. After a silent visit to the chamber of illness she stole back to her couch. The memory of the minister's prayer comforted her but she felt that he was far away from her on a different plane, a man who had been brought up to godly things, and who could not possibly know the common feelings of a soul like hers. Yet ever her spirit turned back to the words he had spoken; and once, as morning almost dawned, she slipped from her couch to her knees and prayed, "Our Father in heaven, help me find Thee."

Then she lay down and slept.

Chapter XVIII

Slowly but surely Mrs. Wetherill rallied. Little by little the stricken limbs responded to commands from the feeble brain, and it became apparent that she would get about again.

Constance daily rejoiced. She had not known how much her grandmother was to her until it seemed as if she were about to lose her. It seemed as if no discouragement were too great to be borne now, if this dear one could get well. She came and went with sunny face and cheery manner, and her grandmother was able at last to smile when she entered the room.

Miss Stokes had become a fixture and a comfort. Her wages were not so exorbitant as those of a city-trained maid or a trained nurse; and Constance felt that the arrangement was quite possible, for now the railroad junction was operating and the number of patrons increased daily. The tea room took quite a start, and promised to do well. Perhaps the old lady's illness and the settled presence of Miss Stokes, a well-known and dependable person, gave prestige to the enterprise. There was promise of one or two settled table boarders.

Moreover, within a week after Mrs. Wetherill was taken ill a rumor spread abroad that a fine boarding school for boys was to be built a mile from the edge of town. It caused quite a stir among the business men of Rushville. Silas Barton had set about an enlargement of his quarters. Some said he was going to add a restaurant, with all the latest improvements; but that had not reached Constance's ears as yet, and so did not trouble her.

She was much needed downstairs in these days; for, though she did not go into the dining-room unless it became actually a necessity, it was necessary for some one to be in the kitchen to keep things from burning, and often to cook something ordered while Norah was waiting upon the table. It became apparent that more help would soon be needed. Constance pondered for a time, and the result was that Jimmy was put into a white duck coat and properly clothed as to his reluctant feet, which did not enjoy shoes and stockings in summer time, and was pressed into service. And a fine little waiter he made, business-like and energetic, though he would have made the hair of old Thomas, the Wetherill butler, rise on end with horror.

Traveling salesmen and railroad men stopped every day at Rushville now, for there were changes to be made in the freight-house and station, and there was talk of a branch road to connect with another through road to the great Southwest. These men naturally drifted to the drug store first; but afterwards most of them had found "The Cedars," possibly through some word of Holly's or Jimmy's, and after one trial came back every time, for solid silver, cut glass, comfort, and good cooking were not to be found at the soda counter of the drug store.

The walls of the old house were thick, and the floors sent up no echo to disturb the old lady who lay there carefully tended and guarded from everything which could trouble her. She knew not that the family plate of the Wetherill's was being desecrated in the hands of taxi-drivers and drummers and railroad laborers, nor knew that her daily bread came from a business carried on by a descendant of two fine old families.

As she grew better and could say a few words, she came to ask for the minister and to look for his daily visit. Always before he went she asked him in her stately, gentle way to pray; and a peace settled down upon her at his first words.

There were long talks between the minister and the proprietress of "The Cedars," on religion, poetry, art, music, and back, always back to religion again. He brought her some of his theological books to read. Constance was gradually growing to feel that the question of personal salvation was the most vital one in the world. Her companionship with John Endicott was not like that she had ever had with any other young man. He came and went informally, because her grandmother enjoyed his coming; and it was natural to drop into the back parlor for a few minutes after he came downstairs, and leave a new book or a paper that contained an article he thought she would enjoy. Often she would play for him scraps of beautiful melody or some stately masterpiece of an old composer; and he would close his eyes, lay his head back in the soft chair, and rest.

Once when she had finished a prelude of Chopin, which he had come to call "The Prelude" because he liked it so much, he suddenly said,

"Oh, if we could have your playing in our church!"

Constance turned gravely toward him and considered it. Here, perhaps, was work she might do to get virtue to her soul. She remembered how she had been sorry that Lent was over, because she thought it might ease her troubled soul to deny herself something. She tried to tell Mr. Endicott now how she had felt, and he quoted these words:

> I dare not work, my soul to save;
> That work my Lord has done;
> But I will work like any slave
> For love of God's dear Son.

He quoted it gently. And then he said:

"My friend, don't make that mistake. You cannot work to yourself righteousness. This gift of life is to be had for the asking, not by doing anything to earn it. But, sincerely, you do not know how much help you might give us by coming over there and playing for us. The good lady who has been playing is going away to keep house for her brother; else I do not know how we could get rid of her; and as yet there has been no talk of any one else. If you will agree to do it, I will forestall any such unpleasant occurrence by announcing your willingness. There are a number of atrocious players in this town, and I shiver to think of one of those at that poor old organ. You might *get* some help, too, for I do not believe we can come into contact with any body of real Christians, no matter how plain or illiterate, who will not help us in some sense to come nearer to the Lord and Master of us all. I have learned a great many lessons from dear old Mr. Mather and his sweet little wrinkled wife. They are almost on the town, they are so poor; they have none of the beautiful things of life, and their past is full of losses; but they are so happy and peaceful, and speak with such triumph of their heavenly home and their expectation of soon going there, that I love to sit and talk with them."

Constance watched his face as he talked, noticed the lights that played over it, and the kindling of his eyes; and, as she had often done before, she compared him with Morris Thayer.

At last she spoke.

"I will do it if you think it will help. I should like to help in any way I can. I could not take that class of girls that Jennie spoke about, because I should not know how to teach them, not yet, at least; but I will help in any way I can; and, if you would like me to do anything else, or if you can use our big dining-room for a social gathering sometime, if grandmother is well enough to bear the noise by and by, I should be glad to help that way."

His face lighted with pleasure. What a wealth of help she could be! How he had sighed for just such help as this!

That was the beginning of new things in the way of music for the little church. The woman who was going away was glad to resign her position at once, and Constance took charge the following Sunday. The organ had been tuned by a man sent for from a neighboring town; and, though it was by no means in perfect working order, yet it was wonderfully better. With confidence and skill Constance touched the keys, and brought forth a different sound from any they had made in years. The people stirred, sat up, and stared; and the choir opened its mouth, and sang as it had never sung before. The loungers from across the street loafed over to look in and see what was going on, and thereafter the beautiful organist became an added attraction to the church.

It was discovered presently that the choir had abilities, and Miss Wetherill had a voice. Little by little she took control of the singing in the church until there was a revolution. Constance found that Jennie's voice, while somewhat strained from having sung too high as a child, had a pretty quality for an alto, and she set to work to give her some hints and practice with her.

Her own voice had received rare cultivation, simply because she had loved music and had delighted to sing, and even in her music-surfeited circle at home she had always been listened to with pleasure. Therefore it was no wonder that the first time she sang a solo in church the congregation sat spellbound. It was only a gospel song she sang, but the minister had chosen it to follow his sermon, and it made a wonderful impression. They sat hushed and tearful. Even Mrs. Bartlett, with hymn-book ready for a closing hymn to be sung by the congregation, glanced up over her spectacles, and watched the sweet-faced singer to the end. Her comment after church in a condescending tone was, "Yes, she has a right pretty little voice."

Jimmy sat in the back seat entranced. He fairly burst with pride, and he watched his goddess from the moment she opened her mouth until the service was over.

And so the summer passed, and the autumn; and the winter came upon them. The town had accepted the fact that Mrs. Wetherill was a helpless invalid, and required the frequent attendance of the minister upon her; although the gossips' tongues still wagged.

The choir had developed into a well-trained band, who met once a week with their leader, and were getting lessons in all sorts of things besides music, from manners, to the arrangements of their respective hair and apparel;

or even now and then a lesson in art or literature, as it happened that their attention would be directed to a picture or a book in the pretty room where they met. It is safe to say that few of them had ever before been in a room so beautifully furnished. Constance was using her belongings for the Master's work, though some might have thought she was doing it for the minister's sake instead.

More and more had these two grown to enjoy each other's society, though neither confessed it.

The minister, fully knowing what he was about, fully realizing the danger to himself in this sweet companionship with a girl born and bred so differently from himself, yet held himself in check, and enjoyed every moment spent with her to the full. It was to him as if God had let an angel from heaven come down to help him in this, his first poor charge, in a little country village. She even put her influence upon the village gossip and the petty church quarrels, like a calm, cool hand upon a fevered brow; and with her superior way of looking at things made some of the foolish tongues ashamed, and turned them to ask forgiveness.

Sometimes in his lonely moments the minister would sit in his dark, musty study, with his face buried in his hands, and imagine for just a little while what it would be to have such a helper with him all the time; his, to call his own; the gift of God. But this he felt could never be. She was of another world than his. She had always lived there; she would eventually go back to it. She had told him her story, and he would not question further; but he felt certain that some day there would come some one from out that other bright, easy world, who would claim her as his own; and she would smile brightly, bid them all good-by, and leave them. It could not but be so. They would find her out somehow, and that time could not be far away. Rushville would not have her always.

Then he would shake himself free from such thoughts, and plunge into his work with his whole soul again, Constance helping him.

Early in the winter there were special meetings held in

the old church every night. People came in from all the country round about, and the Spirit of the Lord seemed to be upon the community. Every night the minister preached his simple gospel sermon, and every night Constance sang. It was as she sang these songs to others, of the precious Jesus and all He could be to them if they would only come to Him, that she came to know that she was Christ's herself, body and soul, for time and for eternity.

It was then that Jimmy came to the minister one day, choking and embarrassed, and said: "I've made up my mind. You kin put me down. I'm a goin' to b'long. Mebbe you couldn't a' fetched me in alone, but you 'n' her together kin do anythin' yer a min' to."

And the next communion Jimmy, and Jimmy's brother, and Jennie, and a number of others stood up in the church to acknowledge before the world their allegiance to the Lord Jesus Christ.

But there was one person in the town who did not love Constance, and who would not be won over to her charms, and that was Silas Barton. In the first place, she had come into town and calmly set up rivalry of his business; and, next, she had dared to ignore him utterly when he had made some advances toward her.

But the last and greatest offense was that she had been the cause of his own public ridicule, and that he could never bear. There were those who had stood in the crowd the day that Jimmy whipped Lanky, and cast it up to the bootlegger that the minister had openly rebuked him and walked away unharmed. So now Silas Barton hated the minister, and hated Constance Wetherill; and he stood back in his rage, and vowed to have vengeance upon them. The poison in his brain worked slowly; but it was of a deadly kind, and, when the venom did appear, it would take a startling form. So he turned over and over various schemes and plots, until one took form so vile and so altogether demoniacal that it seemed it must have emanated from the pit.

And thus matters stood when Morris Thayer came seeking the woman whom he would make his wife.

Chapter XIX

Morris Thayer stood upon the forlorn little platform, and looked about him dubiously. He was fresh from an elaborate toilet and immaculate from the hands of the two porters. There was not a hair awry, nor a stain of travel upon his sleek person. He looked well groomed and well fed, and altogether well pleased with himself. And indeed he was, for he considered himself to have been very bright to have discovered Constance's retreat, though the truth of the matter was he had not been the discoverer at all. He had told his man of the state of the case, and put the matter into his hands. That knowing and wily servitor straightway set himself to find the old butler who had lived with the Wetherills, and through him had ferreted out the abiding-places of all the servants who had left there.

At last he had come to Norah's home, where were still a few little brothers and sisters left to tell tales, and one of them let out unsuspectingly that their sister Norah had gone back to live with the pretty lady who sent the grapes and flowers to their little dead brother, and that she was in a place called Rushville. The man professed great interest in their sister, whom he said he had seen when waiting for a note for his master; and so he found no trouble in obtaining Norah's address. The whole thing had been so neatly done that Morris Thayer, when he landed in Rushville, felt reasonably certain that he should find Constance there, and that she would have received no warning whatever of his coming.

For Constance had been away just long enough for Thayer to have discovered that the world without her was null and void. He had never been denied anything in his life before, much less anything so desirable as this altogether desirable heiress; and why should he be denied now, when all that was needed was a little strategy? If he had not that, his man had. Money would buy anything, even brains. But, in order that he might come into town as quietly as possible, he had reluctantly left his man at home, thinking it better to be stealthy about things, since Constance chose to be so shy in her flight.

Morris Thayer had almost never traveled without the company of his man. He had not felt the loss very deeply while upon the train, for the generously-tipped porters had easily made up for that; but, now that he was stranded upon this bare platform with a large suit-case and bag at his feet, he felt suddenly at a loss what to do next. Ordinarily the man would attend to that, and he would step into a car out of sight of the vulgar gaze of the bystanders.

But now it was quite evident that no car would walk up to him and offer to shelter him from the public gaze, and that he needs must make a move himself. He looked about him, and perceived a line of more or less deeply interested observers, with hands in pockets and eyes upon him. They seemed to have nothing better to do than to look him over, and actually they did not seem in the least impressed. But something must be done. He felt out of patience with Constance for coming here. What could possibly have attracted her? He hoped she was not going to prove troublesome in such ways. He would have to put a quietus on her if she did, for he abhorred such little backwoods holes.

Clearing his throat and raising his gold-rimmed eyeglass the traveler approached the line of bystanders. One of them happened to be Holly Beech, who sat astride of a paint-keg, in his shirt-sleeves as usual chewing vigorously on a fresh quid of tobacco.

"Wal, I swow!" ejaculated Holly, "Ain't that purty now? Can't find his mamma, can't he? Gosh! Where do

they make them things? Up to the city? Hold me, boys;
he's comin' this way!" This all in an undertone that caused
the crowd of bystanders to go into a sort of dumb ague
of laughter.

Morris Thayer paused before Holly, half indignant that
he did not rise:

"Oh, I say——Could you tell me where to find a
hotel?"

It was the same question Constance had asked a few
months before, but he had not even so sympathetic a
company of listeners as had she. There seemed to be
something in the question itself that irritated all Rush-
villeites.

Holly shifted the tobacco to his left cheek, and paused
in his chewing while he scratched his head thoughtfully.

"A *ho*-tel, d'd you say? Now I thought I'd seen one
round somewheres, but mebbe I'm mistaken. Say, boys,
you don't know of no vacant *ho*-tels handy by, do ye?"

The crowd suppressed their feelings for the sake of
hearing the rest of the performance. Morris Thayer was
annoyed. He wished he had brought his valet. He essayed
to explain in a patronizing tone, for he did not care to get
into an altercation with such a burly-looking individual.

"You do not understand, my man. I don't want a vacant hotel. I an not trying to buy one. I want a place
where I can put up, and get something respectable to eat,
you know."

But Holly scented condescension, and, if there was
anything in the wide world he hated, it was to be looked
down upon.

"Oh, I see!" he said, rubbing his chin thoughtfully.
"I'm glad you explained to me, brother. I might uv made
a bad mistake, an' sent you where you wouldn't want to
go. Well, now, brother, there's two places where you kin
git somethin' to eat in this here town. I ain't so sure they
kin put you up. 'Tain't so easy to put up nice, tidy men
like you; but they'll eat you fast 'nough. One place is over
there to the drug store. They have toasted cheese sandridges an' soft drinks, an' some that ain't so soft. I used
to eat there myself before the new tea room come. I guess

that's about your size, ef I ain't mistook. You want one o' them there tab dinners. They're high art, they are, ice cream an' sugar plums an' salads an' all sorts of filimijiggers. Just suit you. Go right over there, brother, an' tell her I said you wanted one o' them there dollar dinners. Yes, that's the place over there behind them big trees; 'The Cedars,' they call it. You'll find it O.K. fer sure. You don't want me to go 'long an' open the gate fer you, do ye, brother? Yes, that's the way! Sure!"

Morris Thayer felt very uncomfortable. He vowed he would never come away without his man again. He gathered up his suit-case and bag, and looked unhappily around for a boy or a porter to help him, but none appeared; so he was forced to carry them himself. It seemed a long, hard walk across that wide, snowy space and down the long path to the house. He felt that Constance should appreciate his coming after her at so great a cost.

Once seated in the palm dining-room, he looked about with approval. Everything seemed in good taste. The room was not built for the purpose, of course, and lacked a good many modern appliances; but he liked the air of refinement, and felt at home at once when he noticed the service with which the tables were set out. He was glad to find so respectable a place to eat in this forlorn-looking town. He ordered a hearty meal, and enjoyed it, wondering why it was the salad made him think of one night when he had taken dinner at the Wetherills'. Miss Constance had worn a gown of pale-blue georgette, and looked like a beautiful goddess in a cool cloud.

It happened that Jimmy had been sent upon an errand at some distance, and Constance was occupied with her grandmother, so that Norah served him herself. She recognized him at once, and instinctively was on the alert to protect her mistress. She had been in the kitchen in New York, of course, and the young man had never seen her in the Wetherills' household. He would not be likely to recognize the Wetherill cook; but Norah had heard all the gossip of the servants, and well knew that this young man was an ardent admirer of Constance. She had often seen him from a window as he drove down a side street, and admired him. But her mistress had told her that she was not to tell a living soul about their reverse of fortune. It was not likely that this young man knew, and he should never know from her. Moreover, Constance had not seemed to wish to have her friends find her, and there must be some reason for it. That being the case, Norah meant to guard her. Not a word did she utter save those absolutely necessary; and, when the young man said that he wished to find out the address of some friends who lived in Rushville, and asked her whether she knew everybody there, she told him she was a stranger, and that he had better go to the post office to inquire. The post office was at some distance from the station, by a freak of the planners of the town, and Norah hoped thus to gain time. She knew Constance would start in a few minutes with the minister to a funeral in the country, at which she was to sing. She resolved not to tell her of Mr. Thayer's visit until she returned.

The young man decided, from her description of the walk, that it must be a long one, and made up his mind to take a car from the garage, which she said was near by. So a few minutes later he bundled himself into the car which he had selected as being the least objectionable vehicle for hire, and was driven to the post office, where he was again under a battery of eyes, among them Jimmy's.

Morris Thayer's ideas of drivers had been so shaken by the man in his shirt sleeves that he was in a most irritable mood, and it was with difficulty that he calmed himself to make inquiries. He was finally driven back to the place from which he had come, and landed at "The Cedars" once more. With astonishment he surveyed his surroundings. Could it be possible that this plain country place held the priceless jewel of which he was in search? He could scarcely believe it, and thought he must have been misdirected.

Norah appeared deferentially, and seemed surprised to see him again; but, when he asked for the Wetherills, she told him that Miss Constance was out. He then asked for Mrs. Wetherill; and Norah, much perturbed, went

up to see whether the old lady would have him come upstairs.

Bewildered, the young man followed her a few minutes
later to the pleasant room, where amid her accustomed
luxury the old lady sat, smiling and beautiful as ever in
her city home, only more fragile-looking. She welcomed
him with her stately courtesy, apologizing for being unable to rise. She told him of her sudden illness, the result of the news of a favorite cousin's death.

Morris Thayer was shocked that he had not heard, and
begged to know whether there was anything he could do
for her. Would she not like him to send home for her
family physician, a private car, some of her friends, some
fruit, flowers, medicine, or wine, anything? He felt
greatly distressed as it dawned upon him how serious a
thing this had been, and yet Constance had not let him
know. She had evidently been offended with him for
something. What could it have been? How annoying! He
did all that he could to show how anxious he was to help,
and exercised the power of his handsome eyes and gracious manner with the old lady, in which art he excelled
at all times.

Mrs. Wetherill chatted with him pleasantly, childishly,
of herself, her illness, all that had been done for her, of
the minister to whose praises she constantly recurred until
Morris Thayer felt almost personally bound to thank the
kind old saint (of course he was old—all ministers were
old in Morris Thayer's idea) who had evidently been so
good to those who were so soon to belong to him. Mrs.
Wetherill said that Constance was gone with the minister to sing at a funeral. Then she launched into a sweet
little story of how his prayers had helped her.

Morris Thayer frowned over the funeral, and said:
"Aw, you dawn't say so!" to her account of the prayers,
and remarked, when she gave him opportunity, that of
course it was very kind of Constance to go and sing for
the minister, but he really ought not to have asked it.
It must have been very trying to her to have to attend
a funeral of a stranger.

Mrs. Wetherill smiled, and looked at him contentedly.

She felt that the trouble between him and Constance was
all over now, and they would probably return to New
York at once; but it suddenly occurred to her that if they
did she would miss her new minister so much. She began
wondering whether she could not get him a better parish
in New York and so have him all to herself; and, pondering in her weakened state, she wandered from her visitor's words, and made no answer to his questions.

Miss Stokes, rising, suggested grimly that it might be
well for Mrs. Wetherill to rest now, as the doctor did
not allow her to talk long at a time. The visitor frowned
and withdrew, having been informed that it would be six
o'clock before Miss Wetherill could return.

What to do with himself this young man did not know.
He was seated in the library downstairs, for Norah would
not open the inner sanctum for anybody but the minister, without Constance's order. He wandered about, per-
plexedly staring at the pictures on the walls, pronouncing
them good, very good, wondering how such things came
to be out here in the country. This must be a most extraordinary tea room. He glanced across the hall, and
saw some real Oriental rugs, antiques, too. He was considered a connoisseur on rugs, and often went with his
friends to help them select some. He put on his eye-glass,
and studied from afar the ocean painting, and wondering why it seemed so familiar, and whether the Wetherills
did not have one something like it in their home? Strange
there should be one here also!

It must be that Constance had heard of this place as
being most extraordinary in the midst of the quiet country. But why on earth did she choose to remain after the
winter had set in and the season at home well begun?
The old lady was evidently well enough to be moved if
she were taken in a private car. Of course he would in-
sist that they do so at once.

He had communed thus within himself a long time it
seemed to him; he studied the view of the road and all
the books in the room, though he did not care for reading, and was exceedingly weary of himself. He concluded
it was about time to do something. He felt that he would

like a glass of wine to steady his drooping spirits, and
hailing Norah from the doorway as she passed with her
tray he asked to see the wine list.

It was with something of scorn that Norah informed
the young man that they had no wine list and never would
have in that house, so long as it was run by the present
proprietor. She advised him to go to the drug store as
she understood you could get anything you wanted there
if you went about it in the right way.

Morris Thayer was annoyed, he scarcely knew why,
but he took Norah's suggestion, and sauntered slowly
over to the drug store.

Silas Barton stood gloomily at his own door as Morris
Thayer crossed the street, picking his way elegantly over
the snowy road. He watched Thayer's progress, and took
his measure. He was not a stupid man, and he had one
evil purpose in view now, toward which he made everything work. Because this man came from "The Cedars,"
and because the man who drove him to the post office
and back in search of the Wetherills had come straight
to the drug store and told the story as soon as he had
landed his passenger, Silas was deeply interested. His
plans were ready. He was only waiting a proper time and
way to spring them upon his unsuspecting victims, and
here seemed to be the very man who would help him.

He slid his hands into his pockets with a quick, stealthy
movement, and watched the man as he came nearer, as
a spider might watch a fly drawing closer and closer to
its web. Yes, he was coming in. Silas drew a long breath,
and put on his most deferential air. He knew how to serve
such men. Had he not been bartender in a great city hotel
at one time until he drank so deeply that he was discharged?

Morris Thayer gave his orders. He was a connoisseur
also at mixing drinks, and in his club boasted of not a
little fame in this line. Silas obeyed quietly and deftly,
getting out his best articles and endeavoring to show that
he understood his business; but behind it all there was
something deeper. He wished if possible to draw this gentleman out. Not with insulting sneers did Silas open the

conversation; he knew better. He knew how to insinuate himself into the good graces of such a man as Morris Thayer. There was deference, but there was also a certain amount of confidence given and taken, a flattering show of the knowledge of the kind of life to which the stranger was accustomed, carried on by a laugh, a shrug, a wink, and a few insinuations.

Under the mellow influence of liquor Morris Thayer became affable and unsuspecting. He admitted to being a very intimate friend of the lady across the street. In Silas's mind that was a distinct point gained. It would not do to insinuate anything against this lady, of course. He did not wish that. It was enough that such a man was her intimate friend. Morris Thayer did not know perhaps how fully he had also let the bootlegger into the knowledge of his own character and habits of life by one or two sentences which showed he was not all pure and noble. Just a condescending comradeship, the city man regarded it; any man would say as much before other men, and some would boast about it. He thought nothing of what he had said, as he sauntered back again to take his hateful little revenge upon Norah, eat his supper, and wait for Constance; for he had decided within himself that it would hardly do to present himself to her before eight o'clock now, as she had not been at home to invite him to dine with her.

Silas Barton had watched him from his narrow little eyes that glinted with the fire of hate, and saw, complete, a story that was to make the town too hot for the minister and the new owner of the tea room.

Constance, all unconscious of the threads that were forming themselves into a net for her unwary feet, was at that moment hurrying into an apron to help Norah, for a party of ten men had arrived on the five o'clock train and ordered dinner to be served at six, as they must leave again at seven.

Chapter XX

The ten men had just taken their seats at the largest table when Morris Thayer entered the dining-room for his evening meal. Holly sat over in the farthest corner, with his arms comfortably spread about a generous platter of nicely cooked ham and eggs, a point of vantage from which he surveyed the room with content. A man and two women with long black veils sat at one of the tables by the front windows. They had just come from the funeral, and were going to take the seven o'clock train.

These were hurrying times in the tea room. Norah had been obliged to give up waiting and go to cooking again, for the funeral party demanded certain things that were not on hand, and Holly's ham and eggs had delayed the dinner. Norah grumbled to the fire about Holly's taking this particular night to order ham and eggs when he usually wanted roast beef, and there was roast beef in plenty without extra cooking.

Jimmy was doing double duty. He slipped around among the tables as if he went by electricity.

Thayer surveyed the situation gloomily. He preferred the room to himself. This company did not suit him, nor go with the rest of the furnishings of the room. Holly's red, recognizing grin was particularly obnoxious. He half turned to go away, and then reflected that he must dine somewhere, and this was convenient. There was nothing for it but to sit down. He selected a table near the front windows, as far from the obnoxious Holly as possible, and summoned Jimmy peremptorily.

"These here railroad gentlemen's got first choice," said Jimmy pertly. "You'll hev to wait. Norah'll get round pretty soon."

Thayer explained to the small waiter that he did not wish to be waited upon by the woman with red hair and an Irish brogue. He desired Jimmy to say so to the proprietor, and to have another waitress sent to him.

Jimmy looked him over contemptuously. He measured him by his unfailing model for all men, the minister, and found him falling far short. He sniffed, "All right," and was off like the wind, and announced breathlessly to Constance, who was just putting on a cap and cuffs preparatory to waiting upon those ten men:

"Thur's a pain-in-the-neck in thur says he wants *you* to wait on him; says he won't hev Norah; she's got too red hair. Shell I tend to him? He's fierce, he is. 'F I's you, I'd let him whistle awhile."

Constance colored. She dreaded all the more to go into the dining-room, supposing some country loafer was there who desired to compliment her; but, telling Jimmy to wait upon the man, she summoned all her courage, and took up her tray filled with smoking dishes.

Morris Thayer did not see her when she first entered; he was examining his fork.

Now, if ever a staid old family fork with a great engraved "W" on its polished surface got up and winked at anybody, that fork did. "You and I have met before," that fork said. "Don't you remember? Think of the most delicious squabs, mushrooms, truffles, salads, you ever tasted"—and Thayer put on his eye-glass and took up the fork curiously.

"Strange!" he said to himself. " 'W.' That is very strange, and the pattern seems familiar. And the spoons, too! Ah—how can this be? A very odd coincidence, extremely odd."

Then he glanced up, and saw Constance's dainty figure as she glided about, deftly waiting upon the big table. Constance had been much too busy to look at him as he sat in the distant corner.

Thayer sat, fork in hand, and stared at Constance. He

could not believe his senses. It was she—and yet *was* it?
The plain black gown, the apron and cap, badges of ser-
vitude. Could this be a part of her benevolence, as well
as attending funerals with saintly old ministers? Or was
she becoming insane? It was high time her philanthropy
ceased.

By the time she returned from the kitchen with a second tray full he had decided that he must not let her see
that he recognized her. It would be embarrassing to them
both. He must eat something, and get out of here as
quietly as possible, and then send for her to see him. So
he dropped his eyes discreetly whenever she came that
way, though he could not forbear watching her covertly
from under a sheltering hand. Most fortunately for Constance she was unaware as yet of his presence.

Jimmy suddenly appeared at his elbow for orders, and
he asked him at once who was the lady that waited on
the big table.

"That's her! The boss!" said Jimmy proudly. "She's
runner of this here tea room and she's a Jim dandy! Now,
d'you want anythin'? Fer you gotter be mighty quick
'bout it. My time's val'able. Don't no grass grow under
yer feet round here. Hustle's the word."

Thayer managed to order something, assisted by the
indefatigable Jimmy, who always tried to see that the bill
would be of adequate size. He ate very little, for his appe-
tite had somehow deserted him; so he soon paid his bill,
and went into the room across the hall, whence he en-
deavored to call a servant.

Jimmy was in the kitchen when the library bell rang,
and remarked, as he made a dive toward to door:

"There goes that mud again. He'd orter know better,
when I told him how busy we was!"

He soon returned, however, with a puzzled frown,
bearing Morris Thayer's card. "He says he's gotter see
you," he said, handing the card to Constance. "I told him
I was your agent, an' you was busy fryin' crokays; but
he said give this here to you right away. He's a chump,
he is. He's fierce. I don't like him. Want me ter put him
out?"

Jimmy's red little face bristled with irritation. He saw himself for the moment sitting astride the chest of the city gentleman and browbeating him. His recent victories had somewhat swelled his head.

But Constance's face was flaming with color and turning white by turns; she found herself trembling like a culprit caught in the midst of her evil deeds.

Morris Thayer had found her out at last! Morris Thayer here, and she in this array and waiting upon a lot of railroad men! There was no chance to equivocate, no chance to hide behind blind phrases. Her secret was out. She must confess, and see him turn upon his heel after giving her her due of pity.

Then her strong common sense came to the front, and her new views of life began to assert themselves.

Well, what matter? He was not worth sighing over if he was made of that kind of stuff. Besides, she was away from New York now, where she would not need to see their pity; and she could brave it better. At least, that was something to be thankful for. But oh, if she did not have to go in there and talk to him! She laughed nervously over Jimmy's offered aid, and wished she dared accept it. A sudden thought of Endicott and a wish for his presence came to her; then she was instantly glad he was not here, for what could he do?

She looked helplessly around the room at the things that were to be done, and then with firm lips set to work again.

"Tell him I cannot come at present, Jimmy; he will have to wait."

Then she went on with the croquettes, which required swift attention; and meanwhile her thoughts worked rapidly.

What should she say to him? Did he know everything, or nothing? Had he seen her in the dining-room? Very likely. She had been too busy to notice him, and too annoyed by having so many eyes watching her at her unaccustomed task to look up more than was necessary. He must have sat alone over in the corner by the window. What had he come for? How should she meet him? She

must go upstairs and dress, of course; and yet it would
take time, and she could not be spared.

Just then Norah grasped the situation, and came to
the front.

Now it must be confessed that Norah's conscience had
troubled her that day. She meant to pray all the saints
to forgive her that night as soon as her schemes were carried out; but she craved indulgence for the sin of deception for that afternoon because she had not told
Constance at noon that Thayer had been there, and had
let her drive away with the minister, knowing that she
was to be gone until evening, without so much as opening her lips on the subject. Just why she did it she had
not exactly known at the time. She realized afterwards
that it was because she liked the minister and wanted to
see him and her dear mistress keep on having good times
together, instead of having her go back to New York and
marry Mr. Thayer.

She had hoped he would be discouraged and go away,
and, even after he asked for Constance's grandmother,
Norah hoped he would take the four o'clock train and
get out of the way. She was therefore much put out when
he remained; and, when he asked about the liquor, she
grew angry. He was no fit man for her Miss Constance.
She would like to tell him so if she dared, but she did
not. Now, when she was caught at last, her wrath broke
forth.

"The iverlastin' spalpeen, hes he coom back agin? Bad
look to the loikes uv him. Miss Connie, ye must joost
rin oop the back stairs, an' get yersilf fixed up foin, an'
he'll niver know the diffrunce." Then she insisted that
she could do everything now with Jimmy's help, as there
was only the dessert left to serve, and she hurried her
mistress upstairs, charging her to put some powder on
her face and never to tell about the tea room.

But Constance, as she groped her way through the dark
staircase, made a great resolve. She would face her own
life honestly, and she would tell Morris Thayer just how
things were. What was there to be ashamed of, and why
should she, a follower of the meek and lowly Jesus, be

afraid of what any wealthy friend should say or think of her? She breathed a quick cry for help as she went into her room, and then swiftly removed all traces of the kitchen and her recent employment.

But, when she went to select a dress in which to appear before her former admirer, she hesitated. She naturally thought of some of her pretty evening gowns, rich and elaborate. But why should she, a poor girl now, seek to hold her former position and appear as she used to? Would it not be false to dress thus? It was not in keeping with her work to wear pale-blue evening gowns that cost several hundreds of dollars each, or decorate herself with strings of seed-pearls. With sudden impulse she reached for the little white gown that she had worn the first night in the house. Norah had washed it and made it look like new. It was simply made and easily donned. She put it on quickly, and ran downstairs before she would have time to change her mind.

But, though she wore a plain little white gown, she wore her old New York air and grace as she came quickly forward in her sweet way to greet her unwelcome guest. And so much did the little white gown change her from the deft maid whom he had seen in black, with white apron and cap, that he thought at once he had been mistaken, and that that had only been some poor country cousin who looked like her. Also, it was good to him to see the face at last for which he had been so long in search. So he held the hand she gave him a trifle longer than propriety required, and looked down into her face until her color came, and almost the tears, too; for to have him look at her like that upset her well-founded ideas of him.

"I have found you at last," he said with that more than flattering intonation that made him so great a favorite.

She led him into the inner room, partly because she wished to be away from possible interruptions, for there was no knowing what Jimmy might take it into his head to do; and partly because she wished to relieve the embarrassing situation.

The young man looked about again wonderingly at the

familiar atmosphere that enveloped the place. It puzzled him why this room took him back to New York at once; yet he had not had time to understand that the furnishings were identical with those in Constance's city home.

"What a charming nest you seem to have found! It is so much like your own taste here, that I might almost suspect you of having selected the furnishings. I have been puzzled all the afternoon, trying to understand some things; but since taking supper in the café, and seeing a most lovely waitress with undeniably cultured manners and a likeness to you, I think I have solved the problem. You are staying here in this delightful retreat with some relatives who have lost their money and are trying to mend matters quietly in this way. Am I correct? It is a pity, is it not for people of culture to be in unfortunate circumstances? Now that young girl whom I saw waiting upon those coarse men would, I am sure, shine in society if she had the right attire and a little experience in the ways of the world."

Morris Thayer was always sure of his own opinions. Since he had sent his card to Constance he had thought out this neat little explanation of the whole matter, and held it in abeyance until Constance should come to prove or disprove it. Had she entered the room at once in her waitress's garb, he would not have been so sure; but the change in her appearance, made so quickly, settled the matter for him. No girl who had just been helping ten men to roast beef, mashed potatoes and gravy could possibly change her appearance so utterly, and enter the room in so short a space of time, looking so cool and unflustered, as Constance had done. So, with mind untroubled, he seated himself and proceeded to get to the point at once.

He had long intended that the next opportunity he had of talking with Constance should be improved immediately by asking her to marry him. He would be put off no longer; she must face the question. Of course she did not intend to refuse in the end, and she only wished to tantalize him a little while, or possibly to wait until she had had enough of her freedom. But he was tired wait-

ing, tired being held at arm's length, frozen one day and
smiled upon the next. He would bring her to terms now,
and before she had any chance to answer him or grow
distant again.

Constance stood still as she heard his remarkable explanation, her heart seeming to stop for an instant and
then to go thudding on in wild little leaps. The color came
and went in her cheeks. She felt like laughing and crying
all at once, and she could not command her voice to tell
him how mistaken he was. A sudden weakness had come
over her, and she felt she could not stand up. She hastily
closed the door, and sank down upon the low divan, trying to collect her wits and speak.

But what did that young man do but drop down upon
the divan beside the astonished girl, and reaching boldly
out to take the white hands which lay weakly in her lap?

"Constance," he said, and his voice was low and mu-
sical, "I have had a long search for you. Why did you
run away from me? But now that I have found you I
am going to tell you that I love you, and I wish to make
you my wife."

His voice was alluring, and his eyes spoke volumes.
He had practiced these sentences over and over to himself as he rode along in the train, and now he was pleased
with himself that at last he had actually said them to her,
and had not been put off. He felt that his suit was won,
and he took the shrinking hands into his own smooth
ones confidently, dreaming not of further rebuff.

But his touch seemed to bring her to her senses, and
with a start she sprang back, and drew her hands away
from his infolding ones.

"Wait! Don't!" she said in a pained voice. "You do
not understand," and she moved to a chair opposite to
him.

He was a trifle annoyed that she still held him off, but
he settled down affably to hear her explanation, feeling
sure that her distance would be but temporary. Of course
she would not refuse him. He knew what his name and
standing were. There were a number of other girls as well
placed as was Constance who would have been glad to

have his attentions. She had never shown any dislike for him, and had often encouraged him with her smiles. He was not shaken in his confidence by her sudden action. On the whole, he decided he liked her the better for it. She would be the more wholly his when she had finally surrendered.

"Morris," said Constance, trying to steady her voice, and becoming conscious all at once that she was a different girl from the Constance Wetherill who had last talked with him, "I ought to have explained to you long ago. But I had a foolish idea of trying to run away and hide. Well—I have learned in the past few months that I have nothing to hide——"

The young man looked at her perplexed, and wondered why she seemed so excited. Constance caught her breath and then went on earnestly.

"So please—Morris—forget what you have just said! Let it be as if you had not said it, and listen to what I have to tell you."

Chapter XXI

When the minister had finished his supper, which he had not dared take at "The Cedars" lest he should have to give account to Mrs. Bartlett, he bethought himself of Mrs. Wetherill and his promise to drop in and see her, if possible, before prayer meeting. If he went at once, he would have time for a few minutes there, and then he might just for once walk with Constance to the church. He dreaded to think of her going alone even early in the evening, there were so many loungers around the drug store, and he hated to think of the evil face and more evil words of Silas Barton.

But when he reached the old house Norah informed him sorrowfully that Miss Constance had company from the city, and would probably not be able to go to meeting that night. She told it to him with sympathy in her eyes, as if she would break the news gently, and he half understood her tone, and smiled gratefully; but there was a load of nameless unrest upon him as he went up the stairs to Mrs. Wetherill's room, where it was by no means lightened.

The old lady was resltess. She greeted him eagerly, as if she had been watching for him; and she waited not at all to relieve her mind of its burden.

"I do not think I could do without you," she said in her gracious, motherly way, that somehow comforted his lonely heart; "and I want you to promise me something."

"Assuredly I will if it is in my power," he said kindly.

"Well, then," she said almost childishly, "promise me

that if we ever have to go away from here, back to the
city to live, that you will accept a call to a church there,
and come and be near us."

John Endicott's heart gave a mighty foreboding of evil.
He felt his strength leaping from his finger tips, but he
put forth his self-control and stayed it.

"Are you, then, thinking of going away?" he asked,
and his voice sounded strangely even to himself. Miss
Stokes noted that his lips were white.

"Oh, I suppose we'll have to, now," she said sadly,
"and just as I was so happy to stay, too; but I wouldn't
have Constance know how I feel for anything. But, if
you will go along, I shall not mind. That dear child would
give up anything for my sake, but I do not mean she
shall. You see it is this way. She and Morris Thayer have
been as good as engaged for two years, and he is of a
fine old family, and a very commendable young man,
of course just the one for her. But they had some little
misunderstanding, and she came off here. I never knew
what it was, because she did not seem to care to talk
about it; but I knew all the time that she came here because of it. I was surprised that he did not follow sooner,
for he has been very devoted; but perhaps it was her fault.
She is very proud. But now he has come, and they are
downstairs together. I think they will probably be married very soon, and of course we shall have to go home
for the wedding. But we have friends in your denomination in New York, and I am sure we could get you a better church there than you have here, and then we should
have you near us. You will do that for me, will you not?
You have helped me so very much."

She put out her delicate twisted hand, and it groped
helplessly for his strong one. He took it in a gentle grasp
as if she had been his own grandmother, and said gravely:

"Dear friend, I will do what I can for you. I will go
where God sends me."

She looked at him a moment questioningly, and then
seemed to be satisfied, and he knelt to pray; but his voice
was strained and full of sudden dread.

So it was that he did not wait for Constance Wetherill

to go to prayer meeting that evening, but went alone through the starlight, his head bowed and his whole being saddened as with sudden loss.

It was Jennie who met him at the chapel door, and looked beyond him questioningly.

"Ain't she coming?" she asked. "Then it's true. Si said her beau came this afternoon from New York, but I didn't believe him. Si always says ugly things about her because she won't be nice to him. He just hates her, too, because she runs a tea room. Say, did you see him?"

"See whom?" The minister's tone was actually cold.

"Why, her beau. Si says he was here all the afternoon, and went back to supper there. Si said some horrid things about him. If they're true, she ought to be told."

"Jennie," said the minister in his pulpit tone, "it is growing late, and Miss Wetherill has been detained. Do you think you could play for us this evening?"

And Jennie, much pleased with the honor, fluttered to the organ, and wondered why the minister had seemed not to hear what she said about Miss Wetherill. Was he jealous?

Meantime, in his inner office, back of the drug store, Silas Barton sat intent upon his evil work. He was writing anonymous letters, and the serpent of his wrath lay coiled at his elbow, hissing into his ear more evil plots than his own revenge had dared dream. His eyes gleamed triumph, and his breath came thick as his pen wrote on, almost as if it were drunk with the thought it was conveying. He paid no heed to the noises that came from the outer room, though there were oaths and curses and a sound of loud dispute. It was Holly's voice. Holly was drunk, and Holly was angry.

* * *

The gentle clock on the bookcase in the inner room at "The Cedars" had ticked out another whole minute before Constance spoke.

"Morris, you are mistaken about this place. It is mine. I have rented it and moved here. The tea room is my enterprise, and it was I who waited upon the table in there a little while ago." She paused to gather strength and see just what there was left to tell, but her listener leaned forward on the divan with distress in his face and voice. This was going to be troublesome and annoying, he feared. When girls took up fads they were hard to manage. And girls were doing a lot of unconventional things these days. But to think of Constance Wetherill admitting that she had waited upon a table of men by her own consent! It was impossible!

"But, my dear Constance," he said deprecatingly, "what in the world do you mean? What have you done all this for? Do you not know that all your friends will be amazed, and will think you have taken leave of your senses! It may be interesting to you to play at such things, but it is unseemly for one of your rank and station to so demean herself, even for amusement. May I ask why you have done this most extraordinary thing?" he asked at last, speaking sternly as if he had the right to arraign her.

Constance answered almost haughtily:

"I have done it to earn my living."

"To earn your living!" cried the young man in astonishment.

"Yes, to earn my living, and grandmother's."

"And why, pray, do you wish to do such an extraordinary thing as that? With your fortune and position it is simply insane to go in for a thing of this sort. I know girls are trying to get in the public eye nowadays by doing wild things, running off to Europe alone in airplanes and going into interior decorating and that sort of thing, but I never thought it of you. I wonder your grandmother allows it! With all your money, Constance, it is disgraceful—ridiculous——"

His voice was still stern. He put on his eye-glass and looked at her as if that would help him to understand this unusual state of things.

Constance suddenly felt that she had to laugh. He seemed so utterly horrified over what to her had come to be an accepted fact, and one that did not grieve her seriously any more. But she conquered her amusement and explained gravely:

"Morris, we haven't any money any more. It is all lost."

She said it as coolly as if she were telling him she had torn her dress.

Thayer looked at her aghast. "Lost your money!" he said sharply, "That is nonsense of course. It would be impossible! Of course your father left his estate well invested! Why didn't you come to me? I would have had my lawyer look into things for you! Of course you have been misinformed——"

But just at that instant the door leading into the front room burst open, and Jimmy's head stuck in between the portières.

His round face was red and excited, and his hair stuck up straight all over his head. The words burst from his lips explosively:

"The stores are on fire, an' the church's catchin' fire, too. The minister's up on the church roof. You better come out."

"You young scoundrel, you, don't you know any better than to come frightening a lady in this manner?" cried Morris Thayer, facing Jimmy, who bristled up at him like a small bantam cock with ruffled feathers facing a large mastiff.

"Constance—I beg you will sit down and not be annoyed. There is doubtless no danger. I will step out and see. Sit down and remain where you are, and let me look after things for you."

"I must go to my grandmother," said Constance, breathless, brushing past the young man before half his words were out. With a grimace of triumph Jimmy followed.

Morris Thayer left to himself, wandered out on the front piazza, saw that there was no danger of fire reaching in the direction of "The Cedars," watched the flames idly for a few minutes, and then sauntered in once more to try to understand the new state of things.

Constance, having visited her grandmother's room and found her peacefully sleeping, closed all windows and doors to secure her from any danger of hearing the noises

that were going on in the street, and rushed down the
back stairs and out into the night. The sentence which
had caught her ear and made her heart rise with terror
was, "The minister's up on the church roof."

Straight out to the road she fled, through the snowy
path. The light from the glaring flames fell on her, and
made her look like some fleeing angel in her rosy white.
There was much noise and confusion, and a crowd had
gathered, black against the rose-lit white of the snow
crust. The whole front of the stores was in flames, and
sheets of fire bursting from all the windows. Across the
road stood the old brick church. The moss-grown roof
which Constance had admired so often during the summer, and which for fear of a leak had been carefully
cleaned from snow that would have protected it somewhat now, had caught fire in several places.

High on its precipitous slope, clearly seen against the
star-studded sky stood the minister working with all his
might to save the church. He was hatless and coatless,
and was drenched with water. He was spreading out wet
carpets and soaking the old shingles with water.

Soon a stream from the inadequate engine was turned
on the church and there began to be a little hope for it.

Then came a great cry of horror.

It was a woman's voice, above even the chug-chug of
the little country fire engine. It was Jennie's voice, and
it rose high and clear above all others.

"Si is in there! Save him, somebody! Save my brother!
He's upstairs in the back room!"

"What does she say?" asked John Endicott, pausing
to brush back his hair from his wet forehead. "Her
brother? What! Silas Barton in the building yet? Where?
Where did you say?"

The minister was going down the ladder as fast as he
could while they answered his questions. They did not
realize what he meant to do, else perhaps they would not
have answered them so readily.

The fight in the store had been going on for some time
before Silas Barton aroused from his absorption in his
work enough to realize it.

Holly had been idle all the afternoon, and with Holly
to be idle meant to drink. He was usually good-natured
when he was drunk, and the boys of the village liked to
tease him and hear what he would say. It was a frequent
amusement on holidays. But tonight some little word
dropped by Si had been handed about by some of the
drinkers, a slight forerunner of the serpent that was
meant to uncoil itself upon the morrow. It had reached
the ears of Holly; and, drunk as he was, he was fired
with anger. He came at once to the defense of the one
woman and the one man in the whole town whom he
looked upon as saints.

"Who-who-who d-d-dares t-s-a-y th-th-th-at?" he stut-
tered, reeling into the middle of the room and rolling up
his sleeves until his huge arms were bare to the muscular
shoulders.

No one cared to go very near, but no one was really
afraid of Holly, for he was always jolly when he was
drunk. They went on with the talk, adding to the original story, and exciting him still more; and, when they
would not tell him who had said the vile words first,
Holly suddenly surprised them all by seizing a bottle that
stood on the counter, and hurling it across the room at
them. They dodged and cried out; but the bottle, whirling
on its furious way, struck first, not them, but the great
glass hanging reflector lamp that was suspended from
the ceiling, and flung it to the floor, where it exploded
with a loud noise.

Before any one in the room was sober enough to know
what to do the room itself was in flames. There was liquor enough to feed it, and it burned up rapidly. Silas,
roused at last by the uproar, came to the door, and, seeing the certain destruction of the whole building, remembered a large sum of money and some valuable papers
which he had left in his bedroom that morning. Stealthily,
lest some one should try to stop him, he slid up the stairs,
and began gathering his valuables together and securing
them about his person. But, when he essayed to go down
again, the staircase was in flames, and suffocating smoke
almost choked him. For an instant he staggered and al-

most lost consciousness. Then a draught of air from the back hall sent the smoke away for an instant, and he blindly beat his way back to his bedroom. Blackened and bleared he appeared for a second at the side window, and Jennie who had been standing in horror on the sidewalk, saw him and cried out. Then he fell back out of sight.

They helped the minister drag the ladder for they did not understand what he meant to do until they saw it placed against the burning building; then they tried to stop him. But he was too quick for them, and they were used to obeying him. With commanding voice he said: "Hands off! No, *I* must go, *not* you! You have a wife and children. I have no one!"

There was almost a satisfaction in the minister's tone as he said that. Here, at least, was one reason why he might be thankful for his lonely condition. He might go and try to save this wretched man who was not ready to die. There was no question of any duty to any one else.

So up he went, in long strong strides, and did not know that at the foot of the ladder in the darkness, there stood a girl in white, with anxious face and agonized eyes, watching him while her lips unconsciously moved in prayer for his safety.

The crowd on the street surged around to the side, quick to scent new tragedy, and a sudden awful quiet swept over them, with a quick drawing of breath, as the minister disappeared within the blazing window. And the whisper went around from one awed observer to another that is was *Si Barton* for whom he was risking his life.

Si's boon companions were there, who had spread the hideous stories that he had concocted against the minister; Holly was there, sobered, with a red gash across his forehead and another on his arm. Jimmy was there, breathless, agonizing, adoring, wishing he might have gone along. He would have readily gone now to save both of the men, only the firemen interfered whenever he came near.

Lanky was there, who had said the minister was a coward; and Mrs. Bartlett was there. She reflected with compunction that she had given the minister no pumpkin pie that winter, and he liked it so. If he came out alive, she would bake some tomorrow.

They were all there, and they strained their eyes, and prayed silently with one united breath, while the flames rolled on nearer and nearer to the spot where the ladder stood, and it began to be feared that the wall would fall.

Then, as if a mighty hope had arisen, a murmur went over the crowd; for the smoke in the window began to take form and darken, and there appeared something clumsy and blackened, and some one went up to help. It was all indistinct at first and the crowd scarcely dared moved or breathe, in spite of the fact that they were dangerously near the wall, and it might fall at any moment. They watched the two men drag their heavy, sodden burden, step by step, cautiously, down the ladder, until they were low enough for waiting hands to receive him from them; and then, the minister suddenly sank, and dropped silently among them like one dead.

They carried him quickly away from the wall, and the crowd melted out of danger none too soon as the horrible flame-enveloped structure shivered, leaned, and collapsed. Mrs. Bartlett turned back, marked where the minister had lain but the moment before, and shuddered to think what might have been.

Constance, with heart beating wildly, scarcely realizing where she stood, or what people would think of her, followed the men who were carrying the minister, and commanded them to bring him to "The Cedars." They looked at her respectfully, glanced at the house, seemed to realize that it was the most convenient place, and obeyed her. Afterward the men who carried Silas followed, and laid him on a hastily improvised couch in the library, across the hall from the tea room. But the minister they laid in Constance's room, among the snowy pillows.

Morris Thayer, standing upon the door-step, saw them coming, put up his monocle, as he always did when anything disturbed him, and said:

"Why, they ought not to bring those creatures in here. This is an imposition. Somebody ought to do something!"

Chapter XXII

It was Dr. Randall who stood beside the minister, working skillfully, grave and silent. Jimmy had searched him out among the crowd and brought him at once. Any doctor would do for Si Barton, Jimmy thought, but Dr. Randall must come to his beloved minister.

Jimmy himself stood near, and flew to the doctor's house with messages for his wife to send rolls of antiseptic bandages and ointments, for there was no more drug store now to run to; flew here and there silently in incredibly short spaces of time, carrying out all directions given him; and no one gainsaid his right to be in the sickroom. He shed his shoes and went about with noiseless tread, his little soul filled with anguish. He had brought the minister to Constance when she was in trouble; he would have liked to bring Constance to the minister in his need; but he had no need, for she was there, softly giving directions, pulling down draperies of costly material that were in the way, ruthlessly sweeping the bravery of her beautiful dressing-table into a basket, that the doctor might spread out his various instruments and liniments and arrange his bandages.

Unconscious there amid the beauty of the room which it would have been a joy to him to look into, John Endicott lay, his face blackened almost beyond recognition, his hair and eyebrows burnt, his hands seared, his clothing smoky and torn, and even burned in places. Constance hovered near, her presence like a troubled angel's. The doctor looked on her once, and tried to smile com-

fortingly. It sat hard upon his grim old face, that smile,
for he did not know how to comfort grown people; it
was only kittens and little ones toward whom his heart
could break forth in its naturalness.

Constance could see sympathy in his face, for each
knew that the other loved the man upon the bed; how
they knew they could not tell, but they knew.

The girl sank down in a low chair at the foot of the
bed, and, covering her face with her hands, prayed as
she had never prayed before. She prayed for John Endicott's life, and she knew as she prayed that she loved
him, and that she had never loved any one else in this
way.

Jimmy glanced reverently at her when he came in, lowered his head, and tiptoed out again. He stood outside
the door in the hall with closed eyes as if some one were
uttering an audible prayer; and then his lips stirred softly,
and he grumbled so that it could be heard only in heaven:
"O God, save our minister. Amen."

By and by the doctor touched Constance on the shoulder, and said in a low professional tone:

"He may pull through. His burns are not so bad as
I feared."

Then Constance arose and took heart of hope. She
slipped out into the hall, comforted the forlorn Jimmy
and sent him to bed; she went to the kitchen, and calmed
Norah, who had been working far beyond any girl's
strength; and she sent to see how the other poor creature who was under her roof was doing. Then it occurred
to her that Morris Thayer must be somewhere. It was
mortifying to have forgotten him, and by this token she
knew that he never could have occupied a very large place
in her heart. How far away it all seemed! How strange
that she had ever cared what he, or that little world of
giddy people in which she had moved so long, would
think. She knew now that she had never cared for Morris
Thayer.

But Morris Thayer was still in the flesh, and at present
in Rushville. He was yet to be dealt with, and what
should she do with him? She had provided no guest room

in the house, for she had expected no guests. The minister was occupying her own room, and Miss Stokes had the only other available spot. There were rooms in the third story where Norah slept, but excepting Norah's these had never been put in order. She did not like to put him to sleep on a couch in the parlor; she felt that alone in such a spot he would be as helpless as a baby in a barn yard. There was no boarding-house in the town, save the place where Mr. Endicott boarded. Stay! Why would that not do? Norah said something about somebody's waiting now to ask her about the minister. Perhaps it was opportune.

She went downstairs at once, and there found Mrs. Bartlett seated on the edge of a chair in the tea room, and Hiram, her husband, standing uncertainly behind her, glancing furtively up the stairs and again wistfully out the front door. Hiram was sleepy. He had arisen at five that morning, and had worked hard all day. He had a natural interest in the minister's welfare, but he could wait until morning to find out about it. They couldn't do anything, anyway. But he did not like to say this to his wife. There were tears in Mrs. Bartlett's eyes. She was thinking of the pumpkin pies, and that now it might be too late ever to make them for the minister. She was thinking, too, of how carefully the minister always wiped his feet before coming into the hall. And he always was so polite, too! She arose disapprovingly, as if the minister's plight were somehow the fault of the young woman who was coming down the hall to meet her.

Constance greeted them quietly, and won old Hiram's heart at once. She told them what the doctor had said, and promised to let them know in the morning how he seemed. Then she made her request. Would it be possible for them to give one of the Wetherill's old friends a room for the night?

Mrs. Bartlett would have declined the honor at once as impossible. Her remorse did not reach to friends of the friends of her minister. She preferred to go home, and make a large batch of pumpkin pies, and send one to the minister, though she knew he would not be allowed to eat it. Strange how sacrifice is always pleasanter than obedience to some people!

But Mrs. Bartlett was left no choice in the matter. Hiram was pleased with Constance, and he did a thing which he dared not often do. He took the initiative himself.

"Yes," he said at once, "we'll put him up. No reason why he shouldn't hev the preacher's bed. 'Tain't okkepied tonight. Wisht it was. Just bring him right 'long, 'an he kin go home with us."

Constance thanked him, and went in search of Morris Thayer, while Mrs. Bartlett turned on her spouse an ominous look, and murmured something about clean sheets and a fine breakfast to get. However, Hiram was suddenly absorbed in a study of the palms on the tea room walls, and seemed not to hear. Constance soon came back with the much-bewildered Morris Thayer in her wake. He was carrying his suitcase and bag.

"Evenin'," said Hiram, putting out a horny hand toward the city gentleman, which under the circumstances it was impossible for him to take even if he had been willing to do so.

It was impossible for him to understand the situation thoroughly. He had been informed that he was to occupy the minister's room for the night, as the minister was perforce occupying the only available room in the house. Morris Thayer was helpless in the hands of his friends, and helpless he went out into the night, preceded by the would-be-affable Hiram and his wouldn't-be-affable wife. If Constance had not been so weary, she would have laughed as she watched them away; but instead she only turned with a relieved sigh and sped upstairs.

A few minutes later Morris Thayer, much broken in spirit, and perspiring freely in spite of the zero temperature of the room, sat down upon the minister's bed, and by the light of the glass kerosene lamp with the red flannel wick took a survey of the situation. He adjusted his eye-glass and took it all in, the matting, the rag rug, the hard bed, the cheap bureau, the faded photograph, and the sorry look of everything.

"Impossible!" he ejaculated. "Can any man of education and breeding occupy a hole like this?" He was silent once more while his eyes traveled around the room to make sure he had seen it aright, and then back to the dismal, humpy bed with its patchwork quilt of flowered calico.

"I will never travel without my man again!" he concluded.

Like a prisoner in a cell he prepared himself for rest; but, though he lay down in a gingerly way upon the humps, he slept but little, and the morning found him almost haggard as he came down, declining breakfast and asking Mrs. Bartlett how much he owed her. She set her lips grimly, and answered in low tones, that Hiram might not hear—he was washing his face and combing his hair at the kitchen sink—that it was *a dollar*! When he carelessly threw down the silver disk, she looked at it regretfully, and said to herself that she wished she had made it a dollar and a quarter; she believed he wouldn't have thought it too much. But she hid the dollar quickly, for Hiram was hospitable and benevolent, and would think she should not have asked for a cent. She grumbled all the while they were at breakfast because she had cooked two extra eggs with the best ham for their guest, and now it was wasted.

During his night's vigil the young man had done some serious thinking. He had gone over the whole story that Constance had told him, and little by little the fine courage of this girl had dimly dawned upon him. Not that he was able to appreciate it to the full, but he saw that she had an element of greatness in her that he could feel was worthy of praise. He was horrified that her money was gone; for he was a luxurious creature himself, and spent a great deal, and the thought of her wealth had been a comfortable one. Indeed, he had pitied many other men who married girls without fortunes, and congratulated himself that he was feathering his nest well; but now that the question was put to him whether or not he would give up Constance, he found that he could not let her go. He was surprised at himself that this was so.

He was pleased at it as an indication of nobility in himself, not recognizing the truth that it was rather merely the desire of a spoiled child to have always what it craved in spite of everything. He told himself that he was benevolent, and would prove it. He would take her in spite of her poverty, and help her hide it from the world.

There was an undercurrent, too, of satisfaction in the thought that this would give him a certain power over her. If he married her, poverty and all, she would never dare to lift her handsome, haughty head again to him in defiance. She would not hold him at arm's length any more. She would be his to do with as he pleased, to go where he willed, and to be what he suggested.

With these worthy sentiments in his mind he took his way to "The Cedars" in the early morning, and after having breakfast in what Jimmy considered a heartless hearty way he sent for Constance. Jimmy thought no one ought to eat or sleep until the minister got well.

Constance came down pale and tired-looking, with dark rings under her eyes; and Morris Thayer thought her more interesting than ever. He came to the point at once, and graciously told her that he had decided not to let her change of fortune make any difference in his intentions. He would marry her, anyway, and he would like to have the marriage almost immediately. He wanted to get her out of this terrible hole and back to her proper sphere.

There was a slight condescension in his voice, and Constance would have been angered by it, had not her thoughts been so wholly on another subject. But her cheeks burned when she heard his cool disposal of herself, as if the matter were settled. When he paused to look her over critically with his practiced eye, as he would have looked at a fine car or a yacht, he had just purchased at a great price, with which he was thoroughly satisfied, she spoke quickly: "I am afraid Morris that you did not understand me last night. The money has nothing to do with my marrying anybody. I could never marry *you* Morris, for I do not love you. I appreciate, of course, the honor you have done me but please put that out of your mind forever, and let us just be friends."

He could not believe her at first, and attempted to argue the matter; but Constance was unmoved. He was dumfounded. He could not believe that any girl in her senses would refuse him, especially a girl in her present circumstances.

It was in a driving sleet that he walked away from "The Cedars" crestfallen, reluctantly followed by Jimmy, borne down by the weight of a heavy suit-case and bag, who took out his displeasure in making wry faces at the young man behind his back. Jimmy set down his burdens hard on the platform, and fled the spot without taking the money which the astonished Morris Thayer offered him.

"Well, that chump's out ther way, enneyhow," he remarked to Norah with satisfaction when he arrived in the kitchen. "Wanted to give me a quarter. H'm! I wouldn't soil my hands with one o' his'n. He needn't think he's got a show beside Mr. Endycut."

And Norah responded fervently as she peppered a kettle of soup:

"Right you are thar, Jimmy, me bye. The saints be praised ef he's raelly gawn! Now, ef the blissed man'll awnly git well!"

Such love, such prayers, such care could scarcely help bringing a man back from death's door, and John Endicott began to rally at last. Constance with gentle ways was in and out of his room, bringing cheer with her whenever she came. Sometimes she read to him, and he would lie and watch her changing face, and hungrily learn by heart the love of her look; but always when she glanced up and met his smile it was a sad one, and she thought he was mourning for his mother.

One day when she had been reading and he watching her thus, he suddenly put out his bandaged hand, and said:

"Ought you not to be downstairs, or away somewhere? Is not your friend waiting for you?"

Then Constance looked at him with amazement and asked for an explanation.

"Why, your friend. Your grandmother told me all about it the night of the fire. She said you were soon to be married, and you would all go back to New York. She wanted me to promise to go, too, and take a church there."

He smiled sadly as if to turn her thoughts away from himself. But she laughed a clear happy, merry laugh.

"Did grandmother tell you that? The blessed old dear! Oh, what a lot of trouble she has tried to make for me! Now I shall have to tell you all about it."

How it happened they never either of them knew; but, as she talked, John Endicott's eyes drew Constance's nearer and nearer to his own, until their faces were close together.

Miss Stokes came softly to the door to tell Constance her grandmother would like to see her, but stepped aside and wiped away a glad tear in the darkness of the hall, and then went back and told Mrs. Wetherill that Constance was very much engaged at present. She stood by the window for a full half-hour gazing into the snow-capped cedar, reflecting what true love could mean, love such as those two in there could feel for each other.

The doctor came, walked boldly in, and caught them so, her face against him, his bandaged arm about her, as she knelt beside the bed. He laid his rough hands on each head with a gruff blessing, and then stood back, and said:

"Now he will get well. I've known he needed something all along, but didn't have it among my medicines."

Constance with rosy face and joyous eyes laughed out her own sweet silvery laugh, just for very joy. It echoed down to the kitchen, and made Jimmy and Norah smile understandingly to each other, and it sent a tiny echo to the room below.

Down in that lower front room the poor burnt, scarred fragment of a wretch was lying, slowly crawling back to a life of pain and remorse. Over his head lay the man whom he had called a coward; and giving him her bounty was the lovely woman whose fair name he had meant to smirch with the pitch of the lower regions; and there he lay helpless, his lower limbs hopelessly paralyzed, his right arm amputated—the hand that had written those vile letters had been burned off—his whole visage disfigured; the mystery of life in an almost dead body. There he was laid, to learn the old, old story of salvation by the Redeemer, through his own story and that of one who had risked his life to save a man who hated him. By and by, when he was able and the minister was better, there would be sweet music in the next room to his, and the old, old story would be sung to him. The hard heart that could not be reached by preaching and praying and warning would gradually be melted by suffering and love. But now he lay there, miserable, with his pretty young sister to wait upon him, and all his brazen courage vanquished.

Far away in New York, Morris Thayer was trying to get used to not having his own way, and was becoming a sadder, if not wiser man. He could not understand why Constance had refused him.

Chapter XXIII

The spring had come, and all the cedars were tipped with brighter green in tender, spicy outputs. The willows down by the pond were draped in their lacery, and there were violets everywhere over the lawn, under the trees, and down on the path to the old summer-house.

By some mysterious metamorphosis a change, too, had come upon the "haunted house." In fact, it was no longer known among the villagers as "hanted." It was spoken of quite respectfully as "The Cedars." Whether that was the work of Dr. Randall or Jimmy or the minister—whose voice still spoke with command from his sick-bed—or the combined work of the three, is uncertain. Through the long weeks of anxiety when the minister lay at death's door, and later when he was slowly and painfully creeping back to life, the people, even Mrs. Bartlett, had learned to respect the sweet-faced girl who always came down when they called to inquire after their pastor. She told the pleasant little messages he sent them in such a way that they fairly seemed to have heard the minister himself speaking them, and knew how his smile had looked as he gave the message. It was next best to talking with himself.

No more slurs and slights were given her, and the visitors always walked with solemn faces and awed tread as they passed the door of the front parlor, where lay for many weeks the racked form of the poor wretch who was doomed to live out the remainder of his days in helpless pain and regret.

"She needn't to 'a' done it," said Holly, shaking his head wonderingly; "and, ef she'd 'a' knowed what he said about her jest 'fore the fire, she wouldn't. She'd 'a' sent him away ef it *did* kill him to be moved."

"No, she wouldn't 'a'," responded Jimmy stoutly. "She'd 'a' did it—done it, I mean—all the more."

Jimmy was getting some perception of his need of an education.

So little by little the villagers had taken in Constance, and she was growing in their regard until there was danger that she might eclipse even the minister, who was now a hero in their eyes.

As John Endicott grew better, and was at last able to come downstairs, he spent hours in Constance's own little sanctum, the old back parlor. Constance often played softly to him, and sometimes sang. Occasionally he would join in a rich baritone with her sweet soprano, and they would sing together magnificent strains from the old masters, or sweet old hymns that both loved. The doors would be left open that Grandmother Wetherill might hear, and Jennie as head nurse in the front parlor fell into the habit of opening the door into the hall to catch more sound than could come through the double doors, heavily hung with portières. She had discovered that her brother lay with closed eyes and some semblance of peace upon his brow while the music went on, and that he seemed disappointed when it ceased. Once, one Sunday evening, the last Sunday before the minister was allowed by the doctor to go back to his church services, the two sang hymns for a long time. The last one they sang was:

"Come home, come home! You are weary at heart,
For the way has been long, and so dreary and wild,
O prodigal child, come home, O, come home!"

They sang several verses, and after the first Si asked to have the door opened wider. When the singing was finally over, and the minister had gone upstairs for the night, Jennie closed the door again softly; and, as she came back, she thought she saw a tear on her brother's

cheek. It startled her so that she went and sat down for
a full minute to think before she went gently about getting him ready for the night.

After that there were long talks with the minister on
days when Barton was not suffering unusually. There
were confession and forgiveness, and Si told the minister the story of his hard young life until John Endicott
wondered no longer at the hold the devil had upon him,
but marveled over the love of God in sparing him and
giving him another chance.

It was a poor, wrecked life, only a piece of a life, that
Si had to give to the Lord; but the minister made the
way so plain that the poor, broken creature could but
thankfully accept the wonderful forgiveness and salvation.

There came a day in the early springtime, the first communion Sabbath when the minister was able to be with
his people again, when all the town were assembled in
and about the pretty stone church with its scarred and
mended roof. The members of the church were there,
for their hearts were very tender with thanksgiving over
the spared life of their beloved pastor. The people of the
village were there out of sympathy with the church-
members and general good will toward the minister, and
perhaps, too, out of curiosity, for a strange rumor had
been going around town. The drug store loungers and
station habitués were there because they had been especially invited by the man who had done his best for five
years to ruin them. Lying upon his bed of pain, his right
hand gone forever, Si had laboriously tried to write with
his left hand. He had written in ragged, irregular, almost
unintelligible, lines—that were pitiful when one remembered the bold, dashing hand in which he had formerly
signed his receipts.

"I want you to come to church next Sunday for Jesus
Christ has forgiven my sins and I am going to take Him
then before men as my Lord and Saviour."

Those were the words, that Si sent out that startled
many hearts. Some of them regarded the letters with horror and a half-superstitious fear, laying them aside with

awe, vowing not to go near the church, and shuddering
at the thought of death. Some of them drew their rough
hands across their eyes, and cleared a strange huskiness
in their throats, and said, "Gosh! but ain't he down?"
Some of them, the youngest, and the older boys, looked
shamed and serious, and were gentle all that day. But
they all came, every man of them, and took front seats
like invited guests, crowding out some of the rightful oc-
cupants, much to their unrighteous indignation. They had
some curiosity themselves that day, and thought they had
a right to first places in the synagogue like the sulky
brother of the prodigal. But they were there, and heard
every word.

Jennie had opened the window and wrapped the invalid so that no breath of cold could reach him. He lay
with closed eyes, listening to the sweet sound of the music
in the church over the way, and letting his heart come
near to the great, forgiving heart of his Maker.

The windows of the church were open, too; and now
and then Si's old friends would glance with awe out toward "The Cedars," knowing that Si would be listening.
It was like a realization of the presence of the dead.

They sang the hymn, "Just as I am," or rather Constance sang it as a solo. It was the first time she had sung
in public since the fire. She sang every verse, and the
words rang deep into the hearts of those rough men and
boys on the front seats. Holly cleared his throat loudly,
and shuffled his big feet around. He looked down at his
hands. He somehow never seemed to have realized before how poor and wretched he must seem before God.

After the singing of those wonderful, humble words
the minister read Si's confession of faith. It was simple,
framed from the agony of his soul and body, word for
word as the minister had written it down from his own
lips. It sounded like Si, only a new Si, a Si that talked
of things heavenly with the same voice in which he had
spoken of things devilish. They had listened to him so
long that they could understand him now, even though
he had been lifted to heights far beyond them. They wondered, and trembled before a God who could cast out

the devil from Si. One by one every head went down,
and the tears rolled down their cheeks as the minister announced that the session had talked with the writer of
that confession, and felt him to be truly a Christian; and
he had been admitted into fellowship as a member of
their church.

There were others who stood up then as their names
were called, and assented to the covenant; and, as they
bowed their heads, and said, "I will" to the solemn questions, it seemed to those men on the front seats as if they
could hear the echo of another strong commanding voice
from the unseen candidate for membership, saying "I
will" with the rest. Then they dropped their eyes, and
no man looked at his neighbor.

That had been a wonderful day. Jimmy's heart had
fairly burst with the greatness of the occasion. He felt
that new worlds were opening before him. As he walked
home from church that evening at a respectful distance
behind the minister and Constance, and looked up to the
clustering stars, it almost seemed to him he could see angels flitting back and forth to heaven with torches, and
hear their praising voices over the "one sinner that repent-
eth." Jimmy felt that to be a Christian was the greatest
thing in the world. Tonight there had been born within
him a desire to be a minister some day like John Endicott,
and to "turn many to righteousness."

Jimmy was happy, happy, happy that night!

It had needed only Constance's little whispered word
at the door—as he lingered to see whether there was anything more he could do for her that night—to put him
into the seventh heaven.

"Jimmy, I want to tell you that Mr. Endicott and I
are to be married soon. It will be announced tomorrow,
and everybody will know it; but I thought I should like
to tell you myself first, because you are my friend, you
know"; and she smiled her brightest smile upon him.

Jimmy's face had lighted up with joy. He could not
think of anything nicer than to have these two, who were
both so dear and so good to him, become one. He tried
to stammer out his feelings, and Constance understood,

and added in answer to his wistful question as he went down the steps after saying good night, "Yes, of course you may tell the boys."

After that the days had passed in a whirl of pleasant occupations. A great many new things happened. For one thing, "The Cedars" took on several alterations without and within. A coat of beautiful creamy paint on all the woodwork changed the appearance of the house entirely, and made "The Cedars" stand proudly out toward the road with a new air. Vines were trained over the pillars. The minister did that with Jimmy's help.

Another event was that Jimmy was to have an education. He had protested that it was hardly worth while, and he could not be spared; also, that he had had all the schooling he desired to acquire; but Constance took him into the back parlor, and had a long talk with him one day, all about his hopes and plans, and the man God had meant him to be when He put him into the world. Jimmy issued from that parlor a sober and thoughtful boy, resolved to have an education if it cost him his life. An education was a necessity, it seemed; and therefore, though it was a hard prospect, he meant to go through with it, and do it thoroughly, too.

But most exciting of all was the little white cottage that was day by day growing on the vacant lot next to "The Cedars."

After many consultations with the minister and Constance, Jennie sitting by with pink cheeks and breathless wonder, the plan was made and Si signed a contract with a good builder to put him up the daintiest, prettiest white cottage with green blinds that a carpenter could build. It had as many bay windows as Jennie asked for, and there was a large, light room on the first floor, with windows along one entire side looking toward "The Cedars." This was to be the room where Si would spend the rest of his painful days until God should say, "It is enough," and call him up higher. Already Jennie had planned many a little comfort and pleasure to make the days of her brother bright, and in this Constance was a willing and unfailing helper.

There was also a large ell, connected with the little white cottage. It was the delight of Jennie's heart, and had been evolved from Constance's fertile brain. This ell contained a large room with windows all about, and an inviting doorway opposite to the station platform. This was to be a dining-room, and it was fully as large as the dining-room at "The Cedars." Back of this was a large kitchen and pantry, and all was to be thoroughly fitted up with conveniences for cooking on a large scale. This was to be the new restaurant, and Jennie was to run it.

In the moments when she could be spared she was already learning wonderful things of Norah in the art of cookery, and had engaged Jimmy's mother as a regular helper in the new enterprise. Jimmy's mother had been called in to help during the siege of nursing at "The Cedars" and was well trained by this time in cooking dainty things at five minutes' notice; for the tea room at "The Cedars" was still going on.

The minister had wished Constance to close it at once, but Constance had persuaded him that it would be better for Jennie if she could take the work with a good business well started, and not have a break in which travelers would find there was no place where they could get a good meal in the town. So with the help of others the work had been quietly carried on, with the expectation that Jennie would take it up when Constance was married.

The white cottage grew, and became an abode, and Jennie flitted back and forth, preparing everything; in her face a glow of joy that comes from lofty purpose. Jennie was no longer a butterfly.

Tenderly they carried the poor, racked body of the man over to his new home, and made him comfortable; and he seemed content in spite of his suffering. He was to be the brains of this new business, and Jennie was to manage everything. Sometimes it all came over him, what he had intended to do to injure these two grand souls who were caring for him now and giving him back as much of life as was in their power; then his heart was overwhelmed with gratitude. Of him truly it could be said

that he was a "new creature in Christ Jesus." Jennie marveled over it every day. His old cronies marveled every
time they passed the neat white house; and Holly Beech
marveled when he stepped into the sunny, airy room of
the invalid to get his daily orders, for he was general fac-
totum, as well as admiring slave of Jennie.

Chapter XXIV

Meantime "The Cedars," its rooms left free once more, began to make changes also. The tea room formally changed hands as soon as the new building had its long dining-room plastered. After all, it did not take much work to make the great dining-room into a charming living-room. The little tables sank back into their proper places; the Persian rugs asserted themselves; the chairs from Constance's sanctum, with a good many others, which had been put in the third story, came in to fill the empty spaces, until in two days not a villager would have recognized the place where he had been wont to come in an ecstasy of delight for a dish of ice cream. More pictures were brought down and unpacked, and costly bric-à-brac. Rare curtains draped the windows; quiet elegance reigned as if by right, where a temporary democratic freedom had held sway.

Jimmie, sent by Norah to carry some article of furniture down to the great room from the attic, paused on the threshold as he had done once before, not knowing that there had been another change, and held his breath. A chill struck him. There was a something beautiful and apart in this room now, something that made him feel he must not enter—not yet. He reasoned it all out afterwards, that evening, on the back-door step. It was something that belonged to an education and undoubtedly he must have an education.

During the next few days the front room, which Si had occupied, and which before that had been the library or office, became a luxurious library indeed. All the fine volumes that had been in the Wetherill house in New York took their places in well-ordered groups behind sliding glass doors about the walls. The large revolving bookcase, the great carved rosewood desk with rolling top and many drawers, the leather desk-chair, all were suggestive of a minister's study. In fact, John Endicott's worn and much-used volumes took their places, a few every day, side by side with the Wetherill ones in half-calf and Russia bindings.

Mrs. Bartlett had again become the nominal landlady of the minister, but the constantly diminishing bookcase reminded her that her time for pumpkin pies was short, and the pumpkins had not yet come. She took it out in lavishing upon him the best strawberries and peas the market afforded, and never grudging anything, even a smile now and then. She was always feeling uncomfortable about that dollar she took from Morris Thayer for his night's lodging, and wanting to make it up in some way. The result was, she spent it a number of times over, till she was almost getting into the habit of being generous.

The back parlor that had been Constance's sanctum was changed into a beautiful dining-room, and the dining-room upstairs became, as it should be, a bedroom. The third story was put in order, and Norah began to breathe more freely, and feel that things were more suited to a member of the house of Wetherill. She sadly regretted that there was so much necessary scrimping, but this was better than having Miss Constance keep a tea room. What a pity ministers had such small salaries and had to work so hard!

Just as spring was ripening into summer, on a rare day in the last of June, Constance was married.

Until just at the last it had not seemed possible to have the wedding a public affair. Indeed, both bride and groom would personally have preferred having it as quiet as possible, but there were others to be considered besides themselves. There was the loving, adoring church, all eyes and ears to see "how he looked" and "how she looked," and "how he acted" and "what she wore," and

live over again their own private romances in the faces
of this dear couple who belonged to them. The minister
knew they would each one feel personally aggrieved that
they could not be present, and yet he could not ask it
of Constance to be married in the church, because of the
state of her grandmother's health. It was Constance who
thought of it, whose quick perceptions knew how Mrs.
Bartlett and Holly Beech and Jennie and all the rest
would feel it they were left out; and her own heart drew
her to give up her personal pleasure in the matter.

Of course, the grandmother must be present. But, as
the warmer weather drew on, Mrs. Wetherill improved
in a most surprising way, and Dr. Randall told Constance
he did not think it could hurt her in the least to be carried over to the church for a little while. In fact, if it
pleased her, it might only do her good. So, one morning
when Mrs. Wetherill seemed to feel pretty well, Constance broached the matter gently, and to her surprise
found her grandmother quite expecting the wedding to
be in the church.

"Of course John will want to please his people, dear,"
she said, "and you should always study to please your
husband. I always did. It's right and best. Besides, I've
had no opportunity to meet his people, and I should like
to see them, they have all been so kind. Then, too, it's
not as if we were in our own home here—we're sort of
boarding—though it's been quite comfortable all winter.
You think you wouldn't care to go back to the house in
New York for the ceremony? Well, I don't blame you.
It's been shut up so long it would be quite a nuisance
to get it into working order again; and, if you don't mind,
I'm sure I do not. A wedding in a church is always
proper, dear, and especially fitting for a minister. Yes,
I think I might easily go."

And so it was settled, and the village and the church
threw themselves into violent preparations for a real
church wedding peculiarly their own.

The women met, and selected a committee of decoration, and the committee planned elaborate decorations
that would have done justice to a third-rate undertaker.

Fortunately Jennie had been put upon the committee, and, coming in late, was rather dismayed at the arrangements. She was so far educated in taste that she now knew that Constance would not appreciate her name and the minister's done in purple and white everlastings and intertwined on a background of artificial moss swinging in the air above her like a coming doom. Jennie listened, and finally spoke.

"Say, those kind of pieces are real fine, but I jest believe she'd like it better if we put real flowers around. When I come over here, I stopped and asked her what her idea was, and she said she wanted you to fix it the way you liked it, but she would suggest to just have it simple flowers and greens. She likes the flowers that grow in your gardens. Why don't you take honeysuckles, and roses, and white pinies, and white hollyhocks, and jest fill it up all white and green in back of the pulpit?"

And so they planned. Jennie contrived to keep things within some bounds, though the result perhaps was not just what it would have been had Constance done it herself. But Constance loved the people, and it mattered not to her.

The day was perfect, the sky shining clear, and the birds doing their best at the wedding-march.

They carried old Mrs. Wetherill over early in a wheeled chair, and made her comfortable close to a bower of white roses, and her old eyes were not so critical as to distinguish between roses and white hollyhocks and candytuft. She had reached the stage of her journey when she was quite satisfied with things as they were, and did not wish to pull them to pieces because they were not just as she had always had them.

Jimmy stood at the front gate in a new suit earned by himself, and bought in New York by Constance. He regarded the village boys on the curb in front of the church across the road with a great look of condescension. They openly admired and envied Jimmy. Why had not *they* carried Miss Constance's bundles that day a year ago instead of squabbling over marbles? Then they might, too, have walked in fine array.

At five minutes before ten the up-train from the city came in. Jimmy looked at the passengers scornfully. Poor things, they had to travel on! They had no knowledge of the great event about to come off, and they had no right to look so carelessly over at the crowd already standing about the church. They were outsiders.

Two men were getting off. They were elegantly dressed; at least one was. The other had a slippery look to Jimmy.

They glanced about to get their bearings. Then the more elegant of the two pointed over toward Jimmy and "The Cedars."

"They'll find they're mistook this time," murmured the boy to himself. "No late breakfasts ner chops to be had here any more!" Jimmy stood up straight, on guard. He enjoyed the situation. He hoped they would come over. He would show them!

They came. Jimmy watched every step with indolent disdain and studied indifference.

But they were not noticing Jimmy, and he planted himself more apparently in the gateway.

The two men were closer now. Jimmy eyed the elegant one keenly. Could it be? Yes, it was! His heart throbbed painfully. Here was possible danger and a chance to show himself a hero. Here, yes, surely here was the old lover returned; just on the brink of the marriage, five minutes before the ceremony, come to stop the marriage and claim his own! It was like the yellow-covered book that Jimmy's sister borrowed from Eliza Whitmeyer last winter.

The evening before, Morris Thayer, lately arrived from Europe, where he had gone to heal his rudely broken heart, had attended a dinner, at the home of one of his mother's friends, where, he was told, two heiresses of unimpeachable beauty would be present. He had found the heiresses already well appropriated, and the only other young woman present very dull and reported poor; so, when his old friend, the Wetherills' lawyer, entered the room, he settled down to a business talk with him.

It was just after the ladies had left the table that the lawyer turned to him and said:

"By the way, Thayer, you'll be glad to hear the good news. You're an old friend of the Wetherills. I suppose of course you knew of their misfortunes. I was not supposed to tell, but you of course were in the secret. Well, I have just found out that some old stock that Constance's father bought years ago—stock in a silver mine—has risen in value, and is pouring in untold wealth. She will have more than ever before. I had an opportunity to buy in the old home, which was sold three months ago, and I bought it. I've just sent her word about it this evening. She had no idea there was any such chance."

Now indeed was Morris Thayer on the alert. He had spent a great deal of money on his trip abroad, having lost heavily in gambling; and he had come home determined to find and marry a rich wife. If it should prove to be Constance he would be well pleased. Somehow he could not quite forget her.

His thick skin had long ago healed over any wounds she might have given his conceit, and he really had no fear but that he might win her if he only put himself out to do so. He had not half tried before, of course; but now it would be something worth while, and—he would take his man with him!

So he telephoned from the club to his man to pack a suit-case and bag, and meet him at the station in time for the next train going Constance-ward; for he reasoned that, if the lawyer had but just written Constance, he might reach her before the letter, and so not seem to have come for financial reasons.

But, when Thayer and his man reached the station, they found that the time-table had been changed that very week, and that the late train was fifteen minutes earlier than they had supposed, and had already left the station.

The next train was very early in the morning; but hard as it seemed, Thayer decided to take it. The lawyer had said there was a great deal, millions, perhaps, in that silver mine. It was worth while. He had never taken so much trouble before for any one. Constance certainly ought to appreciate it. He began to feel a little abused.

But he did it, slept all night at the club, and, irritable and sleepy, was driven in a taxi to the station at the last minute, and was put on the train by his man, who always carried out his orders even if it did go against the grain.

But the unusually early rising, and the unpleasant journey had not improved Morris Thayer's temper. He was disposed to growl at everybody and everything. When he finally reached his destination, he felt like sitting down in the road like a spoiled child and demanding that Constance come out to him. But his man had his orders, and together they walked toward "The Cedars."

They paid no more attention to Jimmy than if he were a cobweb stretched across the path. They would have gone right over him, or brushed him away like a fly. But Jimmy bristled all over with fear and wrath and protectorship.

"This is private property, sir. You can't come in here that way."

"Isn't this a tea room, kid? What are you talkin' 'bout? Get out o' the way!" responded the valet, giving Jimmy a shove from the path. Morris Thayer had confided the whole story of his former visit. It was always best to give his man every fact in the case, and then he knew what to do. He felt now that the man had showed remarkable brilliancy in recalling this fact about the tea room. He never would have thought of it if he had been alone.

But Jimmy was blazing. His new suit had been handled roughly, his sacred wedding-clothes!

"No, this here ain't no tea room any more. It's private property. The Wetherills lives here."

The man looked significantly at his master. The tea room was already a thing of the past! Had the news of the silver mine, then, preceded them?

"Well, sonnie," said the man, taking a new line, "it's Miss Wetherill we've come to see. This gentleman is a dear old friend of hers. Just you step aside. I know what I'm about."

"Not much he ain't no dear old friend," said Jimmy

irreverently, standing his ground; "and she can't see him. She's very much took up with other things at present. *She's engaged!*" He added the last two words in sudden remembrance of what Constance had taught him to say when he had waited upon the door for her sometimes.

"Well, that's all right, sonnie; you jest run along in and tell her who's here, and she'll see us all right."

Jimmy eyed the house furtively. The car was standing at the side door behind a cedar. Jimmy could see the minister already in the little chapel door, glancing over. It was time the bride was coming. Could he parley a little longer? Then he caught a glimpse of a white dress, a vision of a cloudlike veil, and he drew a sigh of relief. A moment more, and all would be safe. He would hold the fort until she was in the church.

"Well, I s'pose you ken see her ef you wait long 'nough. At present there's a wedding goin' to be in about a minute, and she's got to be at it. I can't break in on weddings," said Jimmy philosophically, watching the steady progress of the car down the cedar-lined drive a few paces from them.

"A wedding?" said Morris Thayer.

"Whose wedding?" he asked sharply, suddenly suspicious.

The car had reached the side door of the church now. Jimmy eyed the man suspiciously, and grew wary.

"Why, the minister's wedding, course."

"Aw! The minister's!" said Morris Thayer disinterestedly, dropping his eye-glass.

"What's that got to do with Miss Wetherill, kid?" sneered the man. "Get out o' the way. We want to see Miss Wetherill."

"Well, she ain't here," said Jimmy, leisurely stepping aside and waving his hand magnanimously; "but, ef you want to see her so awful bad, you kin swing on the gate till you see her go by, or step over to the weddin' an' look at her. She's in the church by now, an' I reckon you'll find her easy 'nough ef you know her so turrible well. Anyhow, I'm goin' over, an' you kin come, too, ef you like."

With which astonishing invitation Jimmy vanished over into the crowd, and was soon worming himself to the front of the church, breathless, and feeling himself a hero and a diplomatist. Those two men could never get inside the church in time to forbid the marriage now, for the strange minister's voice was already repeating those mystical sentences that would make Constance Wetherill and the minister one.

Hardly knowing what to do, the two men elbowed their way through the crowd, and struggled into the church just in time to hear the words, "What God hath joined together let not man put asunder"; and Jimmy, turning a triumphant, searching eye for two visitors, saw them as they caught sight of the bride's smiling face when she came down the aisle, leaning on the arm of her husband.

And so it was that Morris Thayer attended Constance Wetherill's wedding.

In deep discomfiture he wended his way home without having discovered himself to the bride, and magnanimously covered his defeat by sending her a solid silver punch bowl as a wedding present.

Novels of Enduring Romance and Inspiration by

GRACE
LIVINGSTON
HILL

☐	26364	**THE GIRL FROM MONTANA #66**	$2.75
☐	26561	**A DAILY RATE #67**	$2.75
☐	26437	**THE STORY OF A WHIM #68**	$2.75
☐	26389	**ACCORDING TO THE PATTERN #69**	$2.75
☐	25253	**IN THE WAY #70**	$2.95
☐	26610	**EXIT BETTY #71**	$2.75
☐	25573	**THE WHITE LADY #72**	$2.95
☐	25733	**NOT UNDER THE LAW #73**	$2.95
☐	25806	**LO, MICHAEL #74**	$2.95
☐	25930	**THE WITNESS #75**	$2.95
☐	26104	**THE CITY OF FIRE #76**	$2.95

Prices and availability subject to change without notice.

Buy them at your local bookstore or use this handy coupon for ordering:

Special Offer
Buy a Bantam Book
for only 50¢.

Now you can have Bantam's catalog filled with hundreds of titles plus take advantage of our unique and exciting bonus book offer. A special offer which gives you the opportunity to purchase a Bantam book for only 50¢. Here's how!

By ordering any five books at the regular price per order, you can also choose any other single book listed (up to a $4.95 value) for just 50¢. Some restrictions do apply, but for further details why not send for Bantam's catalog of titles today!

Just send us your name and address and we will send you a catalog!

Experience all the passion and adventure life has to offer in these bestselling novels by and about women.

DON'T MISS
THESE CURRENT
Bantam Bestsellers

☐	25800	**THE CIDER HOUSE RULES** John Irving	$4.95
☐	25675	**BEACHES** Iris Rainer Dart	$3.95
☐	25801	**DARK GODS** T. E. D. Klein	$3.95
☐	25570	**JEALOUSIES** Justine Harlowe	$3.95
☐	25571	**MAXWELL'S TRAIN** Christopher Hyde	$3.50
☐	25944	**PRETTY IN PINK** H. B. Gilmore	$2.50
☐	26554	**HOLD THE DREAM** Barbara Taylor Bradford	$4.95
☐	26253	**VOICE OF THE HEART** Barbara Taylor Bradford	$4.95
☐	25547	**SWEET REASON** Robert Littel	$3.50
☐	25540	**MOONDUST AND MADNESS** Janelle Taylor	$3.95
☐	25890	**PLEASURES** Diana Sydney	$3.95
☐	05097	**THE SISTERS** Robert Littel (A Bantam Hardcover Book)	$16.95
☐	25416	**THE DEFECTION OF A. J. LEWINTER** Robert Littel	$3.95
☐	25432	**THE OCTOBER CIRCLE** Robert Littel	$3.95
☐	23667	**NURSES STORY** Carol Gino	$3.95
☐	24978	**GUILTY PARTIES** Dana Clarins	$3.50
☐	24257	**WOMAN IN THE WINDOW** Dana Clarins	$3.50
☐	24184	**THE WARLORD** Malcolm Bosse	$3.95

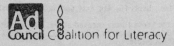